WILL O' THE WISP POINT

XANN-SHAPELLA SMITH

This book is a work of fiction. Any reference to historical events, real people, or real places are used fictitiously. Other names, characters, places, and events are products of the author's imagination, and any resemblance to actual events or places or persons, living or dead, is entirely coincidental.

Copyright © 2019 by Xann-shapella Smith

All rights reserved. No part of this book may be reproduced in any form or by any electronic or mechanical means, including information storage and retrieval systems, without written permission from the author, except for the use of brief quotations in a book review.

Cover design by Doug & Sherry Walker and Xann.

ISBN:
978-0-9992027-2-2

*For my fabulous dairy-farming parents
who never asked why I wanted to
major in theater and film.*

PROLOGUE

From the ocean's view, the Bloom Lighthouse is a welcome sight to professional mariners and weekend boaters alike. The stories the old guide could tell. It was built strategically atop a tall cliff which enables the lantern's light to be seen for miles. It stands as a warning as well as a nostalgic nod to a bygone era. The lightkeeper's house is small by today's standards—just two rooms attached to the tower. Left to the viewers' imagination, the tiny house would most likely be romanticized as a cozy refuge on a stormy night. This makes perfect sense as lighthouses have become a modern-day symbol of tranquility and mystique.

This particular lighthouse has been passed down through the family for generations and is currently cared for by William Bloom. When his parents named him William, they had no idea it meant "resolute protector or guardian." They wanted a proper name that would ring with sophistication in the ivory towers of higher education and be taken seriously in the upper echelons of high finance. Much to their dismay, Will took the meaning of his name to heart. He became a paramedic, implementing the oath to 'serve unselfishly… to help make a better world for all mankind.'

For nearly twenty years, Will has made the lighthouse his home and the small coastal town of Will-O'-the-Wisp Point his family. He can't remember when the dividing line between community and family grew too faint for him to recognize. He's always lived a modest life with simple wants and needs, and a belief that money was only good for the good you could do with it. His grandparents taught him that.

Till now, he's been content to live alone on the edge of a cliff with the ocean as his closest neighbor. Recently, however, contentment has begun to lose its luster. He's all but forgotten what it's like to have conversation over a meal at his kitchen table, or to think out loud and have someone respond, to share his life with someone other than his dog. So Will developed a plan to pursue a romance and set the plan in motion. Then something unexpected happened.

CHAPTER 1

The recorded sound of a female dance instructor's voice filled the light keeper's small living area. The teacher's dramatic delivery of perfectly-enunciated words elevated the learning of the tango to an art form. Clumsily trying to match his feet to the cut out footprints duct taped to the floor, William Bloom, Will to his friends, was doing his best to follow her directions. It was nine o'clock at night and he was still stuffed from Thanksgiving dinner. Unbuttoning his flannel shirt, he tossed it onto the table, leaving him in a cooler undershirt. He continued to rewind the tape to the same point and start again, hoping that her frequent positive comments were a sign that success was imminent. Finally, he reached the same instruction point he had yet to surpass—a tricky step that eluded him. As usual, his feet became tangled and all seventy-two inches of him hit the floor.

"*Remember, there is no one perfect tango, but many perfect moments,*" recited the teacher with exact timing. Lying flat on his back, Will continued to listen to the tutor's voice coaching him through the speaker. "That's it!" he yelled. Resolute, he crawled to his feet and yanked the cord from the wall. "Like feet are meant to do that."

Grabbing ahold of the eighties-style cassette player, he tucked it beneath his arm like a football and opened the door. Unable to resist the opportunity to run free, his golden retriever nearly knocked Will's feet out from under him as he rushed into the storm. "Junior, wait!" he shouted, throwing his raincoat over his head and picking up the flashlight.

As he made his way toward the cliff, he could hear his dog barking through the storm, but his only focus was how far he could lob the cassette player over the cliff and into the ocean. Once he reached the tossing point, he swung his arm back like a discus thrower ready to launch, but Junior's barking had become so incessant that it ruined the moment. Shining the flashlight in the downward direction of his dog's nose, he saw something white on the rocks below. On a dead run he returned the cassette player to the house and grabbed a rope from behind the seat of his truck. As he tied the rope around the base of a boulder, he heard a sound traveling in the wind. The familiar strain resembled a voice pleading with the sea. With his knot securely tied, he began lowering himself down the muddy trail toward the rocks. Nothing could slow his descent.

Getting closer to the water, the beam from his flashlight revealed a body. He'd seen a few wash ashore in his line of work, but never this close to home. Reaching the rocks, he tied the rope around his waist for security then knelt down next to the presumed corpse. Turning the female body over and lifting her into his arms, he was taken back by her beauty even under such terrible circumstances. Her skin was cold from the frigid temperatures and covered with abrasions from the abuse she'd taken in the swirling sea. The lack of clothing made her even more susceptible to the jagged rocks near the coast.

Although she appeared dead, he placed his fingers against the front of her neck to feel for a carotid pulse. Surprised to find one, he mentally shifted from a body recovery mission to lifesaving mode. Her pulse was faint, but present. He was running out of time. Ignoring his training and the use of a back board, he wrapped his rain coat around her body then gently placed her over his shoulder. With both hands he pulled himself back up the slippery trail, losing his footing from time to time. Eventually he made it to the top of the cliff and leaned against the boulder. At thirty-five he was in the best shape of his life, but the physical exertion necessary to climb the trail took more out of him than he realized.

After steadying himself, he moved to the older model pickup truck and carefully laid her on the seat. "You're going to be all right," he said reassuringly. "We're close to the clinic." Running to the house, he put his dog inside then hurried back to the truck and started the engine. A ways from the house, he found the road blocked by a large tree taken down by the storm. There was no way around it. As a paramedic, he began prepping mentally for what he could do as he reversed backwards. He could get the chain saw and cut a path through the tree. By the time he did that, her hypothermia would probably lead to heart failure. He needed to get her warm before her condition became fatal.

Taking her in his arms, he carried her into the house. Once he reached the bedroom, he yanked the covers back on the bed and tenderly laid her down. As he removed the raincoat, the brighter light revealed abrasions and cuts across her back and limbs. In an attempt to conserve heat, her body naturally reduced blood flow to her skin, keeping the bleeding at bay. He would deal with the wounds once her life was no longer in danger. Covering her with several layers of homemade quilts, he ran into the small bathroom and turned the hot water tap on in the old tub.

Letting it run, he hurried into the kitchen and pulled two hot water bottles from beneath the sink then returned to the bathroom. The water had reached the perfect temperature so he filled both rubber bottles. Then he grabbed a couple of hand towels and returned to the bedroom. Wrapping a towel around each bottle, he placed them between her upper arms and the sides of her body. Her skin had a blueish-gray tint to it, telling of a dangerously low body temperature. Running back into the bathroom, he grabbed an electric thermometer from the medicine cabinet. When he returned to the room, he stripped everything off except his long underwear bottoms and crawled under the quilts. Wrapping himself around her, he began to quiver. "Oh! You're so cold!"

As a distraction, he went on to professionally explain what was happening as though his patient were conscious. "I can't get you to the clinic. There's a tree in the road. I have to warm your body temperature or you're not going to make it." No longer able to talk because of the chattering of his teeth, his mind raced with proper treatment protocol for hypothermia. His patient looked to be in her mid-thirties and healthy. That would help.

Once he gained control of his own shaking, he placed the thermometer in her mouth. While he waited, he slid her wet blonde hair off her face and listened carefully to her breathing. It was shallow and slow. He found her weak pulse and counted it off. The alarm sounded on the thermometer, showing a dangerous seventy-eight degrees. Realizing her heart could stop at any minute, he held her closer, placing the side of his face against hers.

The next couple hours felt like the longest of his life. The only treatment he could offer was the heat from his own body and it seemed to be working. Her temperature improved each time he checked but at a very slow rate. With each degree of improvement her pulse grew in strength. The steady improvement gave him hope. He planned to tend to her wounds once her temperature warmed to a safer degree, but the physical exertion of the rescue had drained his own body of strength. Although he fought to stay awake, the adrenaline rush that had kept him vigilant had faded. Eventually Will drifted off to sleep beside her.

CHAPTER 2

*D*awn came as a jolt to Will's system. Staring at the woman lying next to him, he quickly recalled the frantic rescue. With his arms still wrapped around her, he could tell her body temperature had warmed. Gently touching his finger to her neck, he timed her pulse as he listened to her breathing. Happy to find everything normal, he breathed a sigh of relief. He'd feared the worst but somehow she had survived.

Crawling out of bed, Will threw on a sweatshirt and pulled yesterday's jeans over his long john bottoms. As he crept toward the door, he caught a glimpse of himself in the mirror. His messy brown hair was pointing in every direction. Nothing ten fingers couldn't fix as he combed them through his hair. Picking up his leather work boots, he quietly walked toward the wood stove.

The house was chilly, a sign that sometime in the early morning hours, the last ember had gone out. He built a fire using kindling and some dry wood that he brought in the day before. With the draft wide open, the blaze took off immediately. Taking a moment to warm his hands, he glanced at the mysterious woman as she rolled over in bed —another good sign. For Will, there was nothing more rewarding than saving a life or helping those in need. It was the gift that kept on giving, usually in the form of baked goods.

Walking into the kitchen, he picked up the land line phone and called his friend Jack, an officer in the local branch of the Coast Guard. It was his duty to report the woman who washed ashore. He was certain someone would be searching for her. Leaving a message on his voicemail, he hung up the phone and stared out the window. He still wanted to get his patient to the clinic to be checked over by a doctor but the downed tree stood in his way. The tree was a towering white pine with plenty of limbs attached. Grabbing a homemade muffin from a 'thank you' plate, he poured some milk into a small Thermos, added several heaping tablespoons of malted powder and placed it on the counter near the door.

His dog was already waiting to shoot through the door as Will gave him a quick pat on the head and whispered, "Are you ready, Junior?" The dog answered by wagging his tail faster. "Let's go." Will opened the door and watched him run as he reached for a denim jacket. The weather was running mid-fifties during the day and cooling into the thirties at night, so layering a padded vest over a light jacket would suffice. After putting on his baseball cap and tucking a pair of work gloves into his back pocket, he grabbed his muffin, gave his Thermos a shake and left the house.

A morning after a good storm was one of Will's favorite things to experience. The air was crisp and clean and the birds were chirping through the trees. It was just how he liked it on a late-autumn morning. After placing his breakfast on the seat of his truck, he faced the top of the lighthouse. The light had done its job just as it had for decades. Saluting the beacon, he turned and walked toward the shed near the house.

Tossing his chainsaw, tool bag, bar oil, gas jug and splitting maul in the back of the truck, he drove to the downed tree and fired up his saw. Before he could get close to the large trunk, he had to limb the tree. Not an easy job with a tree as large and full as the one before him, but he began making considerable progress. Once the limbs were cut away, he packed them to an open area and piled them on top of each other for a future bonfire.

An official Coast Guard truck rolled up on the other side of the tree. Jack Segal, a salty, sea dog nearing retirement, stepped out of the truck and walked toward the downed tree. Placing his foot on top of the log and his forearm across his bent knee, he waited for his young friend to return for more limbs. Dropping by the lighthouse on his way to and from work was a favorite pastime of Jack's. Although Will was a grown man, he felt a responsibility to keep an eye on him.

Happy to see Jack, Will waved on his way toward him. He was a trusted friend and in many ways, a second dad. Wanting to take a break, he straddled the log next to Jack and pulled off his vest. He'd warmed up plenty with all the work. "What brings you by so early?"

"Just left work. Thought I'd check on your mermaid."

"She seems to be sleeping comfortably. I plan to take her to the clinic as soon as I get the road cleared."

Jack whistled loudly, calling to the dog. "Come here, Jack Junior." Once his namesake arrived, he indulged man's best friend with a vigorous frisk. "That was quite a storm last night. We were measuring six-foot seas. It's a miracle she survived."

"I'm as surprised as you are," agreed Will.

"I thought you were taking this old tree down last month."

"I got busy."

"Thelma's washing machine? Hank's water heater? Harriet's garage door? Or another sink? Most likely Ruby's. You're trained to save human beings, not appliances."

"I'm still trying to get to the sink."

"And I'm still trying to get to bed," said Jack as he lobbed a stick as far as he could, giving Junior something to chase. "Too many parties of 'giving thanks' on the high seas last night."

"You're a trained officer in the Coast Guard, not a babysitter," responded Will, giving back the same advice he had just received.

"Fair enough," Jack replied with a chuckle as he walked back to the truck.

"Any word on who she is?"

"No one's reported anyone missing," replied Jack.

"That doesn't make sense."

"There was a lot of traffic on the water last night. A lot of highfalutin' celebrating. She probably got tipsy and fell overboard."

"How do you not report that?"

"They probably don't even know she's missing. Or worse yet, they don't care," said Jack as he crawled in behind the wheel. "We could post her picture on the news."

"Let's keep it quiet until we talk to her."

"Your call. Well, kid, I better get. The wife was not happy I missed Thanksgiving dinner. Do you want me to bring you up a plate?"

"I'm good. I made the rounds in town yesterday. A lot of good eating and leftover turkey for sandwiches."

"You know she'd have my head if I didn't ask."

"Thanks for stopping by, Jack."

"I'll let you know if I hear anything. Say 'hi' to that father of yours when you head home for the wedding. Remind him he still owes me that pair of boots."

"I always do. Enjoy the leftovers."

"Oh, I plan to. It's always tastier the next day," he hollered out the window as he backed around and drove down the road.

Turning back, Will was surprised to see the mystery woman walk out of the house wrapped in a quilt. He watched curiously as she walked toward the cliff and knelt at the edge. Her long blonde hair floating back and forth with the breeze. Unsure of her state of mind, he decided to check on her before returning to the log. As he neared the cliff, she appeared to be in a trance of sorts, staring out at the ocean. "How are you feeling this morning?" Receiving no response, he tried again. "Is everything all right?" Still no response. "You're really lucky you know. You took a beating against the rocks. It could have been a lot worse," he said, squatting next to her. "My name is Will. William Bloom. I'm the one who found you. Actually, it was my dog, Junior. Jack Junior."

Candace continued to stare into the ocean.

"I couldn't get you to the clinic last night because of the tree blocking the road. I'm working on clearing a path, then I'll take you in to see the doctor." Pausing for a response, Will waited for a few seconds. "Were there others with you? Is there someone I can contact?"

Hearing the sound of the telephone ring through the open door of the lighthouse, Will stood up and ran toward the house. Reaching inside, he grabbed the telephone receiver and pulled it out of the house so he could talk while keeping an eye on his guest. "Hello. I don't know if I'm going to make it today, Ruby. How did you hear about her? Yes, she's alive. I'll try to stop by tomorrow," he said then hung up the phone and shut the door. The woman on the cliff had sent a clear message that she didn't want to talk, so he walked back to the fallen tree, started the chainsaw and continued to cut the log into pieces.

Two hours later, Will was still unable to get her to talk, so he made a couple sandwiches and carried the lunch to the edge of the cliff. Sitting down next to her, he left enough space between them to put her plate and bottle of water on the ground. "I made you some lunch. Turkey sandwich," he said, diving into his as he waited for her to react. He was hungry from a morning of physical labor, so he had to pace himself to keep from devouring his meal too quickly. "I love sandwiches. You get everything you need in every bite: bread, cheese, veggies, meat. All the major food groups. I could live on 'em. Actually, I do live on 'em," he concluded between bites. Tossing his dog a piece of the crust, Junior happily gobbled it down and waited patiently for another. "Your body needs that nutrition and water. Especially the water." Shoving half of the last bite into his mouth, he tossed the final piece to Junior and gave him the paper plate to clean up the crumbs. "If you're smart you'll eat," he said, intended as motivation.

Without warning, Candace threw her arm out from under the quilt, picked up the plate and hucked it over the cliff.

Junior raced to the edge of the cliff and stared over the edge, longing for the sandwich quickly being consumed by the water below. Turning back, he found his master just as shocked as he was.

"I didn't ask for your help and I don't need a doctor," said Candace resolutely. Fighting back the tears, she wrapped the quilt over her shoulder and continued to stare out at the ocean. "Just leave me alone," she softly pleaded.

"Come on, Junior. Let's do as the lady asks." Confused by what he considered to be irrational behavior, he picked up his paper plate and his water bottle and rose to his feet. On his way to the tree, he mentally searched his training and experience for an answer that would explain her reaction.

WITH NIGHT CLOSING IN, Will nervously paced the kitchen floor. Each time he passed the small kitchen window, he parted the curtains to see if she had moved from the cliff. Still she sat, wrapped in the same quilt and refusing to move. Throughout the afternoon, he offered food, drink and clothing to make her comfortable, but she refused to acknowledge him or go to the clinic to be checked out. He was trying to give her the space she needed, but at the same time, he felt responsible for her care. The wind had picked up as a predecessor to the storm rolling in from the ocean. Once raindrops started hitting the glass, Will knew what he had to do. Leaving the house, he marched toward her. "You either get up and walk to the house or I'm carrying you... again!"

With a look of protest, she stormed back to the house. Will followed, entering the open door just in time to see her walk into the bedroom and slam the door behind her. Perturbed by her rudeness, he reached for the handle of the bedroom door, but stopped himself. Instead, he knocked on the door and waited for an answer. As expected, nothing happened, so he slowly opened the door and peeked inside.

Candace stood facing the outer wall, staring at an old painting of a ship caught in a storm, being guided by the beacon from the lighthouse. The sound of the wind swirling around the house brought the painting to life.

"I don't expect you to thank me for saving your life, but you could at least try to be civil," said Will, then he closed the door.

No sooner did Will shut the door, but Candace opened it. "Thank you? You want me to thank you? For what? Sticking your nose where it doesn't belong?" With her voice starting to crack from the rush of emotion, she slammed the door.

Trying to distract himself from her response, he turned to his nemesis: the cassette player. Pressing the play button, he found his footsteps and waited for instruction as he tried to control his breathing.

"Give and take must be shared by you and your partner. A man may lead, but the woman chooses her response."

Rolling his eyes, he quickly shut it off. The last thing he needed was another voice telling him what to do. Storming back to the door, he opened it to find her sitting on the bed still wrapped in the same quilt. "I don't know what went on out there and I don't know how you ended up on my beach, but the least you could do is show some respect while you're in my home." Before shutting the door, he noticed her wipe a tear from her cheek, causing him more confusion than before he entered. Will pulled a clean dish towel from the shelf and walked toward her. He wasn't sure if she'd take it but he offered it to her anyway.

She accepted the gesture and used it to wipe her eyes. "Thank you."

His frustration turned to sympathy as he sat down behind her. He wanted to console her but had no idea what to say. He was great at stabilizing bodies in emergency situations, but when it came to emotional stuff, he was lost for words. "If you were bleeding, odds are good I could stop it." Reaching out, he touched her shoulder, but she quickly pulled away. "Speaking of bleeding, since you refused to go to the clinic, I need to tend to your wounds."

"I'm fine."

"You're not fine. Some of those cuts looked pretty deep. I don't want infection to set in. Why don't we start with the ones on your back?"

"I'll tend to my own wounds."

"Unless you're a contortionist... that's going to be difficult."

"Just leave me alone," she begged. "Please, go away."

"You'll be in less pain."

"What do you know of pain?"

"I've seen a lot of it. There's no reason for you to keep suffering. Unless that's what you want."

After considering his words, she yielded to his care. "All right."

"I'll grab my first aid bag," he said, leaving the room.

Candace timidly lowered the quilt to her hips, revealing her naked back. Returning to the room, Will saw that the extent of her injuries was worse than he thought. Open cuts leaking fluid, large abrasions and smaller scratches covered her back. The bruising had begun to show its coloring as well. "The rocks and the reef did a number on your back. I should have taken care of this earlier." Gently, Will cleaned the wounds and used his expertise to care for them. During the process, he noticed marks and scarring on her back from older wounds but chose to overlook them for the time being.

Once the wounds on her back were properly treated, he moved to her legs. Fortunately, none were so deep they required stitches, so he used butterfly bandages to close the gaps. A half hour later, he felt good about her care. Bringing her a glass of water and a dosage of pain killers was the last of his treatment. While she took her medicine, Will reached into his bag and pulled out a generic toothbrush wrapped in plastic then laid it on the nightstand. "You never know when you're going to need one," he said as he stood up. Opening a drawer, he picked up a pair of red flannel pajamas and placed them on the pillow in front of her. "When you get dressed, I'll take the quilt and soak the bloodstains over night. Before leaving, he offered a positive thought. "Even the worst days come to an end." Then he closed the door.

Candace pressed the dish towel against her face to mute the thundering release of emotion. The mishmash of feelings fighting for recognition was more than she could contain. After a while she gained enough composure to carefully dress herself without messing up the bandages. Then she picked up the quilt and opened the door. "Where would you like me to put it?"

"I'll take it," he said, wrapping it in his arms.

Without a word, she returned to the bed while he walked into the bathroom and turned the cold water on in the tub. Will was satisfied he had done all he could for his patient. The next step was up to her.

CHAPTER 3

Waking up on his dog's twin bed in the kitchen, Will pulled Junior's paw from the front of his face and sat up. "How do you sleep on this thing?" Irritated by the sound of squeaking coils, he stood up, allowing the dog to stretch himself out on the thin mattress. As he passed by the open bedroom door, he noticed the room was empty. He wondered if she'd left during the night. Grabbing the receiver from the wall phone, his initial thought was to call the police. Realizing he had zero information, he stopped himself from calling dispatch.

Will continued to look for clues, possibly a note. Entering the bathroom he found nothing but the quilt soaking in the tub. He stuffed it into the small washing machine and started the load. When he returned to the kitchen, he noticed the tea kettle was hot. Will moved to the window and parted the curtain. The woman he had rescued was standing at the cliff's edge, wrapped in a different quilt and drinking from his favorite mug. Taking it as a sign of progress, Will and Junior left the house to join her.

Standing side by side, he waited for her to speak first—a lesson he learned during the previous day's interaction. Looking down, he noticed she was wearing a pair of his old tennis shoes. They had to be at least two sizes too big, but she had them laced as tight as they would go.

"My name is Candace. That's all I can tell you," she said in a tone much kinder than the day before.

"Okay, Candace. Can I interest you in some breakfast?"

"I'm not that hungry."

"Well, I'm starving. More importantly, I need to get the taste of dog paw out of my mouth," he responded as he and Junior turned to walk back to the house. "If you change your mind, you're welcome to join me."

Candace took another sip from her mug while watching the fog lift from the ocean. It was a beautiful morning for starting fresh. All she needed was the courage to do it. As patches of blue sky began to appear, so did the genesis of a positive thought. Maybe she was a little hungry after all.

Walking back into the lighthouse, she quietly shut the door behind her and surveilled the room. Will was busy cooking at the stove with his back to her while listening to the morning news on a local radio station. To her left was the old-fashioned twin bed, occupied by a dog with zero interest in getting up. Showing his contentment, the golden retriever patted his fluffy tail against the mattress, flirting as he stared at the new guest. Candace sat down beside him and gave him some love as she continued to take in the details of the small room. With the exception of a kitchen table surrounded by four old chairs, there was no formal sitting space. The stove, with several feet of counter space on each side, lined the inside wall leading her eyes to an old refrigerator facing them at the end of the room. The white fridge and stove looked to be decades old, but together they had a certain retro charm. Lining the outside wall on the right was more cupboard space, cluttered with everyday items and a stack of unopened mail. Beneath the small window was an old farmhouse-style, double kitchen sink with a built-in drain area on one side. The white color of the sink, countertops and cupboards brightened the one-window room.

But the most interesting part of the house was what she spied through the open door at the end of the room: a spiral staircase. Wanting to see where it led, Candace pulled the quilt off her shoulders and walked toward the doorway. She was still sore from her near-death experience so she knew it would take her awhile to get to the top.

As she passed behind Will, he caught a glimpse of her out of the corner of his eye. She was wearing a pair of his worn jeans and a red flannel shirt. Stepping back, he followed her with his eyes as she began her slow climb up the stairs. The smile on his face indicated his relief. Today was definitely starting out better than yesterday. His smile quickly disappeared as he considered her possible motivation for climbing the tower to the light. With the exception of a name, he knew nothing about her. If she had a death wish, leaping from the tower would be a good way to make it happen. Turning the heat down on the cast iron griddle, he put a lid over the eggs and hash browns to keep them warm then followed her up the stairs.

Entering the lantern room that housed the lamp and lens, he saw the glass panel door open. She had found her way to the gallery, an open platform-style balcony that surrounded the outside of the light. Turning around, he watched her circle the rear of the light and make her way back to the ocean side. It appeared she was only interested in the view. Just to be on the safe side, he crawled through the small opening and walked toward her. "She's got an incredible view, doesn't she?"

"It's gorgeous."

"I've got some hash browns and scrambled eggs waiting on the stove… if you've changed your mind about breakfast. I'm no chef, but I do all right in the kitchen."

"Thank you."

"It's no problem. Cooking for two is as easy as one."

"I meant… 'thank you' for saving my life," she said, gripping the railing for enough support to get through her serving of humble pie.

"That's what I do."

"You pull a lot of naked women out of the ocean?"

"I'm a paramedic. The only one in town. So you did good."

"I did good?"

"You picked the right beach to wash up on."

"Did I?"

"You're alive, aren't you?"

Conflicted inside, Candace responded to Will's rhetorical question with silence.

"Do you need to call someone... to let them know where you are?" asked Will, taking a chance to find out more about what happened the night she washed ashore.

"No."

"Someone's got to be missing you."

"There's no one to call!" denied Candace, her voice raised in volume. "Please, don't ask me that again!"

"Okay." Will turned to leave the platform.

"I'm sorry. I'm not usually like this. I'm just a little on edge from everything that's happened."

"I shouldn't be poking my nose into your business," he said, offering her an easy out before he climbed back through the open glass panel. As Will made his way down the spiral staircase, he realized what was keeping her on edge. He recognized the symptoms of post traumatic stress disorder thanks to a series of state-wide training courses for treatment of PTSD. Avoidance in talking about the incident, behavioral changes from the norm and mood swings were all obvious signs. He was no mental health professional but was familiar with the five levels of PTSD. The best he could tell, she was experiencing what was termed: a normal stress response.

If that were the case, recovery would come naturally the more she explored her emotions and worked through the traumatic experience. Talking about the incident from a place of honesty and sharing how she felt would add to the healing process. Until Candace asked for help there was little he could do from a medical perspective. Beneath the outward manifestations, he knew there was more going on than he was privy to—deep emotions that could lead to personal harm or even suicide if left bottled up. As his feet met the floor, he looked up at the light. For now, he would offer friendship and the help she needed to get back on her feet. That and a tasty breakfast.

FEELING regret for snapping at him, Candace watched Will disappear down the stairs. Her frustration seemed to come in tsunami-sized waves, entirely uncontrollable at times. She wanted to say something or do something, but nothing came. She wasn't emotionally prepared to give him what he wanted, nor could she recall the details of that night. As hard as she tried to remember, her memory was blank. Will had a right to ask the questions, but the answers he was looking for weren't that simple. The last thing he deserved was to be the target of her instability. The fact that he was willing to be on the firing end of her volatility was another sign of his kind character.

Turning her attention back to the horizon, a sudden gust of wind rushed by her, causing her to grab onto the railing to keep from being blown away. It was instant exhilaration, making her feel alive. The ocean had always been a place of harmony and peace—the perfect setting for retrospective thinking. But this was a new day and she wanted desperately to be done reviewing the mistakes of her past. Being rescued from the verge of death gave her a second chance to live her life. A new starting point. As exciting as that sounded to her imagination, she was scared to death. She had no idea where to begin.

She had one person in her new life—the man who rescued her. So far, he'd bent over backwards to help and she had yet to reciprocate. She needed help and he was the only one offering. She wanted to return the kindness he had shown, to genuinely thank him for his care. That would require lowering her defenses, as well as an attempt to fix what was broken inside her.

Resolved to at least try to let someone into her life, she crawled through the glass pane door and shut it snuggly then made her way down the spiral staircase. Entering the kitchen, she found Will loading his plate with breakfast. She noticed a place set on the table for a second guest. Smiling at his continued thoughtfulness, she walked toward the kitchen and leaned up against the wall. The pain of the wall pressing on her sores caused her to quickly straighten up. Trying not to miss a beat, she changed focus. "That smells amazing."

"There's plenty here," he responded, keeping his eyes focused on the griddle.

"I am a bit hungry."

"Have a seat."

Turning off the radio, Will reached behind him and picked up her plate, then proceeded to arrange a grouping of hash browns and scrambled eggs, with a few slices of tomatoes as a delicious garnish. Turning around he put the plate in front of her and placed his across the small table. Then he moved to the fridge and pulled out a jug of milk and bottles of ketchup and jam. The toaster popped the bread up in perfect timing and he placed one piece on each plate then sat down to eat.

Candace watched with curiosity as he smothered his toast with a healthy dose of butter, then a thick layer of strawberry jam. Taking a bite, he moved onto dressing the rest of his plate with his condiment of choice. Squirting an interesting pattern of ketchup over his hash browns and eggs, he was careful to ensure equal coverage. Then he dug in with enthusiasm.

Noticing how quickly he was going down on his toast, she left the table and put two more slices of bread in the toaster.

"Hungrier than you thought?" asked Will.

"I think we both are," she replied, sitting back down and buttering her toast. Normally her breakfasts consisted of a meal replacement shake and possibly a banana. She forgot what it felt like to eat a real breakfast. The combined flavors were music to her taste buds as they continued to eat in silence. The feeling of being watched caused Candace to look toward the floor, instantly connecting with Junior's longing eyes. He'd been trained as a gentleman and waited patiently for her to respond. Unsure of the protocol for feeding pets from the table, she ignored his request and continued to eat.

"Milk?" Before she could answer, he placed his fork down and filled both of their glasses. After drinking a quarter of his glass, he went back to eating. Sipping from the top, Candace followed his example, but at a slower rate of consumption. She could tell he was used to eating quickly so he could get on with his day. The toaster popped the bread up and Will beat her to the counter, plopping one piece on both of their plates.

"I don't think I have room for both," she responded.

"Okay," he said, buttering both pieces and placing them on his plate.

She couldn't remember a time when she'd been so entertained at the breakfast table. Instead of dinner and a movie, it was breakfast and live theatre. Placing the last bite in his mouth, she watched him wipe up the juices and left-behind fragments with the remaining piece of toast and wash it down with the rest of his milk. Glancing down at her own plate, she was only a quarter-way through.

Leaning back, he patted his stomach, completely satisfied. "So... what's next for you?" he asked with some trepidation.

Candace took her time to think before reacting—proof that she was making an attempt at trying. "I seem to have arrived without a contingency plan."

"Did you leave it on the boat with your clothes?" joked Will, before he thought about the consequences.

"Of all the paramedics in the world, I get rescued by the funny one?"

"We're all funny. It's a job requirement."

An awkward silence fell over the table as neither had a segue to help move the conversation along.

"I need to run into town to take care of something. You feel like going for a ride?" asked Will.

"I don't want anyone to see me."

"I won't be long. You can stay in the truck if you like."

"Don't you trust me here alone? Are you afraid of what I'll do?"

"It's just a ride. Let's not make it more than that," he said as he left the table and walked into the bedroom. Scooping the three novels from the nightstand, he walked back into the kitchen and left them on the counter near the door.

Candace watched as he gathered his plate and placed it in the sink. "I see you like to read."

"I've probably read every novel in the local library. I borrowed these from a lady in town." Will decided to up the stakes as he walked back into the bathroom and pulled the quilt from the washer. "I'm going to hang this on the line to dry. I'll wait for you outside." Opening the door, he left the house before she could answer.

Losing interest in her breakfast, she turned toward the drooling dog. The look of anticipation was almost more than she could stand. Clearly, he favored the possibility of leftovers to racing from the house when his owner opened the door. Placing the plate on the floor, Junior cleaned it up in no time flat, leaving no evidence of a half-eaten breakfast. Patting the dog on the head, she picked up the plate, rinsed it off with hot water and left it in the sink to be washed.

Through the window, she watched Will hang the quilt on the clothes line. It was sunny but still cool. She wondered if it would dry. Her mind started to ponder other curiosities about Will until she broke free from the distraction. She knew she had to make a decision: step into the world and see what was out there or hide out in the lighthouse like an ostrich with its head in the sand. Everything inside her screamed: "Ostrich! Ostrich!" Turning away from the window, her eyes fell to the cutout footprints taped to the floor. They seemed to be leading to the door. It was the sign she needed. Putting one foot in front of the other, she followed the footprints to the partially-opened door.

Still uncertain of her next move, Junior made the decision for her as he raced through the opening, causing the door to fly wide open. She watched as he jumped into the back of the blue, three-quarter-ton pickup and readied himself for a thrilling ride.

Thinking she decided to go with him, Will walked around the side of the truck and opened the passenger door. The pressure was on. The only thing she could do was walk to the truck and lift herself onto the seat.

"Buckle up," he advised before shutting the door. "Safety first." Candace did as he requested then waited for him to get behind the wheel before asking a favor. "I don't want anyone to know that I washed up on shore."

"Only two people know and I trust them both," said Will as he started the truck and drove toward the road.

CHAPTER 4

The scenery was fresh and breathtaking as they headed down the rural coastal road. Neither of them had much to say, so Candace spent the time soaking in the beauty of the ocean and trees. Eventually, they passed a sign that read: *Welcome to Will-O'-the-Wisp Point.* "What a strange name for a town," she thought to herself. She had no idea what it meant, but she tucked it into the back of her mind for a future conversation.

The town was small and seemed like a sleepy place to live. Main street appeared to be where most of the shops were located. Candace had plenty of time to study the business names due to Will's strict observance of the twenty-five-mile-an-hour speed limit. People waved to Will as he passed by and he waved back with a smile. Candace couldn't help but notice the curious looks on their faces as they stared at her as well.

A large Christmas tree being erected in the town square caught her eye. The men securing it in place all waved to Will and he honked back at them. "That's Joe and the rest of the volunteer firefighters that I work with. We get tasked with putting up the tree each year, as well as star placement and lights. The community adds the decorations."

"Why aren't you helping them?"

"They said they could handle it this year."

Candace knew she was the reason he wasn't joining in on the tradition but that was his decision to make. She was just along for the ride.

Pulling up to a large Victorian-style home, Will turned off the truck. "This shouldn't take too long," he said, picking up the books and leaving the cab.

Candace watched him grab his toolbox from the back of the truck, then moved over and rolled down the driver's-side window. "I think I'll take a walk."

"Go for it," said Will as he passed by. "It's hard to get lost in this town."

Returning to her side of the seat, she glanced up at the second-story window as she reached for the door handle. A dark-haired young woman peered through a small opening in the curtains. She disappeared as soon as eye contact was made. "Strange," she whispered to herself. A knock on the front door returned her attention to Will standing on the porch. A beautiful older woman, possibly late-fifties, with salt and pepper hair opened the door and stepped outside. Candace instantly fell in love with her outfit. Dressed in a red, bandana-print shirt dress with a concho belt at the waist and a dark blue jean jacket, she was the opposite of what Candace expected to see. Her rustic-brown ankle boots added the perfect touch to her ensemble. This was a woman who knew what she wanted. Curiously, Candace watched and listened from the truck as they greeted each other.

"Good morning, Ruby."

"A fine morning to you, Will. Wasn't that a magnificent storm last night?"

"Magnificent's a pretty good description."

"Is that our lost girl?" she whispered.

Candace heard the inquiry and quickly left the truck. On her way around the back, she heard Will's reply.

"Her name is Candace and she wants to keep things private."

"I haven't told anyone."

That was the last thing Candace heard before she walked out of range.

Will and Ruby watched her walk down the sidewalk as they continued their conversation. "You never told me how you found out about her?" asked Will.

"I went for a walk last night. I saw your light where the beach ends near the cliff."

"You were out during the storm?"

"I know that beach like the back of my hand," she responded, keeping an eye on Candace.

"I brought back the books you lent me."

"There's plenty more where they came from." With Candace getting farther away, Ruby had to act fast. "You know where to find them and the sink. I'll be right back," she responded, picking up a waist-high, stylish walking stick with a gold ball at the top as she left the porch. On the outside, Ruby's beauty was remarkable—almost ageless in appearance, but her health had been in decline for months. As much as she hated using it, the need for a walking stick was essential when leaving the house.

Candace found two benches in a park nearby and chose the one facing town for her resting place. That way she could see if someone happened upon her. An autumn breeze rushed by and she closed her eyes to enjoy the sound of the leaves blowing with the wind. While her eyes were closed, her mind slipped back to the night in the ocean. Little by little, she was beginning to piece things back together. She recalled sinking into the cold water and how shocking it was at first. She remembered slipping into the quiet darkness. The silence was unexpected with the storm raging above. She thought of how the sea wrapped itself around her, rolling her body back and forth. Oddly, she recalled how peaceful she felt.

"Do you mind if I rest a bit?" asked Ruby as she sat down next to her.

The sound of Ruby's voice abruptly ended the memory she was experiencing. Trying to avoid conversation, Candace kept silent as she stared into the distance. The last thing she wanted were people probing into her life.

"Seems quiet today," Ruby continued as a second breeze kicked up, causing more of the dead leaves to wisp past the bench. "I see the wind's changing direction. Probably blowing something in from the sea." Not getting a response from the stranger, she tried a more direct route. "My name's Ruby Stratton. It's imperative that we speak."

"Not to be rude but I'd like to be alone."

"We have to talk about why you're here."

"That's really none of your business." With that said, Candace stood up and left the bench. Finding herself heading down Main Street, she had no idea where she was going. Her only motivation was the avoidance of the woman in pursuit. Eventually, Ruby caught up to Candace and pulled on her arm from behind. "Please slow down."

Begrudgingly, Candace heeded her request and waited for her to come face to face. "Why are you following me?" she whispered, trying not to draw attention to herself.

"I want to hire you," Ruby responded, trying to catch her breath.

"I don't fix sinks or anything else."

"I assume you're unemployed."

"Presuming to know anything about me is your first mistake."

"I thought we could just talk."

"That's your second one," said Candace as she walked away.

"Wait, please! It pays extremely well... Ten thousand dollars."

Candace stopped for a moment to consider the offer. Then she returned to Ruby's spot on the sidewalk. "Ten thousand dollars?"

"I'm good for the money, but I won't pay until the job is done."

"Ten thousand won't even buy me a reliable car," replied Candace, beginning what she hoped to be a negotiation. She knew no one would offer that kind of money without having a lot more at their disposal.

"Then I'll double it."

"Just like that?"

"Just like that."

"Then triple it," demanded Candace as a test to see how far she would go.

Looking across the street to Godfrey's Bakery, Ruby spied four women staring back at them through the window. They were all lined up, sipping their coffee. The time for wheeling and dealing was over. "Done."

"So what do you want for that kind of money… a kidney?"

Keeping her eyes glued to the bakery, Ruby knew their conversation had to end once the door opened and Louise Godfrey stepped out onto the sidewalk. She was the owner of the baked goods establishment and unofficial leader of the gossip mongers that congregated at her shop each day.

"We'll discuss it tomorrow," said Ruby, noticing Louise crossing the street toward them.

"I didn't say yes."

"You didn't say 'no' either. Be at my house bright and early," she responded as she turned to speak to the bake shop owner.

The last thing Candace wanted was more interaction with strangers so she started down the sidewalk and disappeared into a nearby alleyway. Fortunately, the passing cars stole Louise's attention away as she crossed the street. Candace was able to make her escape unnoticed, leaving Ruby to fend for herself.

Ignoring Ruby, the bakery owner stepped onto the sidewalk, looking for Candace. "Where did she go?"

"Good morning to you as well, Louise."

"Good day."

"Is that a new sign on your bakery?" asked Ruby, attempting to divert her attention from searching for the newcomer.

Offended by the question, Louise turned her attention back to Ruby. "It's six months old if you consider that new."

"My, how time flies," responded Ruby. She remembered the day the sign was changed. It made the front page of the paper. The insult of using the sign as a distraction also gave her an unexpected pleasure. "It sure is a lovely morning."

"A bit brisk for my taste."

"We are heading into winter."

"I prefer the spring."

"I've always liked the fall."

"It's a bit cold for my taste." Having had enough small talk, Louise turned her attention back to the stranger. "The woman you were talking to... is she a friend of Mr. Blooms?"

"I couldn't say."

"She rode through town with him."

"Did she?"

"She arrived at your house with him. You didn't notice?"

"I suppose she did."

"You followed her to the park and sat next to her."

"Did I?"

"You were just having a conversation with her," noted Louise, growing more frustrated by the moment.

"Indeed I was," replied Ruby, refusing to give her one morsel of information.

"Yet you have no idea what her relationship is with Will?"

"I wouldn't tell you if I did."

"And why not?"

"That's her business."

"You don't chase a person down the street without an objective in mind!"

"Whether or not I have an 'objective' is my business, Louise."

"As a business owner and President of the Chamber of Commerce, it's my business to know other people's business. It's also my duty to welcome people. Being informed is part of the process."

"A process you've certainly perfected."

"Excuse me for having a sense of community."

"Is that what you call it these days?"

"You haven't changed a bit. Even with the recent death of your husband."

"The death of MY husband!" replied Ruby in no uncertain terms. "One day, Louise, you're going to have to get past the fact that Wally fell in love with me, not you. As for change... you try losing the same husband twice." With that said, Ruby turned to leave.

Realizing she went too far, Louise extended a provisional olive branch. "I just pulled some bread from the oven. If you're interested."

Ruby hadn't purchased anything from her bakery in at least fifteen years. She found the idea of walking into the town's gossip hub to be repugnant. The last thing she wanted was to change that pattern. Turning back to her old rival, she responded to the gesture. "My wallet's at home. Maybe another time."

"With the weather turning cold, I got a bit overzealous this morning. I made more than I'll ever sell. One loaf on the house?"

Ruby recognized the only way to end the conversation was to graciously accept the bread. "That's very kind."

Immediately, Louise stepped from the curb and crossed the street. Ruby slowly followed, stopping at the bakery door. There she waited for Louise to return with a loaf of bread, neatly tucked in a paper bag.

Hidden behind a sign in the alleyway across the street, Candace watched the exchange in front of the bakery. Covertly, she had listened to their conversation and was impressed that Ruby had her back. As Ruby left the door of the bakery, it was Candace's turn to do the stalking. Staying out of sight, she followed Ruby past the park and back to her neighborhood. Their previous conversation made her curious and Candace wanted to know more. She studied her every move. Her slow walk and occasional stop to catch her breath caused Candace to conclude that her health wasn't very good. It could be a number of things. Her body looked to be in great shape, and although she had some gray in her hair, her face hardly had a wrinkle on it. Her biggest question of all was what she expected for that kind of money.

Once she reached the house, Candace hid behind a large tree. She watched Will leave the house carrying his toolbox just as Ruby turned into the driveway.

"That was quick," said Ruby.

"Looks like the entire faucet is shot."

"Whatever you think is best."

"I'll pick one up at the hardware store and be back either today or tomorrow."

"Captain Bob knows the type of sink I have." Passing by, Ruby turned back and shoved the bag of bread into his hands. "Take this. You'd think after running a bakery for forty years, the woman would have learned to bake."

Will took hold of the bag and tossed it into the cab. "Thanks, I think."

"Cover it in gravy and it might go down smoother," suggested Ruby as she slowly climbed the stairs to the porch. She was running out of energy fast so she kept moving.

Noticing that Junior had no interest in eating the bread, Will ignored giving the dog a command to leave it alone and followed Ruby back to the porch. An idea hit as his eyes made contact with an old bicycle leaning against the banister. "About that old bike... do you still want to get rid of it?"

"Take it. These legs quit turning wheels and heads a long time ago." Worn out, she entered the house. Will pulled the old bike from the tall grass that had grown through the spokes and packed it toward the truck.

Having seen enough, Candace hurried back to the park where she found her empty bench. She didn't know what to think of the bizarre encounter with the Stratton lady but it definitely gave her something to consider. Then again, maybe not. Her thoughts changed direction as Will's truck pulled next to the curb in front of her. She waited for him to lean over to the passenger side door and manually roll down the window.

"I need to pick up a faucet at the hardware store. Want to go with me?"

"I'm really tired. Would you mind taking me back to your place first?"

"Sure. I'll pick up the part on my way to Ruby's tomorrow," he responded, pushing the door open from the inside.

Candace walked to the truck and crawled in, accidentally slamming the heavy door. "You don't have to change your plans on my account. I'll be fine on my own."

"Ruby's in no hurry to get it done."

"What's she like?"

"Ruby? She's always been good to me. Why?"

"She offered me a job."

"Doing what?"

"She wouldn't tell me."

"You're welcome to stay at the lighthouse as long as you need to."

"I'm not sure what I need," said Candace, clicking the seat belt into the lock.

"One thing you need are your bandages changed. The ones you can't reach. I'll take care of that when we get home."

"Yes, Doctor," she replied, knowing the importance of avoiding infection.

Looking at the new selection of books setting on the center of the seat, Candace was tempted to leaf through them as Will pulled away from the curb. She chose to stare out the window instead. Although the shoppers walking along the sidewalks had changed, their reactions were the same. Will returned a courteous wave to all the folks as he drove by, while Candace studied the looks on their faces. Will-O'-the-Wisp Point rarely saw the arrival of new people so Candace was the newest curiosity.

Staring straight ahead, her inner dialogue presented the question: "How did I end up here?" In a way she was referring to the town, but the question begged a larger answer. Retracing the circumstances of her life, she found herself going back to a simpler time, before she washed ashore in Will-O'-the-Wisp Point.

CHAPTER 5

From the time she was a young girl, Candace had big plans for her life. She loved to dance, and although her parents were lower-middle class, they were able to scrape enough money together to enroll their only child in classes at an early age. Candace was dancing before she could read or write. She studied everything from ballet to tap with the instructor who ran the only studio in town, Ms. Hildebrandt. This lovely woman had spent several years on stage as a professional but her career was cut short by an injury. Her tragedy was a gift to their small town. She was the perfect mentor for a young girl.

Candace soon became her golden child, the star of every show and the captain of the dance team. She received several scholarships which she used at the local junior college to earn an Associates of Art degree, her emphasis being dance. She was the hometown superstar and everyone believed she was destined for fame and glory. Leaving her family and small town behind, she traveled to the city and began life on her own.

Auditions quickly opened her eyes to the competition she faced. Hundreds of dancers just like her were trying for a handful of roles being offered on a regular basis. She was cast in a small show here and there but the money was not enough to live on, so day jobs that worked around rehearsal schedules were a must. Still, she was building a performing arts resume. Years went by and she continued the same process, holding onto her dream with both hands as the discouragement built. It was the same story shared by many.

At first she would return home for the holidays with exaggerated stories of success. Her parents and community couldn't have been more proud. But as the years progressed, her trips home lessened until they stopped all together. Using excuses of work over the holidays made it appear okay. The facade of a successful life continued.

One day close to Christmas, her agent called her into her office for what she thought was a strategy meeting for her career. She hadn't talked to her actual agent since she was reassigned to a junior agent two years earlier, so she was excited to get the call. Walking in the door, she shook her agent's hand with confidence. She wanted to send a signal to the successful business woman that she was still working as hard as she could. Candace's agent had her take a seat in the sitting area away from the desk. After a kind welcome and inquiry into how things were going, her agent changed the direction of the conversation. "Where do you see your career going, Candace?"

The last thing Candace wanted to do was answer truthfully, so she put on her positive face and responded. "There's some great shows announced for next year and I'm really excited about the possibilities. I've been working hard on new audition routines and I think this coming year will be a good one for me. I've also heard of some slots opening up in a couple dance companies."

"Remind me how old your are?"

Her agent knew exactly how old she was, but Candace responded without missing a beat. "I'll be thirty in February."

"In my experience, it's much harder out there for dancers who haven't seen real success in their twenties," she said as she leaned back into the chair and crossed her legs.

"I'm in great shape. I work out and practice every day."

"I'm not saying you don't have great discipline and commitment. Those are two of the reasons I've represented you for so long. I like you as well. But this is a hard industry where only a few rise to the top."

"I can do this. I know I can."

"Have you considered other ways to use your talents to make a living? Teaching is one."

"Teaching?" asked Candace, trying not to react to the lump growing in her throat.

"I've watched you help others perfect their moves while waiting around at auditions. You have a knack for it."

"I suppose I could try to find a part-time job teaching."

"You have a two-year degree. You may want to consider going back for a bachelor's and teaching certificate."

Candace had nothing against teaching, but performance was her true passion. "I can't afford that right now."

"Surely there would be grants available for someone like you."

"I suppose," Candace responded, her head growing foggy at the sound of 'someone like you.'

"When we first met, you told me about all your dance performances growing up. A town with an active community theatre like that would allow you to perform while making a living using your talents in teaching. Moving home might be a good thing for you."

"What exactly are you saying?"

"At the end of each year, I clear the books, so to speak. I've kept you on for a long time, but at this point, representing you is just taking up space."

"You can't drop me. Without an agent, it'll be harder to get auditions for professional shows."

"There are a lot of agencies in this town."

"You know how difficult it will be to get representation."

"I see we've set up two more auditions for you. That's two more chances. If you get cast before the end of the year, we'll talk. If not, consider this our last meeting."

"Please don't do this."

"We all come to points in our lives where we need to reassess,

Candace," she advised as she walked her to the door. "It's decision time. That can be a good thing."

Candace walked through the door, allowing it to shut behind her, and made eye contact with the receptionist who gave her a sympathetic smile. Her walk through the lobby seemed to take forever as employees of the agency passed back and forth. To them, she no longer existed. Stopping at the glass entrance doors, she glanced at several young girls sitting in the waiting area reading old copies of industry magazines. She recalled sitting there once herself, full of hope and prospects. And now it was 'decision time.'

The next day came the first of two last auditions. Everything was riding on her getting cast. She did everything she could to be prepared. She'd worked for this director the first year she moved to the city and it showed on her resume. It was only as an ensemble dancer but she hoped he would remember her. He had risen in fame over the years so this could be the key to turning everything around. As she walked onto the stage to begin her audition, his assistant read her name and told her to continue. The director didn't even acknowledge her presence or look up from the paper he was reading. Still, she gave it her all. She did not receive a callback.

The audition went long, and by the time she arrived at work, she was two hours late. Her boss handed Candace her final paycheck and told her she was late for the last time. Candace pleaded for him to reconsider, but the holidays were a busy time and he'd already hired a replacement. The check she was holding was not enough to pay the rent in her rundown, one-room apartment and she was already behind. It was snowing by the time she left so it was a cold walk home in her dance clothes and jacket.

Things went from bad to horrible when the landlord told her she had one more week to pay the back rent or be evicted. Even if she found a job that day, she wouldn't see a paycheck for two weeks. It was decision time and Candace had finally been humbled enough to call her parents. She spent most of the conversation in tears and her parents just listened. They had no idea things were so rough for their daughter. As soon as the phone call ended, they packed the car for the eight-hour drive.

The next morning, Candace prepared for her last audition. She would give it one last chance. It had snowed all night and was still coming down. She hadn't received word that the audition was cancelled so she headed out. "Maybe less people will show up," she thought to herself as she trudged through the snow. Her audition was flawless, but still no callback. With an apathetic 'thank you,' the assistant director brought an end to her representation and possibly her dreams. She was crushed. On her way through the lobby, a man approached. "Excuse me, Miss Hart. It is Miss Hart?"

"Yes."

"I thought you were great in there."

"Thank you."

"My name is Dante Donadio," he said as he took her hand in his. "I'm an investor in the arts. It's a hobby of mine. I've seen you audition several times and I'm always surprised to see you not cast. You're very good."

"Seems I'm never the right look," she responded, pretending to be in good spirits.

"If they can't see how beautiful, graceful and talented you are, they're crazy."

"I don't think beauty and grace have much to do with being cast as a background dancer."

"If you ask me, you're star material. But I'm just the money man."

"That's nice to hear. Especially today of all days."

"Can I buy you lunch?"

"I can't. I'm expecting my parents to arrive at any time. I have a lot going on today. I'm sorry."

"Here's my card. Give me a call when you have more time and we'll do lunch."

"Thank you," she said as she watched him walk out of the building.

The walk home was a rough one. She wished her mind could let up as easily as the snow had. Today she officially lost her agent and faced being evicted from her apartment. Yesterday she lost her job and at age twenty-nine she was being rescued by her parents. Just as she reached her apartment building, her phone rang. It was her uncle calling. "Strange," she thought to herself before she answered. The news was tragic, causing her to drop to her knees.

Candace jolted back to reality with a loud gasp.

"Are you all right?" asked Will as he pulled up to the lighthouse.

Refusing to let him see the tears forming in her eyes, she quickly exited the truck and ran into the house. By the time Will entered, she was already in the bedroom sobbing into her pillow. Will took the open door as an invitation to the bedroom. He sat down on the side of the bed and waited.

Although her back was to Will, the movement of the mattress told her he was close. She was surprised by the comfort she felt from his presence. Without word or touch, he had a calming effect. Knowing he was there, waiting to help, was exactly what Candace needed. "About those bandages?" she asked, looking for a transition that didn't involve pouring out her heart.

"Whenever you're ready."

"I'm ready." Candace pulled a tissue from the box and slid backwards to the edge of the bed. While Will retrieved his medical kit, she unbuttoned her flannel shirt and lowered it to her waist in preparation. Picking up a blanket, she covered her front out of respect for herself and her caretaker.

Walking toward the bed, Will looked at her back. It resembled a patchwork quilt of horrors. Large blotches of dark blue and purple signified where she'd taken the hardest hits. The bandages were securely in place so he wouldn't know the state of her wounds until each one was removed. Looking into the mirror on the opposite wall, he saw Candace staring back at him.

"It's bad, isn't it?" she asked. "I can tell by the look on your face."

"It could always be worse." Kneeling at the foot of the bed, Will pulled a tube of antibiotic cream from his bag and a variety of bandages. "Taking these off might sting a little."

"I can handle it."

"I'll be as careful as I can," he said, tenderly pulling the first bandage from her skin.

"You have a gentle touch."

"Years of practice, I guess."

"I'm sure that's helped."

Will was pleased at the sight of the first wound. "No sign of infection so far."

"I'm a pretty fast healer."

"That'll help." After applying the cream and proper bandage, he moved to the next sore. Candace continued to watch his face in the mirror as he worked. His eyes drew most of her attention. They were full of compassion from somewhere deep inside. Years of experience may have fine-tuned his skill but his ability to care came naturally. It wasn't long before he'd checked and dressed each wound. Standing up, he lifted her shirt and waited for her to put her arms through the sleeves. Then he turned his back to give her the privacy she needed to button. "I'm going to make some lunch. Are you hungry?"

"I'm good. I think I'll just rest."

"There's plenty of sandwich fixings in the fridge if you want to eat later. I'm going to run down to the fire station for the afternoon." Will picked up his bag and walked out of the room.

Candace laid down on the bed and listened through the open door. The sounds of bread being pulled from a bag, the fridge opening and shutting and Junior's toenails against the floor was the perfect accompaniment to send her off to sleep.

CHAPTER 6

*W*ill closed his book and sat up, frustrated from his inability to get comfortable enough to fall asleep. Leaving Junior's squeaky bed, he walked to the bedroom door and pressed his ear to it. The sound of silence answered his question. With Candace asleep he was free to practice his dance steps. Walking to the well-used cassette player, he pushed the play button and got in position. The sound of the female dance teacher's voice blasted into the room. In a panic, he rushed back to the boom box and turned it down. He quietly chastised himself for being an idiot, then rewound the tape and hurried back to the footprints on the floor.

"*Gently step forward with the left foot. Turn to the left and hold.*" Will was pleased with himself for mastering the first two new steps, his hands wrapped around an invisible partner. "*You have the freedom to choose where your steps will lead. Don't be afraid to take risks.*"

The sound of the bedroom door opening behind him caused him to change his stance. Yanking his arms from the air, he reached out to the cassette player and hit the 'stop' button, then nonchalantly filled a glass with water from the tap. Still embarrassed from being caught in the act, he kept his back to Candace as he poured the water down his throat. After a while he wondered if she was still behind him. Turning around, he saw her standing in the doorway. The awkwardness became palpable as he looked around the room for a way out.

"Is the paramedic in need of a rescue?" she asked, helping to break the silence with some humor.

"I'm sorry if I woke you?"

"I needed a drink, but I didn't want to interrupt."

"Nothing to interrupt here," he replied nervously as he watched Candace take a glass from the cupboard and walk toward the refrigerator. "There's a pitcher of cold water in the fridge. But you already know that. I have juice, too, but it's been in there a while." Unsure of what to say next, Will watched her remove the sixty-four-ounce box of juice, take a whiff, then fill her glass half full. After taking a drink, she stared at Will on the other side of the kitchen. Feeling the pressure to confess, Will decided to come clean about the dance lessons."My youngest brother's wedding is coming up."

"How many brothers?"

"Two," answered Will as he watched her walk toward him. "Sam and Henry."

Candace pulled the cassette player forward on the counter and popped out the tape. "'*The Tango Made Simple*.' Is that even possible?"

"The woman should be sued for false advertising," he answered, circling around the table to avoid squeezing past her. On his way, he pulled a socket and ratchet from one of the kitchen drawers then walked to the bike Ruby gave him.

"So which one's getting married?"

"Sam's the batter up. Henry's already married." Turning the bike upside down, he proceeded to remove the wheels as he continued to awkwardly share more information than he intended. "I want to dance at the wedding... not like a performance! I mean... there's this girl. She's Nancy's best friend... Nancy is Sam's fiancee."

Intrigued, Candace drank more of her juice while watching Will's hands work the tools like a professional.

"The family seems to think we'd be perfect for each other... not Nancy... her friend, Jill. That's her name. Jill. She's supposed to be beautiful, classy and comes from a... well-respected family."

"So Jill's got looks and money. Way to go."

Surprised by her candid response, Will dropped the nut he was removing from the bolt and it rolled away before he could grab it.

"Over there. By the bed leg," she said, directing him to the runaway nut. "I can sleep out here if you want your room back."

"I'm good. Junior's doing better at sharing," he responded, standing up and reaching for his coat. "I need a tool from the truck."

"Good night," said Candace as she passed by his newly-acquired stack of books setting on the counter. "Do you mind if I borrow one of these? It might help me drift off to sleep better."

"Go for it."

She placed the quarter cup of juice on the counter, then pulled the bottom book from the pile and leafed through its heavy pages. Candace recognized it was old and probably quite rare. She wondered if Will realized what he had taken from Ruby's home. Rather than a published novel, the book looked more like a family heirloom. "What a strange book."

The book was written in cursive with an instrument that needed to be dipped in ink: most likely a steel-point pen, rather than a quill. The workmanship of the paper and binding, as well as the ink, was evidence it was written in the mid-to-late 1800's.

"I didn't look at the titles," he said. "I just grabbed a handful off the top shelf.

"I'll take good care of it." Before she entered the bedroom, she turned back with a question. "Why the tango?"

"The library had two options. This or the polka. You think I should have gone with the polka?"

"Only if it's a Polish wedding."

"So the polka and tango aren't common dances?"

"The tango more than the polka, but I wouldn't call it common."

"You know something about dancing?"

"Good night," she said, walking into the bedroom.

Will waited for her to shut the door, then turned his attention to his dog comfortably sprawled out on the bed. "Come on, Junior," he called, stepping toward the door. "And no hogging the bed tonight."

The dog responded by cocking his head to the side, almost to ask, "Whose bed is it?" Will didn't answer. Instead, he smiled at his best friend and opened the door only to have it jerked out of his hand by the force of the cold wind coming off the ocean.

Will's attention shifted from the toolbox to the cliff overlooking the ocean. As he walked through the darkness, the thundering sound of waves crashing against the rocks told him everything he needed to know about the weather: another storm was fast approaching. Reaching the edge, he waited to hear the indistinct voice that the wind so often carried with it. In a way it sounded like a woman calling for help, pleading for someone to listen. Maybe it was the ghost of someone tragically lost at sea or a wife left behind to mourn her loss. His grandfather pointed it out to him one night when Will was a boy. Whatever its origin, the cry for help was usually powerful enough to capture Will's attention. But there was no voice tonight.

The last time he heard the voice was two nights earlier when Candace washed ashore. "A coincidence?" he wondered. It was silly to think that one had anything to do with the other, but she was as mysterious as the voice itself and had materialized the same way. He had more questions than answers and no way of finding out more than she wanted to share. All he knew was that a storm named Candace had blown in from the sea and knocked his world off axis.

The dog returned from doing his business and took his usual position, staring out at the sea near his master's feet. With the wind picking up in speed, Will decided to call it a night before the rain hit. The idea of sleeping next to a wet dog did not appeal. Turning his back to the storm, Will fired off a vocal starting gun. "Let's go, Junior!"

Racing him back to the door, Junior won the race resulting in a victory dance of tail wagging and prancing. As soon as the knob turned in Will's hand, the dog pushed open the door and jumped onto his cozy bed. Although it was past his normal bedtime, Will was far from sleepy. Making himself comfortable at the table, he picked up a well-worn deck of playing cards and began the familiar game of solitaire.

CHAPTER 7

Will pulled into the driveway of Ruby Stratton's home and waited. In silence, they sat together in the cab as Candace surveyed the house. She loved Victorian houses and their asymmetrical design. Ruby's home reminded her of a house she used to pass by on the street she lived on as a child: the shingled roof, the double chimneys, decorative trim, bay windows topped with stained glass panels, and of course, a turret. As a kid she used to dream of living in a house like this. Her eyes stopped when she caught a glimpse of the same girl in the same turret window as the day before. The curtain closed as soon as she made eye contact.

"I'll be at the firehouse. It's just on the other side of town. In case you need anything."

"Need anything?"

"You know... if things don't work out."

"You don't think this will work out?" asked Candace, growing uneasy.

"I'm sure it will work out."

"What made you change your mind?"

"I didn't change my mind."

"So you do think this will work out?"

Will turned and looked into her eyes. He recognized the growing look of panic. "Everything's going to be fine, Candace. You're here to find out what Ruby has in mind. She asked you to come by to discuss the details. It's just a conversation."

"Just a conversation," she repeated, in an attempt to convince herself.

"That's all."

"I can do that."

"Of course you can."

Without another word, Candace opened the door and left the truck. Hearing voices from behind, she turned to see two women walking down the sidewalk, staring at her while talking to each other. It's was obvious that she and Will were the topic of conversation. Candace continued to watch them as they passed by the driveway, then she took a deep breath and started toward the house.

Will watched curiously as she rounded the front of the truck and slowly walked up the steps leading to the grand porch. At the pace she was moving, he wondered if she was having second thoughts. His answer came loudly with her three assertive knocks. The door opened instantaneously as though Ruby was waiting for her cue.

Once Candace entered the house, Will had no excuse to stay so he started the engine and backed out of the driveway. Keeping his eyes on the house in the rear view mirror, he slowly drove down the road, increasing in speed as the distance widened.

AT RUBY'S REQUEST, Candace removed the light jacket Will had loaned her and laid it across her host's extended hand. After hanging it in the coat closet, Ruby turned and walked away. "Wait here for me," she said in no uncertain terms as she disappeared into another room. Due to the feeling of being watched from every angle by the dark faces in the portraits hanging on the walls, Candace didn't dare leave the spot where she was told to wait. Her desire to explore would have to be postponed. For now, she would look but not touch.

Much of the large room was hidden in shadows thanks to the thick curtains covering the windows. What she could see clearly was evidence of decades of fine collecting. Old-fashioned electric lamps lit up the details of several sitting areas, each arranged in groupings of well-maintained period piece furniture. It felt more like an antique shop than a living space. The only thing missing were aged price tags hanging from strings with amounts written in calligraphy.

Books filled the shelves to overflowing and were stacked up the side and back of every chair and love seat, along with old issues of classic magazines. It was hard to tell where the top of the book stacks ended and the wooden end tables began. The lacy doilies protecting the wood surface from the lamps and knickknacks helped to differentiate between furniture and reading material.

"Rose is in her room," said Ruby, startling Candace and drawing her attention away from the decor.

"Rose?"

"Come with me."

Candace watched her walk toward the staircase carrying a tray holding a covered dish, a teapot and three dainty cups and saucers.

Moving through the living room, Candace noticed an old wooden Victrola and paused to lift the lid. Inside she found a vinyl recording of Wales folk music setting on the turntable, just waiting to spin. Intrigued, she gently closed the lid and hurried toward the staircase.

She caught up with Ruby halfway up the stairs, both coming to a stop. Candace observed that her host needed a moment to catch her breath. "Would you like me to carry the tray?"

"I'm perfectly capable," she answered, then slowly made her way to the top of the stairs. Before walking down the balcony ahead of them, Ruby took another break to catch her breath.

"Is everything all right?" asked Candace, concerned by her labored breathing.

"I'm fine." After a moment, she continued down the balcony toward two adjacent doors. Choosing the door to their left, rather than the one facing them at the end, Ruby took a deep breath and quietly entered the room. Candace followed.

The sight of the room immediately piqued Candace's interest. She had never stood in a round room. Curtain-covered windows made up the top half of the curved wall that circled nearly three-fourths of the room. Similar to the living room, the curtains were made of a thick fabric. Her bed, dresser and night stands lined the lengthy flat wall. Bookshelves filled the bottom of the curved wall, stuffed full of books and a few knickknacks.

Candace stood in the doorway as Ruby walked around the bed toward the only window in the room with open curtains.

"Good morning, Rose," said Ruby as she packed the tray toward a thin girl sitting at a small writing desk reading a book. Candace just assumed that the girl facing the window was Ruby's granddaughter. Her long dark hair lay loose against her floral nightgown and had yet to be combed. With great interest, Candace continued to watch from the doorway as the mystery girl closed the book in front of her, slid it to her left and waited for her breakfast to be served. "Good morning, Mother."

"Mother?" Candace repeated quietly to herself in surprise. Moving closer to the bed, Candace noticed the window had an unobstructed view of Will's lighthouse in the distance. "What a beautiful sight to wake up to," she thought to herself. Little did she know that would not be the case this morning.

Seeing the reflection of Candace in the glass, the girl quickly turned toward the intruder with a look of horror on her face. Candace was surprised to find her to be older than she thought—possibly in her early twenties. Her maturity level, she quickly discovered, was much younger.

"You have a guest for breakfast," said her mother, wrapping a supportive arm around her shoulder. She was doing everything she could to lessen the fear her daughter was experiencing. "This is Candace."

Reaching out, Rose grabbed onto the apron around her mother's waist. She began nervously wadding it into a ball while the knuckles on her other hand turned white.

Confused by the scene playing out, Candace tried to make sense of what was happening. She was locked into a stare-down with the young woman while the muted sound of Ruby's coaxing filled the background. Someone had to make a move and they both knew it. While still maintaining eye contact, Candace saw something familiar in her face: a deep-seated fear. A chill ran down her back followed by a sick feeling in her guts as Rose slid from the chair and disappeared from sight. Ruby's coaxing turned to pleading as her daughter crawled under the bed to hide.

Finding it difficult to breathe, Candace hurried from the room. She stopped for a moment and leaned over the railing as she listened to Ruby implore her daughter to come out from under the bed—a request that seemed perfectly normal to Ruby or anyone else involved in a similar situation. But Candace saw the fear in Rose's eyes. A fear so disabling it replaced all rational thought. She had experienced that same fear far too often. At least for Rose, no one was pulling her out kicking and screaming.

Refusing to be swallowed up by the darkness of her memories, Candace ran down the stairs. Before she reached the bottom, Ruby rushed to the balcony. "Candace, wait! Don't go!" Her words came too late. Candace hurried through the living room, grabbed her jacket from the coat closet and left the house.

Unwilling to let it end this way, Ruby carefully made her way down the stairs, hanging onto the railing as she went. Her only hope was catching her before she got too far down the street. Opening the door, Ruby found Candace with her arms wrapped around one of the porch pillars, clinging to it for support.

"I probably should have prepared you better," said Ruby as she stepped onto the porch.

"I don't know what you want from me, but whatever it is, you can forget it."

"Rose needs your help."

"From what I just saw, she needs professional help."

"That's out of the question."

"Why?"

"They'd take her from me," responded Ruby as she walked to the railing to steady herself while the adrenaline slowed in her veins. "If it's more money you want..."

"Give it to someone who can help her."

"You can help her."

"I'm not capable of that!" said Candace firmly.

"Yes, you are! I know you are."

"You don't know me!" yelled Candace as she walked down the steps. "You know nothing about me."

"So many people have been lost to the ocean," called Ruby from the porch.

"So many husbands and sons, swallowed up in its watery grave. Now it's seen fit to give one back."

"What are you talking about?" asked Candace, turning to face Ruby.

"I was on the beach the night you washed ashore, pleading in the storm. The ocean listened and sent you to me."

"The ocean didn't send me here. It didn't suck me in and spit me out for you or that messed up girl," she responded as she crossed the yard.

"Fifty-two thousand, four hundred, twenty-seven dollars and sixteen cents!"

"What?"

"That's how much I'll pay you."

"You've got that kind of money?"

"That's all I've got. It's yours if you'll help my Rose."

Before she could respond, Candace took a minute to think—a moment for them to both settle down. She couldn't believe what she was being offered. That much money would go a long way toward starting over. "What is it you think I can do for her?"

"I want Rose to be married to someone who will take care of her," responded Ruby nonchalantly as she picked up a pre-fitted furniture cover and began placing it over one of the patio chairs.

Shocked by Ruby's declaration, Candace walked back toward the porch. "Married? You've got to be kidding. I'm guessing she's never even talked to a man, let alone dated one."

"It may seem like a challenge after what you observed..."

"Challenge?" questioned Candace, trying not to bust out in laughter from the absurdity.

"I know what's best for Rose. She needs to be taken care of by a good person, a kind man who truly loves her. Someone like Will."

"Will has his sights set on someone else."

"You're missing the point."

"I'm not the one missing the point," argued Candace.

"I realize that marriage may seem like an old-fashioned notion to some."

"There's a whole world of possibilities out there for a girl her age."

"Or a world of hurt!" she snapped back.

Incapable of arguing that particular point, Candace chose to be silent. She needed more time to think. Walking up the steps, she proceeded to help Ruby cover the furniture as she considered the offer.

Neither of them saw the curtain move in the second-story window as Rose's hand carefully slid the window open just enough to listen. She had the perfect spot to eavesdrop on their conversation. Her peaceful existence had been turned upside down and she wanted to know why.

Covering the furniture gave Ruby and Candace some time to think clearly. Ruby jumped back in first. "I've protected her since she was a child and I'll continue to do so as long as I'm able. Will you help me?"

"For fifty-two thousand, four hundred and twenty-seven dollars?"

"And sixteen cents."

"I'd be an idiot to turn that down, but the terms have to be negotiable. There has to be another way."

"There isn't," argued Ruby.

"Do you realize what year we're living in?"

"Do you want the money or not?"

"Of course I do."

"Then we have a deal. Here's some spending money in the meantime, Ms...?" enquired Ruby as she reached into her pocket.

"Candace is good enough."

"For the kind of money I'm paying, I deserve a last name."

"Hart. Candace Hart."

Ruby pulled out some cash and shoved it in her hand. "Consider it a bonus, Ms. Hart." Abruptly, she opened the door and entered the house.

"That turned out to be more than 'just a conversation,'" she said to herself, negating Will's previous advice. Her workday had ended before it even began, leaving Candace wondering what to do next as she attempted to make sense of her morning. Walking toward the edge of the porch, she paused as folk music could be heard from inside the house. The sound of string and wind instruments slowly dancing together had a sadness to it. Although she couldn't understand the Welsh lyrics, they added a melancholy to the music. Candace was drawn to the small open space in the curtains. Peering inside, she saw Ruby leaning back on the couch, her hands covering her face in an attempt to silence her sobbing.

Candace turned from the window and hurried down the steps. Just as she reached the sidewalk, she turned and looked toward the second floor turret. Rose was watching her from the window. But only for a second. Once the curtain yanked shut, Candace continued down the street, repeating to herself, "Fifty-two thousand, four hundred and twenty-seven dollars."

Inside the house, Ruby did what she always did to pull herself out of a slump: fill her mind with memories of a happier time. She thought of the day she first met her husband, decades earlier.

SITTING by herself on the beach, a handsome young man happened along. Ruby usually had a remote piece of shoreline to herself so the sight of another person was a surprise.

Out of breath, he ran toward her. "Have you seen a black dog pass by?"

"No," she replied, rising to her feet and walking away.

"Wait!"

Ruby stopped and waited as he requested.

"Are you new in town?"

"I live out of town."

"That makes sense, since I thought I knew all the pretty ladies in town."

"Don't you have a dog to catch?" she asked, then walked toward a trail leading away from the beach.

"Did I say something wrong?" asked the man as he continued toward her.

"I have to get home."

"Can I walk you home?"

"I know the way well enough."

"My name is Wally. Wally Stratton."

"I really must be going."

"Is it possible to know your name before you disappear?" he asked.

"Why would you want to know my name?"

"I have to call you something during my daydreams."

"Your dog is getting farther away," she reminded him, trying to get the stranger to move on.

"Maybe our meeting was the dog's plan all along."

"I highly doubt that."

The sound of a dog barking turned their attention to the black lab on a dead run toward them. "Looks like your dog has returned."

"It's just like him to return to the scene of the crime." The dog instantly took a liking to Ruby and she reached down to pet him.

"That proves it. He set the whole thing up."

"You're impossible!"

"After all the work he went to, are you really going to disappoint him by not telling us your name?"

"My name is... Ruby," she said in protest. "Now I really must go."

"Until we meet again, Ruby, at our special spot."

"Good day, Mr. Stratton," she replied. As she made her way down the trail, she found herself smiling at the encounter, especially his clever humor and quick wit.

The next day she returned to her spot on the beach and to her surprise found him waiting for her. "How long have you been sitting there?"

"Since dawn. I didn't want to miss you."

"It's afternoon. You've really been sitting here all morning?"

"Make it worth my while and sit with me."

Ruby sat near him and waited for him to start the conversation.

"You know what would make this easier?"

"What?"

"A daily meeting time."

"What makes you think I want to share my special spot with you every day?"

"I'm a hopeless romantic," he admitted as they began the first conversation of many to come.

SITTING UP ON THE COUCH, Ruby smiled as she recalled the beginning of a beautiful romance. Her memories were her go-to place when life became too difficult. They were a respite from the world. A distraction she could always count on for relief. Her tears had dried and she was ready to face the rest of the day.

CHAPTER 8

Approaching the firehouse, Candace studied the brick architecture and well-maintained grounds of the old building. Surprised to see the large bay door open as she grew closer, Candace stopped as a fire truck pulled out of the building.

"Done already?" said Will as he walked up behind her dressed in his paramedic uniform and carrying a bag. Jack sat at his feet eagerly awaiting the command to board the fire truck.

"Like you said, it was just a conversation."

"See? Nothing to worry about."

"I wouldn't go that far."

"What did you think of her?"

"Her?"

"Ruby Stratton."

"She's going to take some getting used to."

"Ready to go?" yelled the fireman behind the wheel of the truck.

"We got a call," said Will. "It's not an emergency, but it could turn into one."

"Don't let me hold you up. I can wait."

"I've got an idea. Joe! Get down here."

Climbing out of the back door, a young man in his early twenties eagerly approached Will and Candace. "Yeah, boss?"

"Take the ambulance and drive Candace back to my place."

"I'm fine waiting," she reiterated.

"He'll be back in no time," yelled Will as he ran around the truck and got in the other side.

Candace shook her head at how fast Will could form a plan and carry it out.

"I'll grab the bus," said the young man as he ran into the building while the fire truck drove away. Within seconds an ambulance came to a sudden stop next to Candace. Jumping out of the vehicle, Joe ran around the front and opened her door. "Allow me. I'm Joe, by the way. But you already knew that."

"Why aren't we taking Will's truck?"

"This ambulance is on loan while ours is being repaired. It was delivered this morning. It's a lot newer than our old one. Will wanted me to take it for a test drive to get used to it."

"When you say test drive... how fast are you planning on driving?"

"I only speed in times of emergency. Safety first."

"That's reassuring," said Candace as she crawled in and put on her seatbelt. She waited for Joe to shut her door and walk around to the other side. "Do you like being an EMT?"

"EMT in training. I'm a volunteer fireman. I assist Will when I'm not doing my mail route. If an emergency comes up, the mail has to wait," he said, shutting the door and returning to the driver's seat. "Most people on my route are all right with that... their mail being late. I eventually get it delivered."

"Are you sure Will doesn't need you?"

"Mr. Hanson's wife went off her meds again. It happens every now and then. After Will gets her straightened out, they need to put the satellite dish back on the top of Mr. Hanson's roof. A tree took it off during the storm a couple nights ago. If Will doesn't do it they'll have to wait for the repair guys to come down from the city. He gets over five hundred channels. Imagine that, five hundred channels." Joe continued to talk non-stop as he familiarized himself with the different switches, buttons and levers on the dash of the ambulance. "I heard Will mention Ruby Stratton. Are you a friend of the family?"

"I'm just helping out around the house."

"That's a big house to keep up."

"Do you know her well?"

"She's on my mail route. We talk every now and then. Mostly about the weather," he said as he turned the siren and lights on and off.

"Have you ever met her daughter?"

"A bunch of us used to play together in the park when we were kids. Rose is a couple years younger than me."

"What was she like back then?"

"Like any other kid."

"How long has it been since you've seen her?"

"Yesterday."

"Really?" responded Candace, surprised by the revelation.

"I see her for a brief moment when I deliver the mail."

"Peeking through the curtain?"

"Yep. It's a two-second encounter. Just enough time to smile and wave," he said as he pulled onto the street and headed out of town.

"How long have you been doing that?"

"Since I started my route... about three years."

"And it's never gone beyond two seconds?"

"Nope. I just move on to the next house down the street. I only have so much time to get my mail delivered."

The subject naturally changed to a different aspect of the postal system as Joe drove down the road. Candace knew she was in for a very instructive ride. Joe was a river of information with no dam to slow the flow. On their way out of town they passed a sign that read, *"Thanks for visiting Will-O'-the-Wisp Point."* Candace was curious about the meaning of the town's name so she waited for a break in his discourse of facts. The break never came. Cutting into Joe's recitation of postal details, she changed the subject. "What kind of name is Will-O'-the-Wisp Point?"

"Scientifically, the term will-o'-the-wisp is used to describe swamp gases which ignite into flames over marshy grounds."

"You live in a town named after swamp gas?"

"In folklore, will-o'-the-wisps are mysterious lights that are said to lead people from their well-traveled paths into dangerous marshes. Some people believe the lights to be lanterns carried by malevolent spirits or mischievous fairies."

"So which is it... swamp gas or evil fairies?"

"That's where it gets interesting. Over a century ago, there was a young woman who lived in a far-off land."

"I'm not getting a two-word answer, am I?" asked Candace.

"Why would you want one?" Her blunt response was completely lost on Joe as he continued with the story. "The woman was beautiful, intriguing and some say magical. In fact, she never aged. Because of these qualities, the men in the land were drawn to her. This went on for many years, even decades, which of course upset the women of the towns she frequented, especially the wives."

"Don't take this the wrong way, Joe, but you probably need to get out more," said Candace as they arrived at the lighthouse. Candace opened the door and stepped out of the ambulance. "Thanks for the ride."

"Don't you want to hear the rest?"

"Maybe next time."

Joe watched her walk toward the lighthouse, dumbfounded that she didn't want to hear the rest of the story. "I didn't even get to the good part yet," he whispered to himself as he turned the ambulance around and headed back to town.

Candace closed the door behind her and slowly slid to the floor—an instant reminder of the sores on her back. Resting her head against the door, she allowed her arms to fall limply to the floor. Still feeling the effects from her battle with the ocean, Candace needed all the rest she could get. The outside evidence of her battle with the rocks was beginning to heal, but the real pain came from the battered and bruised muscles beneath the skin. Reaching into her pocket, she pulled out the cash Ruby had given her for spending money. She straightened each bill as she counted. Twenty-five dollars. Staring down at the money, her thoughts returned to the last time she held that same amount in her hand.

S‍ITTING IN A MUSEUM, she reached in her pocket and pulled out twenty-five dollars and a few coins. It was all the money she had left in the world. She'd paid five dollars admission to leave behind the noise of the city. She needed a place to quietly think—to slow time so she could breathe. Although it was an accident, the guilt of her parents' tragic death was almost more than she could bear. Candace had no one to turn to and nowhere to go. She couldn't go home and face the accusing looks of her extended family, nor the disappointment of the town. Word of her epic failure had to have spread by then.

While counting the dollar bills, she found the business card given to her by Mr. Donadio. "He seemed so kind when we talked," she thought to herself. Building up the courage, she pulled out her phone and dialed his number. She was alone in an obscure exhibit room so no one would know if she was using her phone. She hoped he would answer because she didn't know what to say in a voicemail.

"Hello," came a voice on the other end.

"Mr. Donadio?"

"Yes."

"This is Candace Hart. We met in the theatre lobby several days ago."

He remembered her instantly. "I was hoping you'd call. Does this mean you've found time for lunch?"

"Lunch would be perfect."

They arranged a meeting place and during lunch Candace poured out her heart to a complete stranger. He had an apartment he kept for when he was in the city on business, so he let her move in to the guest room until she got back on her feet. He was her knight in shining armor and it wasn't long before they were dating. The first year they were together, Dante made sure she was in every show he financially backed. It felt incredible to finally have success. He was making her dreams come true. As her self-appointed manager, he controlled her finances and schedule. He made sure she wanted for nothing. At first, it seemed harmless enough until she began to ask questions. Her fairytale soon turned to a tragedy and she had no way of escape. The man she counted on for help was not what he seemed.

PULLING herself out of a trance-like state, Candace did the math. She was headed down the same road she'd already traveled. With nowhere to turn, she accepted Will's kindness just as she had done with Dante. The fear of making the same mistake again caused her anxiety to kick in gear. Soon her heart was racing. The last thing she wanted was to incur another debt she couldn't pay. Years of damage to body, mind and spirit had destroyed her ability to trust in others or even her own instincts. Will didn't seem like the kind of guy who would expect more than she wanted to give, but that was all Candace knew when it came to men.

Working to control her breathing, Candace eventually gained control of her fear and began to think rationally. Just minutes earlier, she was ready to bolt and never look back. Thinking clearly allowed her to recognize the need for a roof over her head and gainful employment. Her knee-jerk reaction would help to serve as a warning —to watch for signs she was heading down the wrong path. It was clear she'd have to fight to keep her past from invading her present and future. The last thing she wanted was to repeat the same terrible mistake twice. Giving into drowsiness, she fell asleep sitting against the door.

CHAPTER 9

Candace woke to find herself curled up on her side, her cheek stuck to the floor. Freeing her face from the sticky goo, she grabbed onto the counter top and painfully crawled to her knees, her eyes coming face to face with a bottle of jam that had tipped over. Knowing the spill was due to human error rather than something Junior tracked in helped her feel a bit more human. Pulling herself to her feet, she placed her elbows on the counter and rested her head in her hands. She'd lost two hours—two hours too many to be spending on a hard floor.

While pondering her situation, her eyes toured some of the finer details of the small room. There wasn't a whole lot of wall space for hanging pictures. What was available held old photos of family. Focusing in on a picture of a teenage boy with what looked like his grandparents made her smile. She wondered if it was Will as a boy. Candace had grown accustomed to much grander surroundings, but the homey, lived-in space had a quaint charm to it. Although she'd just met Will, she could see his personality in every corner. This tiny home was the nucleus of his world, and in a way, his oasis. Candace envied that.

Her eyes came to rest on a stack of cassette tapes setting near the out-of-date tape player. "Interesting taste in music," she whispered to herself as she shuffled through the pile, stopping at a copy of a 1960s album of movie themes. She turned the case over and read the list of songs—each one inducing memories of past dance classes from the time she was old enough to walk. Allowing a brief smile, she ejected the dance instruction tape from the player and inserted the old recording of a favorite song. As she waited for the music to play, she pulled the dirty dishes out of the sink and stacked them on the side. Turning on the hot water, she added the detergent and waited. She could at least make an attempt to earn her keep.

Then it started: *Moon River* from *Breakfast at Tiffany's*. It wasn't Audrey Hepburn singing from the window sill, but the gentle, relaxed voice of Andy Williams carrying her back in time to dance classes with Ms. Hildebrandt. Closing her eyes, she slowly moved her head from side to side, arching backwards while holding onto the sink. It wasn't long before the music swept her away and she began slowly dancing around the kitchen table. Moving gracefully, her classical ballet training was evident as she used the backs of the chairs for support. Her sore muscles sounded off alarms but the music carried her through the pain. Her face showed the emotion of being transported to a happier place. Lost in time, she didn't hear the sound of Will's truck pull up to the house.

Junior couldn't wait for the truck door to open so he could search the perimeter of the house for the scent of foreign invaders. "Don't go far," yelled Will as he pulled his bag from the truck bed and walked toward the lighthouse. Reaching for the doorknob, he heard the sound of music. Cautiously he opened the door just enough to see Candace floating on her toes around the kitchen. Stunned by her talent for dance and the beauty of her elegant movement, he found it impossible to look away. This was a side of his guest he had not expected. Her graceful twists and turns coupled with the romantic music and seemingly apropos lyrics of two drifters... 'after the same rainbow's end...' 'waiting round the bend...' instantly captivated him.

Common sense told him to shut the door and leave her to her privacy, but he was enchanted—taking in every nuance of her movement. Her hair sweeping back and forth, falling across her face with each tip of her head. The shape of her outstretched arms. The pointing of her fingers toward invisible objects. It was as though she was telling a story with her body, a story he wanted so much to understand.

Junior's abrupt entrance through the door brought everything to a crashing halt. Their eyes made instant contact, both recognizing the look of alarm they shared. Fortunately, the sound of water flowing from the sink onto the floor gave them an out. Jumping into action, Will shut off the tap as Candace grabbed a couple dish towels and fell to her knees. Will pulled a pile of towels from the drawer and joined her. As they wiped the water from the floor, they took turns looking at each other but avoiding direct eye contact.

"I'll take those. I won't be doing laundry today so I'll let them dry on the clothesline," said Will as he tried to take the towels from Candace's hand.

"No! This is my fault. I'll hang them out," she responded, clinging to the towels.

"It's not a problem. I'll take care of it."

Relinquishing her grip, Will stood up and left the house with the towels as Candace leaned back against the cabinets, covering her face in embarrassment. It wasn't long before Junior offered his condolences by licking the jam off her face. Disturbed by the dog saliva, she batted his head away but Junior refused to leave her side. Instead, he sat down and waited for her to need him. Recognizing his empathy, she reached out and gently pet the top of his head. "I'm sorry. Forgive me?"

Junior rested his chin across her thigh, hoping she would continue to stroke his head, which she did. Will walked back into the house and began awkwardly rocking back and forth on his heels, unsure of what to say.

"How long were you watching me?" asked Candace.

"Long enough," he responded, relieved she broke the ice first.

"What does that mean?"

"Long enough to be impressed."

"I got caught up in the music."

"Those tapes belonged to my grandparents."

"They had good taste," she responded.

"I'm sorry for spying on you," he admitted, sitting down on the edge of his temporary bed.

"This is your home, Will. You should be able to come and go as you please," said Candace as she rose to her feet and walked into the bedroom, closing the door behind her. The dog looked at him intently, questioning his next move.

"I think she needs her space," he whispered. "We're going to respect that. Let's go."

Junior left the house as Will walked to the counter, replaced the tape in the player with dance instruction and carried it out the door.

Hearing the door shut, Candace wanted to see where he was going. She slowly opened the door and found the main room empty so she walked to the outside door and cracked it open enough to find his truck parked in the same place he left it. Opening the door wider, she looked to the cliff then scanned the distance till her eyes reached the forest in the opposite direction. Catching sight of him just before he disappeared into the trees, Candace was satisfied to believe he went for a walk.

Feeling a chill in the air, she turned on the stove to heat the tea kettle. A nice cup of tea would warm her up as she waited for her host's return from the woods and the next uncomfortable moment. It didn't take long for the tea kettle to announce itself with a whistle. Candace had used her time wisely by adding a large teaspoon of honey to the bottom of the cup. Slowly she swirled the boiling water with a spoon until the honey was melted, then in went the peppermint tea bag and a saucer on top to help it steep. It was her mother's method of making tea.

While Candace waited, she returned to the sink. The water was still warm so she released some of it down the drain and proceeded to wash the dishes. She'd forgotten how much she enjoyed this simple chore. The repetitive swirling of the dishcloth against the cups and dishes was very soothing as she stared out the window toward the coastline. It wasn't long before an odd sensation overcame her: the feeling of being home. Quickly, she shook it off. She had plans for a new life and none of those included a man.

Wiping the counter top, she noticed the cord still plugged into the outlet but the tape player was missing, as well as the dance instruction tape. "Oh, no," she muttered to herself, realizing she'd driven him from his own home to practice in the woods. Grabbing her jacket, she hurried from the house and headed toward the forest at the edge of the clearing. Finding a well-worn path, she followed it into the woods. It wasn't long before she could hear the voice of the dance teacher giving instructions. *"Slowly step back with the right foot, remembering to keep the knee flexed while keeping the left foot in place."*

She found herself in the same situation as Will just a half hour ago, spying on him while he danced. The setting was beautiful and serene but the stumps and roots made it no place to practice dance. *"Rotate the left foot counter clockwise and close to the right foot without shifting your weight onto the left foot, keeping your knees pliant,"* instructed the voice from the tape.

"Are you kidding me?" yelled Will, focusing his frustrations on the tape player. "How is that even possible?"

"It's all right to be frustrated," answered the voice from the instructor. *"Just don't give up."*

Candace covered her mouth to keep her reactive outburst stifled as Will looked at the tape player with surprise. Then he diligently tried again. Turning her back, she leaned up against a tree and focused on what she was feeling. It was laughter. Candace had rediscovered what the urge to laugh felt like. It was as though her body and mind were waking up from a coma. The joy soon turned to sadness as she realized how much had been take from her. The slippery slope of emotion continued from sorrow to shame.

Drowning in morose, she turned to sneak down the trail just as the next set of instructions sounded through the trees. *"Those who tango know that it's danced with the heart. Steps must be learned but true passion for the dance, as for anything worth pursuing, comes from within. Don't give up until you find it."*

The words resonated with Candace, stopping her from leaving the forest. She wanted desperately to find her passion, to once again feel her heart beat with enthusiasm. Her dream of becoming a professional dancer was the last time she felt passion for anything. She made the commitment and was willing to put in the time and work necessary. Candace recalled years of choreographing routines, grueling workouts and disparaging auditions. Although she saw small successes along the way, she'd come to view the entire experience, ten years of her life, as an epic failure. An easy thing to do when you're at your lowest point.

As Candace contemplated her past, a ray of sunlight burst through the clouds and fell on her face. The warmth of the sun combined with the dance instructor's intermittent pep talks changed her perspective. "I used to be a fighter!" she whispered boldly. Her lengthy pursuit of a dream proved it. She fought for what she wanted her life to be. It was her choice to make. She gained too much from those years to consider it a failure. Candace stood bewildered, trying to equate her former self to the woman she'd become. Again, the word 'failure' crashed her thoughts. This time she didn't allow it to stay.

"Why can't I get this?" yelled Will in frustration.

Looking back, Candace commiserated with him as he tried to master the same step over and over. She knew how frustrating that could be. More than that, she knew she could help. Taking a deep breath, she entered the grove, resolved in some small way to pay back the man who had bent over backwards to help a stranger. "Is this your dance studio?"

"For the moment," responded Will, surprised to see her.

"Spacious."

"The only drawback is not having my step patterns. They don't stick to the ground very well."

"You could always draw them in the dirt," she joked, continuing toward him.

"I'll take that into consideration."

Candace stopped within inches of him and placed his hand around her waist and took the other in her hand. "Show me what you know."

Awkwardly, Will fidgeted as he tried to hold onto her. "It feels different with a real person."

"The tango was designed for two."

"I'm aware of that."

"The embrace should be more relaxed. Like a hug."

"A hug?"

"Like when you wrap your arms around someone."

"I know what a hug is," responded Will nervously.

"Whenever you're ready."

"Ready?"

"Generally, the man leads the woman."

"Of course." With a sudden lunge, Will yanked Candace to his right as he tried to remember what foot to put where. Mechanically, he moved her around the grove, occasionally stepping on her toes while twisting her back and forth. After a few minutes of jarring movement, a wrong turn led to tangled feet and they both fell to the ground.

"Are you all right?" asked Will, sincerely concerned for her well-being.

"Yup! The stump broke my fall," she responded, trying not to show the pain she was feeling as she rolled onto her hands and knees.

Will leaped to his feet and offered his hands for assistance, which she gladly accepted. Once upright, Candace bent over and arched her back in an attempt to stretch her sore muscles. "I think we should start with a basic dance step first. That way you can feel what it's like to move with a partner before we tackle the tango."

"You don't have to do this. Go back, soak in a hot tub, and relax. "

Candace turned to face Will and held out her arm. "Do you want to learn this dance or not?"

Swallowing his pride, Will took her in his arms the same way he had done the first time.

"A hug, remember?"

Will tried again, but he could tell by her reaction that he was doing it all wrong, so he dropped his hands to his side. "I'm not a dancer. I don't know what made me think I could do this."

"It's just two people embracing each other. Many dance teachers will tell you to hold your partner like a baby."

"I've never actually held a baby outside of emergency medical treatment."

"That's fine. I'm sure you held the baby securely, but gently. Not too loose, but not too tight."

"You're seriously telling me to hold you like a baby?"

"Yes."

"I thought learning the steps was intense."

"The embrace is crucial. It's also important to surrender yourself to your partner. The tango is a very passionate dance. You want to feel something between the two of you. If you can get the embrace right... Jill will be putty in your hands."

"Here we go," said Will, after taking a deep breath. Gently he wrapped his arm around her back just below the left shoulder blade. Then he lifted his right arm and connected with her hand, making full contact with Candace's left arm.

"We're going to start with a simple box step," she instructed.

"I like simple."

"Step with your left foot forward into a closed position. Good. Step back with your right foot. Now step to the side with your right foot into a closed position. Then move your left foot to side. Right foot back, closed position. Left foot forward. Left foot side, closed position. Right foot side. Right foot close, left foot close. And that's it."

"Seems simple enough."

"Good. Let's do it again."

"How's the embrace?" he asked.

"Much better. Left foot forward into a closed position..."

Holding her in the proper position, Will moved Candace around the grove, performing the same steps over and over. The more he repeated the steps the more confident he became. At one point he spun her out and drew her back to him just for fun. The torture he had endured for more than a month suddenly became enjoyable. Their afternoon in the grove produced the perfection of the box step and taught Will how to hold a woman in his arms. It also gave him the assurance he so desperately needed.

Will wasn't the only one who gleaned something from the experience. By giving a gift she didn't think she could afford to share, Candace opened her heart to a measurement of the passion she once felt. For years she blamed dancing for getting her into the terrible situation she had endured. Candace swore she'd never perform again. Dancing through a forest with a relative stranger opened her eyes to a greater truth. It wasn't her love for dance that started her down the wrong path, but her refusal to broaden her tunnel vision.

Leaving the grove, they made their way down the trail. "How did you end up living at a lighthouse?"

"When I was a kid my parents used to send me down here to spend the summers with my grandparents. My grandma was the principal at the elementary school for a long time and my grandpa was the lighthouse keeper."

"So you followed in his footsteps?"

"Oh, no. Everything's electric now. No need for a keeper. The lighthouse has been passed down through the family. It was built by my great-great-grandfather, a retired ship's captain. My grandpa told me it was his father's way of staying connected to the sea."

"Your parents never lived here?"

"Dad was raised here but moved out as soon as he graduated from high school. He went to college, made his fortune and never looked back," answered Will as they reached the lighthouse. "I've still got some daylight hours left so I'm going to split some wood." He placed the tape player on the counter inside the door then walked toward the truck.

"I can help," offered Candace.

"Have you ever split wood?"

"What exactly does that entail?"

"Hop in. My turn to do the teaching."

As they drove to the fallen tree, now limbed and cut up in small, more manageable logs, Candace returned to their previous conversation. " You never answered my question."

"What question was that?"

"How did you end up living here?"

"After Grandpa died, Grandma was alone so I moved down here my senior year of high school to stay with her. She died about ten years ago and I'm still here."

"It's a nice inheritance."

"My dad owns it," he said as he parked the truck near the wood and got out.

Candace followed and watched as he pulled a splitting maul from the back of the truck. Using the largest log for a base, Will placed a smaller piece on top of it and swung his maul through the air. With one strike it split in half.

Impressed by Will's prowess with the maul, she watched him place the second half of the log onto the chopping block and take another swing. "What will you do with all these pieces of wood when you're finished?"

"Burn them in the wood stove to heat the house."

"That one stove heats the whole house?"

"Easy to heat a tiny house," he said while setting up another log and taking a swing.

"You really love this place?"

"I guess you could say it's in my blood. Dad keeps talking about selling it and I keep talking him out of it. He thinks if he sells it I might have to make something out of myself," responded Will as he struck another large piece with even more force than the ones before.

Candace could tell it was a touchy subject by the increased force of each swing. He was taking his aggression out on the wood, relieving his frustration in a productive way. "He's not happy with you saving lives and fixing sinks?"

Feeling slighted, Will split the log then rested his maul on the ground, using the end of the handle for support. "This is my town, Candace. I care about these people."

Then he placed another log on the block and took a swing.

Candace got the message so she moved on to a different topic. "Have you ever met Rose?"

"Sometimes I catch a glimpse of her in the window. I don't think anyone's seen her since she was a girl." Needing to clear some space for more pieces to fall, Will leaned his maul up against a log and started stacking wood in the back of the truck.

"It's not because they haven't been watching. Everyone in this town seems to want to know everyone else's business. Typical."

"What does that mean?"

"People can't be trusted," said Candace, refusing to see it any other way.

"That's a bit of a leap, isn't it?"

"It's true."

"You can't paint an entire town with one broad stroke."

"I'm just calling it like I see it," she responded, allowing her lack of trust in human beings to surface.

"So you're an expert on the topic."

"Life has taught me everything I need to know about people."

"You know what I love about splitting wood?"

"It's a practical workout?" she replied.

"It helps me to think. It's just me and my splitting maul, surrounded by the silence of nature."

Candace leaped from the tailgate and walked toward the house. "I'll leave you to your silence."

Before she got too far, Will offered some advice. "Splitting wood can also be great therapy. You might want to take a swing or two." Smiling to himself, he continued to stack the pieces of wood in the back of the truck as he kept an eye on her until she entered the house. He'd been more direct than usual but didn't regret the advice he offered.

As a paramedic, Will was skilled and very proficient at dealing with physical ailments. Candace's wounds extended deep below the surface. Without her opening the door, there was nothing he could do to help.

CHAPTER 10

It was her second day at work and Candace planned to make the most of it. Carrying the tray of food that Ruby had prepared, she walked up the stairs and across the balcony to Rose's room. With her last experience fresh in her mind, she turned the doorknob with apprehension and slowly entered the room. "Good morning, Rose."

The sight of Candace caused Rose to clutch the book she was reading tightly to her chest. The tension on her face intensified with each step Candace took. Reaching the desk beside her, Candace put down the tray and took a seat in the chair across from her, blocking her exit to the door. "Your mom will be up in a minute."

Rose's level of discomfort was evident by how white her fingers were turning as she gripped the book for dear life. Like a caged animal, she watched Candace's every move, waiting for an opportunity to escape.

"It's a shame you don't open all the curtains. More sunlight would brighten your room." Per normal, she received no response. Hoping to ease her pain, Candace reached out to lift the book from her arms, but Rose refused to let it go. It was her shield and all that was standing between her and the intruder.

"You must read a lot," said Candace as she pointed to the book-filled cases that covered the lower third of the wall. Hoping to show Rose they had a shared interest, she stood up and moved to the bookshelves.

Instantly, Rose darted from her chair, crawled across the bed and ran from the room. She was so fast that Candace barely caught a glimpse of her out of the corner of her eye.

"Rose!" Running after her, she reached the bathroom door just as Rose slammed the door and turned the lock. "Rose. Come out of there. Your breakfast will get cold. Rose, please." After a lengthy attempt to get her to open the door, Candace finally conceded defeat and walked back down the stairs. She could tell that Ruby knew exactly what happened by the look on her face as she entered the kitchen. "Didn't go so well?"

"She's locked herself in the bathroom."

"This won't be easy, but stick with it," said Ruby nonchalantly as she mixed in a bowl.

"I've got nowhere else to be. Since it's only ten o'clock, what can I do to help?"

"I'm not paying you to be my maid."

"I'm pretty much done until she comes out, unless you want me to break down the bathroom door."

"I doubt that would be the best approach."

"Then give me something to do."

"Do you knead?" asked Ruby.

"Need what?"

"Bread. Do you know how to knead bread?"

"I think I can handle it," said Candace as she walked next to the counter.

"Get yourself an apron."

Candace did as Ruby requested and grabbed an apron off a hook near the door. Pulling it over her head, she tightened it behind her and stood ready to help. "Bring on the dough."

"The counter in front of you has been wiped down. Sprinkle some flour on it and start kneading." Ruby watched her apply flour to the counter then drop the ball of dough in the center. She was impressed with how gently she pressed the dough away from her with the heel of her hand then folded it back toward her. She had definitely done this before.

"Thank you for letting me help."

"I could use the extra muscle today," responded Ruby as she sat down at the small kitchen table to catch her breath.

"You're not well, are you?"

"It'll pass."

"For the moment."

"Your concern is Rose, not me."

"Is that why you want Rose married? Are you dying?"

"You certainly don't mince your words."

"Neither do you."

"Your concern is Rose, not me," reiterated Ruby. "I picked up some essentials for you at the store. A couple bras, some underwear and socks, as well as a few other things you probably need. The bag is by the front door."

"You didn't need to do that."

"Are you telling me that Will has a drawer of female undergarments and toiletries?"

"No, he does not."

"I put a pair of canvas walking shoes in there as well. Our feet look to be closer in size than those clodhoppers you're wearing."

"Thank you."

"We'll consider it a trade for kneading the dough. You're welcome to go through my closet and find some better fitting clothes as well."

"Thanks, but I'm fine."

"Fine with dressing like a man?"

"For now," responded Candace. The mindless task of kneading dough gave her time to think about Ruby's question. She wasn't exactly sure why she was so comfortable in Will's oversized jeans and shirt. In a way, she was hiding inside them, dealing with her feelings of being lost. She also knew her sense of self had been stolen. Wearing his old clothes allowed her time to piece it back together naturally.

The last thing she needed was the pressure or expectations of looking a certain way.

"How's the dough feeling?" asked Ruby.

"The texture feels great," responded Candace as she changed focus. "It's got a nice elasticity."

"It's a beautiful recipe. A woman I boarded with when I was younger taught me to make bread. She was extremely gifted in the kitchen. I learned to cook from her."

"Did she live here?"

"Outside of town, near the wharf."

"Can I ask you a personal question?"

"How personal?"

"Is Rose's father in the picture?"

"He was taken from us when Rose was a girl."

"I'm sorry."

"And now you're wondering if that led to Rose's current circumstances."

"I didn't say that."

"You didn't have to. One plus one equals two."

"So did it?"

"Losing my husband changed many things."

"Did you meet here or move to town after you were married?"

"He was born and raised here. This was his family home."

"How did you meet?" enquired Candace.

"On the beach one day. He was chasing his dog when we ran into each other. We started meeting for walks along the beach and the rest is history."

"What made you fall in love with him?"

"That's a little personal."

"Sorry. I'm just curious."

"At first it was his sense of humor. He reminded me how wonderful it was to laugh."

"Had you forgotten?"

"Yes."

"Me too," whispered Candace as she stopped kneading the dough and stared out the window.

"The world can be a dark place without laughter," said Ruby, surprised by what seemed to be a shared experience.

"And after that?"

"He earned my trust."

"How did you know you could trust him?"

"He never tried to change me. We loved with an honesty that allowed us to be ourselves. That's real trust."

Candace dropped the ball of dough into the mixing bowl then quickly removed her apron. "It feels done. I forgot I have to be somewhere," she said walking toward the door.

"Will you be back today?" asked Ruby.

"I'll be here tomorrow," she answered before leaving the kitchen. Within seconds, she'd grabbed her jacket and made it out of the house. The front porch had become her safety zone, the center pillar her comfort object. It was something she could hug tightly while catching her breath and calming the urge to explode. The only hug she'd known for years was the one that came after the threat, after the punishment. The consolation prize designed to wound the inside as much as the outside. Her arms were weights hanging at her side as she felt his crushing embrace. Slowly she would reciprocate, knowing full well what would happen if she didn't. She was trapped in a vicious cycle that worsened each time. Dante's hug delivered the message that she was a prisoner with no end in sight. In a very real way, Candace longed for someone to wrap their arms around her, to feel the safe, reassuring embrace of a friend or loved one. She feared her lack of trust would never allow that to happen.

"Are you all right?" asked Ruby from the open door.

Ruby's voice disconnected Candace from the past. "I'm fine."

"You forgot your essentials."

Still a bit dazed, Candace turned to see Ruby pointing to the paper bag near the door. It was a beautiful large boutique bag with the store name written in cursive: *Leblanc's Embellishments and Remedies.*

Candace wrapped her fingers around the handle and turned to leave. "Thanks again."

"Candace?"

"Yes."

Ruby paused for a moment, then wished her well as she closed the door. "Have a good day." She wanted to say something profound to Candace, but with no context, she feared making it worse.

Walking through town on her way to the fire station, Candace did some window shopping. She looked like the typical shopper packing the bag Ruby had given her. Christmas was everywhere so she decided to take a different route through the backstreets. When she arrived at the fire station, there was no one attending it. Probably a common occurrence in such a small town. Without a ride home, Candace decided to walk. It wasn't so far that she couldn't make it before dark and the exercise would do her good. The sky was overcast and threatening but the view and the sounds made up for it.

About a mile out of town, a truck slowed down next to her. "Can I give you a ride?" asked Jack Segal. He wasn't dressed in his uniform so Candace had no idea he was a member of the Coast Guard.

"I think I'm all right," she replied.

"Those clouds look like they're about to open up."

"It is getting darker."

"Where are you headed?"

"To the lighthouse."

"You must be the newcomer everyone's talking about."

"I guess that's me," responded Candace as rain started landing on the windshield.

"Here it comes."

"Looks like it."

"I'm a friend of Will's," said Jack. "We work together on occasion. Hop in before you get soaked."

"Candace opened the door and crawled into the warm cab, placing the bag near her feet.

"The name's Jack Segal. Nice to meet you," he said as he put the truck in drive and continued down the road.

"I'm Candace. Are you a fireman?"

"Only if they need me."

"So you volunteer?"

"When I'm not patrolling the ocean. I'm an officer in the Coast Guard."

Candace chose not to respond, turning her attention to the passing view. She was afraid of what he might do if he found out she was lost at sea. She hadn't seen any news so she wasn't sure if her boyfriend had declared her missing. The last thing she wanted to do was to be found alive.

"If you're wondering if anyone's reported you missing at sea, the answer is 'no.'"

"Then you know who I am?"

"Will called me the morning after he rescued you. Since no one was looking, we decided to leave things up to you."

"Thank you."

"I trust Will's judgment. He's a good man."

"He seems to be," she agreed.

"I was best friends with his dad growing up."

"Do you still keep in touch?"

"I tried, but friendship is a two-way street. The only thing we share is an ongoing joke about a pair of boots he's owed me since we were seniors in high school."

"That must be some story."

"The stories I could tell," he chuckled as he approached the lighthouse. "There's Will's truck. He must be home."

"Thanks for the ride, Mr. Segal."

"Call me Jack."

Candace smiled and left the truck. She hurried to the house to avoid getting drenched. The house was empty when she walked in. "Will? Are you here?" She walked into the bathroom and sat the bag by the sink then continued her search. Making her way to the bottom of the spiral staircase, she tried again. "Will?" Still no response. His cassette player was on the counter so he couldn't be rehearsing in his outdoor studio. Not that the wet weather would allow such a thing.

The door opened just as she walked back into the kitchen. Junior rushed through the opening and straight toward Candace. He was wet from the rain so she quickly grabbed a dish towel and wiped him down as best she could.

"Thanks for drying him off," said Will as he entered, packing a six-foot Douglas Fir with one hand and a hand saw with the other. "I was hoping the rain would hold off till we got back from the woods, but no luck. Can you grab that bucket in the corner and fill it half full of water?"

Candace obliged as he packed the tree through the kitchen and into the room housing the staircase. Candace joined him, and Will stood the tree in the bucket then leaned the top against the corner. "Thanks. The floor is concrete. I'll wipe it up later after the water drips off the branches."

"Is that what I think it is?" asked Candace.

"Tis the season. I like to put the tree up a little after thanksgiving so I can enjoy it longer."

"Won't it dry out?"

"A fresh-cut tree lasts longer than the ones you buy at a Christmas tree lot. They're cut earlier for shipping."

"When are you going to decorate it?"

"It'll dry off by tonight. I've got to head back to the station," said Will as he walked to the door. "I'll grab a pizza and bring it home for dinner. What kind do you like?"

"I'll just pick off what I don't like." She couldn't remember the last time someone asked her what she wanted.

"And that would be?"

"Sausage and pepperoni."

"I'll do my best. See you later," said Will as he shut the door behind him and Junior.

Left standing in the room with the tree, the smell of the ruffled needles caught her attention. She leaned in closer and breathed deeply. It'd been a long time since she smelled the scent of a Christmas tree. It reminded her of being a kid and going to the tree lot with her parents to pick one out. The memory was nice but didn't last long. As usual, it was chased away by the pain and guilt she still felt about her parents' deaths. Leaving the room, she shut the door behind her to trap the scent inside.

Feeling wiped out from her morning, Candace decided a nap was in order. She was still recovering and could use more rest in the process. It seemed her eyes were shut only for a few minutes when a knock was heard at the door. Crawling off the bed, she walked through the kitchen and answered the door. It was Jack Segal.

"Good afternoon, Candace."

"Hello."

"When I got back to the office I saw a missing person's report on my desk," he said, holding up a form with her picture on it. "I had to perform due diligence and report that you had been found."

Finding it hard to breathe, Candace backed away from the door as Jack walked toward her. "I called the authorities up north and they said your boyfriend's been desperately searching for you. In fact, Dante Donadio's boat is currently docked at our port. He's been trying to find you."

"Hello, Candace," came a familiar voice from the doorway as Dante entered the house behind Jack.

"No. I won't go back!" she yelled, backing into the bedroom with no way of escape.

"Dante's come all this way to find you, Miss Hart."

"Don't let him take me!" she screamed as she ran out of space. Her back was pressed to the concrete wall as Dante stepped in front of Jack.

"I'll give you two some privacy to work this out." Jack walked out of the bedroom and closed the door behind him.

"Don't leave me with him!" she screamed over and over as Dante approached.

"Candace. Candace, wake up!"

Sitting up in bed, Candace found Will next to her. "Where is he?" she screamed. "Where is he?"

"Where's who?"

Realizing it was a nightmare, she tried to collect herself as her mind processed the fact that it wasn't real.

"It was just a dream. Are you all right?"

Still unable to speak, she nodded her head as an answer.

"I'll get you a drink," said Will.

As he left the room, Candace could feel the tears forming, so she jumped out of bed and ran into the bathroom. With the door locked behind her she felt free to fully react to her nightmare.

"Candace. Are you okay?" came Will's voice from the other side of the door. "I'm here... if you need to talk."

The last thing she wanted to do was talk. She needed an excuse to stay in the bathroom. "I'm going to take a bath."

"Okay."

With that said, she turned on the taps and adjusted the temperature. She'd never been so grateful for slow water pressure. The longer she could hide out in the bathroom, the better. Leaning over the sink, she looked at her reflection in the mirror. The fear she felt was an instant reminder that although she'd found refuge at the lighthouse, she still wasn't safe. "Fifty-two thousand, four hundred, twenty-seven dollars and sixteen cents," she said to herself. She would use the money to get as far away as she could.

AFTER A LENGTHY SOAK in the tub, Candace dried herself off and pulled the new undergarments from the bag. It wasn't long till she felt like a woman again, underneath at least. Ruby had purchased everything she could possibly need, including a hairbrush, deodorant and lotion. Ready to face Will, she left the bathroom and walked into the kitchen. The smell of pizza filled the air—a wonderful discovery since she hadn't eaten since breakfast. Looking through the open door at the end of the kitchen, she saw Will decorating the tree. He had it placed in a stand and covered with lights. The star on top was the twinkling type she remembered from when she was a kid. The small room was bright with color but nothing came close to the joy that lit

Will's face. This was pure enjoyment. The last thing she wanted to do was ruin his tradition with her somber mood.

As far as she could tell, he was unaware of her presence so she quietly lifted the pizza box lid to see what was left. A quarter of the pizza was missing from what was clearly the meat side. The other half was full of all the vegetable toppings Candace loved. She smiled at his thoughtfulness while placing two cold pieces on her plate. Then she grabbed a can of ginger ale from the six pack nearby and snuck back into the bedroom. She made herself comfortable on the bed and began to eat. Noticing the borrowed book on the nightstand, she picked it up and gently opened the cover. A yawn told her she might not make it far. Curiously, she began to read as she nestled her head into her pillow.

Can a life still be considered a life if units of time do not pertain? Are birthdays irrelevant if the passing of years has no consequence on your physical being? Could it be this woodland creature spent too much time thinking during the countless years of her existence? Or is it possible the subjects of her contemplation needed to evolve? All questions for further reflection. For now, she will continue her pastime for her thoughts are the only true friends she has.

For centuries, one of Rhue-wyn's favorite thinking spots was the beautiful Ffos Anoddun, a secluded gorge on the River Conwy in the country of Wales. The moss-covered rock walls lined a narrow waterway that ran through a beautiful forest. The music of the gorge was magical as the water moved over the rocks beneath a choir of birds singing in the canopy of trees. The low-hanging branches created the perfect camouflage, and as the seasons changed, so did the colors, transforming the gorge from luscious green to every shade from yellow to red. The forest was the only home Rhue-wyn had known until her curiosity grew beyond its wooded borders.

She longed to step out of the shade and into the sunlight. To walk beneath a full sky instead of the passing glimpses of blue between the leaves. To let the wind blow across the meadow and tangle her hair. To sail a body of water so massive the distant shore could not be seen. What far-off lands would the open sea allow her to visit? What adventures would it allow her to have?

Wanderlust filled her heart, and each time a passerby would take a shortcut through the forest, she would study them intently while others of her kind were content to play mischievous games with them. Playing tricks on humans was a favorite pastime for those who lived in the forest. It would be dishonest to say that she didn't enjoy it herself on a frequent basis. They all possessed their own natural strengths—abilities that were honed and perfected, usually on humans as they passed through. Rhue-wyn's ability as an enchantress was unique and in her opinion the most fun. She was born with the innate ability to mesmerize. Nevertheless, once she set her sights on walking amongst the human race, she kept her distance in order to observe them. As time passed, she learned enough of their ways and mannerisms to fit into their world. At that point she left the forest behind. Her adventure was only intended for a season, but the road she traveled never allowed for her return. She was Rhue-wyn of Nant Ddaear-y-Llwynog and this is her story.

Although Candace found the book interesting, it soon became impossible to keep her eyes open. She drifted off to sleep, allowing the book to slide from her hand.

CHAPTER 11

*D*ay three at work. Candace entered quietly through the back door, crossing through the kitchen and entering the living room. Placing her finger across her lips, she signaled to Ruby to remain silent, then whispered in her ear. "Did Rose ever leave the bathroom?"

"It took me three hours after you left yesterday but I finally got her to come out."

"Do me a favor," whispered Candace.

Ruby listened to her plan and agreed to play along. Putting a limited amount of trust in her judgment, she waited until Candace crept to the top of the stairs and into the bathroom.

Rose waited in her room for Candace to arrive. Her mother had told her that Candace was only trying to help, but Rose wanted nothing to do with this stranger complicating her life. She was on her own and she knew exactly what to do to protect herself. Standing at the window looking over the driveway, she parted the curtain just enough to spy on the street below.

"How are you today, Candace?" Ruby's words echoed to the second floor and penetrated Rose's heart. She opened the door, ran into the bathroom and slammed it behind her. Twisting the lock, she breathed easy until she turned and saw Candace sitting on the back of the toilet.

Candace stepped off the toilet and walked toward her. She'd already tried the nice approach, now it was time to lay out what she expected. "I'm going to talk and you're going to listen. Your mother hired me to do a job and since I need the money, I'm not going anywhere."

Rose slowly slid along the wall until she wedged herself between the sink and the corner, pressing with all her might against the wall.

"I've got nothing but time, so you decide how long this is going to take." Having said her piece, she unlocked the door and left the bathroom. "And the door stays open."

Rose slid down the wall to the floor, allowing herself to breathe for the first time since the shock of seeing Candace. She had underestimated the interloper and now she was in over her head. The sound of the front door shutting allowed her to crawl to her feet and run from the bathroom. She hurried to her bedroom window facing the street and separated the curtains with her outstretched fingers. She only needed an inch or two to find out if her nemesis had left the house. She breathed a sigh of relief once she saw her leave the yard and head down the sidewalk. Before she could close the curtains, she spied Joe entering the driveway.

Dressed in his Postal Service uniform and pushing a rolling cart with a mail bag attached, he walked into the driveway. Rose watched him like a hawk in the sky, wondering if he would look up as he always did. Approaching the porch steps, he glanced toward Rose, smiled and waved. Closing the curtains, Rose turned her back to the window and placed her palm over her mouth to conceal her giggle. One of her favorite moments of the day was getting a wave from the mailman. It made her feel connected to the outside world without having to hear the voices of passersby sharing their cruel analysis of her past and grim predictions for her future. Turning back to the window, she parted the curtains just in time to see him walk down the sidewalk. She watched until he disappeared from view—officially ending her social time.

Checking to make sure the window was closed tightly, she walked across the room to the window facing the lighthouse. Picking up her binoculars, she strained her eyes to see as far as they would allow. The sky was hazy, making it more difficult to see. A quiet knock on the door caused her to quickly lower the binoculars to their resting place. She turned just in time to see her mother enter the room.

"How did it go with Candace this morning?" She asked, walking toward her.

"I hate that she's here." Rose plopped down on her chair and folded her arms as though she were a sulking six year-old.

Ruby picked up her hairbrush and began combing through her long dark hair as they both stared out the window. "She wants to be your friend, Rose. You need to give her a chance."

"I don't need friends. Especially her."

"Having a friend can be a wonderful thing."

"She's not here to be my friend."

"What makes you say that?"

"You shouldn't have to pay someone to be their friend."

Ruby realized she was talking about the offer of money she made to her that first day. Not sure how much Rose heard, Ruby decided to test the waters. "I'm not paying her to be your friend."

"She told me you hired her to do a job."

"I'm paying her to help both of us. She needs the money and I need the help."

"Help with me."

"Give her a chance, Rose," advised Ruby as she placed the brush on the table and walked toward the door. "I'll have lunch on in a few minutes."

"I'm not hungry."

"Suit yourself," said Ruby as she walked toward the door.

Once Ruby left, Rose moved from the chair to her bed. She lifted the glass lid from an old-fashioned jar setting on her nightstand. Reaching in, she pulled out a wishbone. Holding it with both hands, she wanted to snap it in half—to wish Candace would go away and leave her alone. Before she could follow through, the sound of laughter stole her attention. The voices were snickering at her again. In a panic, she crawled over the bed and ran toward the window. Finding it already closed, she fell to her knees, plugged her ears and waited.

CANDACE APPROACHED THE LIBRARY—a small colonial-style, two-story, brick building. She needed to speed things up with Rose and thought she might find a book written by an expert on the topic. Once inside, she stopped to take a look around. The sitting area to her left was furnished with comfortable chairs and lamps for better lighting. It looked like a wonderful place to pass the time reading a good book. As far as she could tell, the library was empty. The only sound she could hear was a voice coming from behind the desk attempting to whisper into the phone.

In front of her was a large display table with an old historical map of Will-O'-the-Wisp Point encased in glass. The map of the town looked to be old, back when it was only a village. A quick glance at the map was all she was interested in as her attention turned to the voice. "I'm telling you, Janice, that's exactly how I heard it. And what about Louise's niece? Such a sad turn of events... You don't say? Where did you hear that? If you heard it from Claire, it's got to be true," said the librarian.

On her way to the check-out desk to ask a question, she saw a large painting of a woman walking on a beach, carrying a lantern. Distracted by the work of art, she began to study the detail. She was dressed in a flowing white gown that trailed behind her on the sand. Candace wondered if she was alive or an apparition. Maybe she was a bride with a tragic story to tell. There was a longing on the woman's face. What was she seeking? Who was she waiting for? Why was she on the beach at twilight? Candace was drawn to her and wanted to know more.

"I'll call you back, Janice," whispered the voice from behind the counter. "May I help you?"

Turning to respond, Candace came face to face with the librarian. The cat eye glasses cocked sideways on her face screamed bookworm. The frames were held securely to her head, stuck through a knitted cap with a fanciful flower attached. Walking toward the counter, Candace saw the antitheses of the stereotypical librarian. Her shiny polyester blouse was a mixture of bold colors with a different-patterned, blue-toned scarf tied around her neck in a bow. Her multi-colored skirt went to the knee, made of the same shiny, manmade fabric. It took a few seconds for Candace to process the mishmash of colors and patterns competing for dominance before she could respond. "I'm just looking."

"If you have any questions, feel free to ask."

"Thank you," said Candace as she moved to the outdated card catalogue system. Pulling one of the drawers open, she used her fingers to go through the index cards and their titles. Every now and then she would glance the librarian's way and catch her staring back. Once she was caught, the librarian would busy herself, pretending she wasn't studying her every move. Choosing to ignore her, Candace found several references for psychology books and went in search of them. Once she reached the section she needed, she was slightly intimidated by the selection. She pulled several from the shelf then sat on a bench and leafed through them. Candace had her work cut out for her.

The librarian's curiosity continued as she purposefully walked back and forth, pushing a cart full of returns as an excuse to spy on Candace. She was dying to know who this woman was and what brought her to town. Being the first to know would be a feather in her knitted cap. She couldn't wait to find out more so she could share the news as an informed citizen of their community.

Finding the books she wanted, Candace replaced the rest and made her way to the counter.

"Oh, dear!" exclaimed the librarian when she saw the large stack of books come to rest in front of her.

"I just need to brush up on a few things."

"Three books is the maximum amount allowed to be checked out at once, unless of course you're homebound."

"Would I be here if I were homebound?"

"We deliver."

"Then I'll take the top three."

"Your card please."

"Card?"

"No books may be checked out without a current library card," said the librarian, pointing to a sign on the wall that stated the exact same thing written in calligraphy.

"Then I guess I'll need one of those."

"Only residents of this town or county have the privilege of owning a library card."

"I'm currently residing in this county."

"Is that so? Well, then... fill out this form legibly. Make sure your address and phone number are current and correct."

"Will this get me a ten percent discount off my first purchase?" joked Candace.

"The books are not for sale." The librarian accentuated her statement by stamping the checkout dates with three pronounced tamps. "I see you have an interest in psychology or a background perhaps?" pried the librarian.

"Or perhaps... I find human nature fascinating."

"As do I."

Candace handed the librarian the form and waited for the next step as she perused the information.

"Oh! You're staying at the lighthouse. With Mr. Bloom, no doubt?" enquired the librarian in anticipation of some cream of the crop gossip to share with her circle of do-gooders.

"Yes. I'm not sure of the correct address."

"I can pull it off his account. He's a regular." Rolling a blank library card into an old electric typewriter, the librarian began typing the information on the appropriate lines. "May I ask how you know William Bloom?"

Recognizing her curiosity stemmed from a gossip's need to feed her addiction, Candace decided to have some fun with the librarian. "Will and I are old friends."

"Really?"

"Yes. We knew each other in college."

"While he was studying to be a paramedic?"

"That's right. But only for a short time because of the accident."

"Accident?" asked the librarian, her fingers coming to a stop. Her attention could no longer be split between two tasks so she turned to Candace to focus on her story. "How awful."

"Then came the surgery... and the long, painful recovery."

"Surgery?"

"If only he'd listened to my advice and left her."

"And who might 'her' be?"

Leaning over, Candace whispered in her ear. "The other woman."

"Another woman," repeated the librarian, delightfully horrified with anticipation.

"Who knew her boyfriend had a gun?"

"A gun?"

"But at least the baby lived."

"A love child," whispered the librarian as though she just learned some top secret information worth millions of dollars on the black market.

"They'll always have the memories of their time spent together in Argentina," concluded Candace, trying her hardest not to laugh out loud.

"Argentina? That explains the tango. The dance of love."

"Unrestrained passion is more accurate. My card?" she responded, leaving the librarian with more questions than she had answers. Candace had no doubt she would fill in the holes with as much sensationalism as possible.

"Your card? Oh, yes, of course, your card." Snapping out of her fantasy she pulled the card from the typewriter and signed the bottom then handed it over to Candace.

"On second thought, why don't you take all the books. If you can't trust a 'mental health professional,' who can you trust?"

"Thank you." Candace picked up the pile of books and left the counter.

"Tell Mr. Bloom not to worry about bringing that dance tape back on time. He can hold onto it as long as he needs it."

Candace stopped to respond. "Why do you only have the tango and the polka?"

"That's all we have left. Some tapes wore out, others were never returned."

"Have you ever considered restocking in a more modern format?"

"You can learn anything on the internet or with an app so what's the point?"

"True," remarked Candace as she walked away.

"I offered to help Will with his dance instruction. He declined," continued the librarian as she hurried around the counter. "Not to brag... but I used to strut my stuff on the dance floor as a teenager."

"Really? What's your favorite dance?"

"Anything disco," she said proudly while performing a few steps from the hustle, to the bump and ending in the disco finger pose. "I used to burn, baby, burn, yeah."

"Maybe you should consider opening a studio," said Candace playfully on her way to the door.

"Maybe I should," the librarian whispered to herself while imagining the possibilities. Once the door shut, she reached for the phone and dialed. Her sole mission was to inform the community. "You're not going to believe what I just learned," she whispered into the phone as she walked toward the window dragging an extraordinarily long cord behind her.

Leaving the library, Candace was surprised to see Will approach the curb in his truck. "Hop in." Placing the stack of books between them, Candace lifted herself onto the seat. As Will pulled onto the street, he noticed the librarian watching them from the window while talking on the phone. "I wonder what's got the librarian all excited," he said, waving at her through the open window.

"Could be a few things," added Candace, with a mischievous smile and a quick wave.

"Maybe she's excited about making a new friend," he implied, hoping to prove to her that not everyone in town was untrustworthy.

"She definitely showed an interest in me."

"See? 'There are no strangers, only friends you haven't met.'"

Choosing to remain silent, Candace allowed Will his perceived victory. She was trying her best to repay his kindness. A less sarcastic view of the place he called home was a good start. "How did you know I was at the library?"

"Mrs. Lazarra saw you go in while she was walking her dog."

"Did she call you?"

"She told Joe when he was dropping off her mail."

"So Joe told you."

"He mentioned it when he stopped by the firehouse."

"And all this happened in the span of a half hour?"

"I guess," said Will, disregarding the point she was trying to make.

Not far down the street, he parked his truck in front of The Cargo Bay, the town's only hardware and more store. From the truck, Candace found it to be a quaint shop similar to ones that existed in towns all across America forty plus years ago. The age of large franchised home improvement stores had replaced the majority of them.

Will left the truck just as an older man walked out of the store, pushing the refurbished bike that once belonged to Ruby. Candace stepped onto the sidewalk while Will and the store owner shook hands. At first glance, he looked like a fit version of Santa Clause with a fluffy white beard and mustache. His red apron and matching colored wool Irish flat cap sealed the deal. "So this is where Santa hangs out the rest of the year," she said, approaching them both.

"A true statement, Lass," he responded with a hint of an Irish dialect and a robust laugh, his handshake just as jolly.

"The days of being a lass are far behind me."

"Not at my age, young lady."

"Candace, meet Captain Bob, the owner of the finest hardware store on the coast."

"It's a pleasure to meet you, Captain."

"Call me Bob. My sailin' days may be far behind me."

"What about the wooden schooner you spend every weekend working on?"

"She's been dry docked at the harbor for a good year now."

"There's still plenty of voyages left in you, Captain."

"Time will tell the tale," he responded. Looking to the opposite side of the street, his attention was stolen by a woman walking down the sidewalk. His eyes lit up with excitement. Poking his head through the open doorway, he hollered to the clerk. "Donna, I'll be runnin' an errand." As he stepped onto the street, he turned back to wish Candace the best. "Enjoy your new bike, Lass."

Candace watched as the captain hurried across the street to catch up with the classy blonde woman in a white sheath dress, knee-length red blazer and three-inch heels. She was perfectly accessorized with dress gloves and a red, wide-rimmed hat. Candace was shocked to find someone so stylish in the small town. "Does she live here?"

Will looked up from examining the bike to see who she was referring to then went right back to his inspection. "That's Fae LeBlanc. She owns the drugstore."

"She looks like she just stepped out of a Saks Fifth Avenue window display."

"She always looks that good. She won some big beauty pageant a long time ago. It must come natural."

"She's stunning."

"So's this bike," responded Will without looking up.

"What did the captain mean when he said, 'Enjoy your new bike?'"

"It's yours. I had him put on two new tires, a bell and a headlight. Think you can handle it?"

"It's been a while," she answered quietly.

"Try it out."

"You shouldn't have done this."

"It was nothing."

"No." she argued, feeling a tinge of panic set in. "This is something."

"Hop on. Give it a spin."

"Maybe later."

"I'll steady it for you."

"I said later!" yelled Candace.

"I didn't mean to upset you," apologized Will, knowing PTSD outbursts rarely make sense to the person on the receiving end. "I'll load it in the truck."

"No! I'll walk it home," she said, opening the truck door.

"I thought it would be a good way for you to get around, since you arrived without a driver's license," he said while she retrieved her books, stacked them in the wicker basket and began to push. "You don't have to ride it home today. We've got the truck."

Candace continued down the street, trying to put some distance between them before the inevitable flow of tears. Turning into an alley, she made her way through town by avoiding the main street. To Will, the bike was nothing more than a practical means to an end. She realized that. But for her, it was the first link in a new chain she felt wrapping around her. Her last relationship had supplied her with many gifts over the years, all coming with expectations and stipulations. The chain she left behind when she washed ashore was the last she would ever wear.

The sound of children laughing captured her attention as she approached the playground of a school. It must have been recess as Candace pushed her bike next to the chain link fence, watching the kids have fun on the playground equipment. It wasn't long before her steps slowed to a stop so she could let some of their joy rub off on her. Happily, some chased each other around the grass, playing a game of tag, while others played a game of kickball. The sight of their innocence began to change her countenance, eventually turning her scowl into a smile.

"I can teach you how to ride," said Will as he rolled up in his truck.

"I know how to ride."

"Then what's the problem?"

"Gifts complicate things," she said, still facing the children through the fence. "Too many assumptions."

"Let's make it a loan."

"Loans are worse."

"How about you borrow it? No strings attached."

"There's always strings."

"Then let's deal, Lady. Five dollars and it's yours. Come on... I know Ruby gave you some spending money."

Candace turned and leaned her back against the fence, crossing her arms over her chest. "Five dollars wouldn't even cover the bell."

"Cough it up or no bicycle. Which means you have to depend on me for transportation."

Reaching into her pocket, she pulled out a ten dollar bill and handed it to him through the open window. "Ten dollars is my final offer."

"I'm pretty sure you don't understand the art of negotiating, but I'll take it," he said, folding the bill in half and putting it in his shirt pocket.

A group of children ran to the fence, individually calling to Will. "Hello, Mr. Bloom." "Hi, Mr. Bloom."

"Hi, guys," responded Will with a wave through the window. The cluster of children ran away as quickly as they had arrived—excited to see their friend from school.

"Looks like you have a fan club," noted Candace.

"I'm always down here fixing something or helping out where I can."

"Your grandma would be very proud of you."

"She loved this school. Educating children was her life's work."

Silently, Candace took a moment to compare her disappointing life to a woman who made such a difference in the world.

"Are you all right?"

"Just lost in thought," answered Candace. "I apologize for my reaction to the bike. You were trying to help and I took it the wrong way."

"I figure you have your reasons. Those wheels will take you anywhere you want to go in Will-O'-the-Wisp Point."

"Thank you. Speaking of that," she said, pointing to the sign. "You wouldn't believe what your ambulance driver tried to tell me about how your town got its name."

"Angry women, an infamous sea captain and lots of skullduggery."

"You too?" asked Candace in disbelief as she started pushing her bike down the street.

"It goes over well with the tourists." Will put his truck in gear and coasted down the sidewalk to continue the conversation. "Actually, it's a great story. A bunch of jealous women pay a ship's captain to capture a mysterious temptress and sail her to a faroff land."

"Sounds expensive."

"After she was abandoned on this very shore," continued Will, using his best storyteller voice as he pointed toward the beach, "the townspeople shunned her because of the fearsome stories the sailors told when they left her behind."

"So what does the woman in the story have to do with the name of the town?"

"You haven't heard the best part," he replied before reverting back to his narrator voice. "For more than a century after her abandonment, people have seen a mysterious light on the beach at night. According to legend, the will-o'-the-wisp is the light from the lantern being carried by the forsaken woman, waiting for the ship to return."

"If the ship's captain and his crew were so horrible to her, why would she want them to return?"

"No one tries to make sense of it. It's just an old story that brings in the tourists. Every summer, people come from all over to walk the beach at night in search of the woman with the lantern."

"Are you serious?"

"It gives a seasonal boost to the economy. We even had one of those ghost finding cable shows come out and film an episode."

"Why?"

"People still claim to see the light from her lantern. Tourists have slipped off the edge of cliffs and nearly drowned in the ocean following the light. At least that's what they claim after we rescue them. I'm pretty sure it's just carelessness."

"Have you ever seen it?"

"I've seen a light on the beach many times. It could be anyone. I think people turn it into what they want it to be."

Interrupting their conversation, Joe's voice came over the radio. "Will, an elderly woman has fallen at Mae's Grocery. Possible broken hip."

Will responded immediately. "Get the ambulance over there, Joe. I'll meet you at the store."

"That doesn't sound good."

"Duty calls. Are you all right getting home?"

"Home?"

"Back to the lighthouse," answered Will, oblivious as to why she asked about his choice of words.

"Don't worry. I won't follow any lanterns off a cliff."

"Then my job here is done," he joked as he turned the truck around and sped down the street.

Candace watched him until he turned a corner and disappeared. "Looks like it's just you and me," she said to the bike. Lifting her leg over the frame, she worked up the courage to ride for the first time since she was a kid. Wobbly at first, Candace course corrected until she got her pedals and handlebars to cooperate with each other. As her confidence and skill level grew, so did her speed.

Passing by the remaining homes and buildings, she headed out of town along the coastline. The wind on her face exemplified the freedom she felt. Standing up, she pumped the pedals hard, increasing her speed to more easily climb the small hill ahead. Once she reached the top, she removed her feet from the pedals, raised her legs in the air and coasted down the long, gradual grade. The sight of the water mixed with the smell of ocean lifted her senses to a whole new level. Riding home at the end of the day would be the perfect way to balance out the frustrations of working with Rose.

CHAPTER 12

Once again, Candace found herself alone at the lighthouse. She parked her bike, took the library books from the basket and walked through the front door. Thirsty from her exercise, she placed the books on the counter and filled a glass with water from the tap. After a lengthy drink, she carried her glass into the bedroom and placed it on the nightstand next to the book on loan from Ruby's collection. She'd only cracked the surface of Rhue-wyn's tale and wanted to know more. Curling up with a good book sounded so enticing. On the other hand, work was calling. She thought of the library books on the counter and how she should begin studying. But the lure of the unnamed fantasy lying within reach was strong. A decision had to be made: textbook reading or fiction.

Grabbing the book from the nightstand, she laid down and pulled a blanket over her lower body. She would reward herself with a little fiction then hit the research books. Opening the cover, she found the page she left off on and began to read.

It was business as usual in the bustling little coastal town while Rhue-wyn watched from the hilltop. The port was busy with goods being loaded onto ships as horse drawn-wagons full of grains and produce waited in line. Rhue-

wyn thought of some of the changes she'd seen during her existence. Steam engines had replaced the use of sails for the most part and ships were being built from iron rather than wood. The exhaust from the coal-burning steamships had changed the smell of the port towns, as well as the sound. In many ways, she missed the simplicity of earlier times.

Commerce bored her more than anything, so she simply avoided it. "There are more pleasing ways to spend my time," she thought to herself as she bit into an apple pilfered from a farmer's tree while on her daily stroll. The bite was crisp followed by a sugary sweetness that brought her mouth to life. The town she currently called home was surrounded by lovely orchards and farms. The harvests were plentiful that year which made for more merriment than usual. A development most pleasing to Rhue-wyn. Of all the towns she had called home, this one was by far her favorite. It was big enough to offer the finer things in life, but not so large to threaten the power of her influence.

For years Rhue-wyn wandered from town to town after leaving her home in the forest. She would stay only until the amusement wore off then be on her way. This nomadic lifestyle helped her avoid questions as to why she never aged: an important detail when keeping your true identity a secret. But more than that, she loved what her entrance into a new town did to the status quo. There was nothing more satisfying to Rhue-wyn than upsetting the social apple cart—a result of the mischievous nature inherent to those of her kind. Her ability to instantly mesmerize turned the heads of every male, giving her the power she sought. Treasures ranging from food to adornment were left at her doorstep by suitors of all ages; married, single and from all walks of life. She wanted for nothing. To the men of the town she was royalty; to the women, she was a menace. The female citizens longed for the day when she would move on and leave their town in peace. But that never seemed to happen.

Finishing off her apple, she tossed the core aside then hopped to her feet. Before she could take a step, her eye caught something of great interest. It was a large ship in the distance that appeared to be making its way to shore. It was nothing like the smaller steam-driven merchant ships Rhue-wyn had seen coming and going from their port. This was a type of ship that once sailed the globe by the hundreds, a ship that experienced the adventures you read about in poems and storybooks—the type of vessel once used to conquer *civilizations and build nations through trade and colonization. Sadly, this majestic lady who commanded the sea for centuries had fallen victim to the Second Industrial Revolution and was now in danger of becoming extinct. That's what made the sight of her so extraordinary.*

The array of white sails blowing the ship toward shore was a beautiful sight, almost hypnotizing as Rhue-wyn sat back down to wait for her approach. After what seemed like an eternity, the large ship came within rowing distance of the shore and began lowering its sails. It was too big for the depth of water in the port, so they anchored farther out. She watched curiously as the sailors lowered two long boats onto the surface of the water. Soon they would row to shore in time for a good meal and some entertainment before the sun dropped in the western sky. "Who were these men and why had they sailed to such a small port?" she wondered. "What stories of adventure would they bring?" She had to know the answers firsthand so she jumped to her feet and ran toward town.

After a quick bath in a nearby stream, Rhue-wyn chose the most extravagant dress she owned, styled her hair just so and danced down the street. The anticipation was thrilling as she walked to a ledge overlooking the docks. The first rowboat had reached shore and she watched curiously as the captain climbed off while his crew steadied the boat. He was nothing she imagined a man of the sea to be. She saw no rough appearance or straggly beard, and no sword hanging from his waist, or any other weapon for that matter. Dressed in dark pants tucked into his boots with a white shirt beneath an open vest, he handed his hat and dark jacket to a member of his crew who waited beside him for further orders. As he surveyed the dock area, it didn't take long for his eyes to make contact with hers. With a tip of his head, Rhue-wyn knew she had won his favor. The game was afoot.

Hearing the sound of a truck pull up to the house, Candace pulled herself from the story and walked to the kitchen window. It was Will. She didn't expect him to return so soon. But when she factored in the amount of time it took her to ride home, as well as the several stops she made along the way to rest and take in the view, his arrival time was accurate. Rushing into the kitchen, she grabbed the pile of textbooks from the counter and placed them on her nightstand. Then she sat on the bed, her back straight with the headboard and opened a psych book. She listened for the door to open and Will to enter the house. Within seconds, Junior was at the side of her bed, tail wagging with excitement.

"Junior, get out of there!" Will called to his dog as he walked toward the room. Junior did as he was told and passed by his master as they met in the doorway. "Hard at work, I see."

"I have a lot to get through."

"Do you mind if I close the door so I can practice?"

"Not at all."

Before Will could close the door all the way, Candace interrupted him. "How much longer till the wedding?"

"One week. It's coming up quick."

"Would you like some more help?"

"I don't want to interrupt your research."

"These books aren't going anywhere."

"I could use some help," Will humbly responded as he reopened the door.

Candace followed him into the kitchen and allowed Will to awkwardly take her in his arms. "I forgot to start the tape."

"Why don't you show me what you've learned so far and we'll go from there."

Mechanically, Will pushed her around the kitchen, trying to remember what he had practiced. After thirty-seconds of movement, he came to an abrupt stop. "That's all I know."

"That's a good start," said Candace, trying to find the positive in how little he knew.

"There's a lot more, isn't there?"

"How long have you been at this?"

"Just six weeks."

"Just?"

"I know... it's hasn't been very long."

Candace was thinking just the opposite but kept her analysis to herself. "I think it would help if we had more room. Do you mind if we move the table and chairs?"

"That's a good idea," he responded, breaking his hold and jumping into action. "Can I ask how you know so much about dance?"

"It was an interest of mine growing up."

"Not that I'm an expert," responded Will, "but you seem pretty good at it."

"Not good enough."

"You're way better than the lady who's been teaching me."

Candace couldn't help but giggle. "It helps to have more than a voice to work with."

"I see that now."

Once the table and chairs were moved, Will held out his hand and Candace gracefully placed her hand in his. Proudly, he took her through the steps he had mastered. His newfound confidence was encouraging so Candace showed him the next step. Again, they started from the top and moved through the next motion. "Good."

"This is definitely easier than the tape. You should consider teaching."

Will's words sent her back to the past. She had always planned to return to her small town and take over for Ms. Hildebrandt after retiring from a long and successful career on the stage. That was no longer in the cards.

"Are you all right?" he asked, noticing her change in demeanor.

"I'm fine. Just a little tired," said Candace as she let go of his hand. "I should probably get back to my research."

"I can take you by the elementary school in the morning and introduce you to the principal. I'm sure she'd love to have you teach dance during gym class on occasion. You could do it as a specialist and make a little extra money."

"Let me think about it," she said, then closed the door behind her. Candace sat down on the bed and stared at the painting of the ship caught in a storm. The only thing visible to the ship was the beacon from the lighthouse. She wished it was that simple for her. Caught in her own storm, she longed for a guide to show her the way. Lying down, she wrapped her arms around an extra pillow and held it close to her chest. As she drifted off to sleep, her thoughts traveled back to the night she washed ashore.

Lightning danced through the clouds, illuminating the water's surface as Dante Donadio's yacht cut through the waves. An endless series of white caps crested high, causing the yacht to seesaw in all directions as booming claps of thunder grew in intensity.

In desperation, Candace burst through the mid-cabin door of the luxury yacht, grabbing onto the railing to keep from going over the side. The powerful wind slammed the door shut behind her, providing a reprieve that would last only seconds.

Her blonde hair caught in the wind obstructed her sight until she pulled it back, revealing blood trickling from the corner of her mouth. The pelting rain helped to cool her recently bruised face as she came to grips with the reality of her choice to escape. Suddenly aware of the bloody steak knife clutched in her fist, Candace dropped it to the deck as she turned toward the back of the boat. Along the way, she noticed a strange sound accompanying the wind—possibly a voice crying for help. Chalking it up to her temporary insanity, she continued toward the back of the boat, pushing against the wind. Using both her hands, she ripped the strand of pearls from her neck, leaving the pieces scattered. One-hundred-mile-per-hour winds couldn't change her direction as she pulled her loose-fitting cocktail dress over her head and dropped it to the deck. Reaching the end of the boat, she became eerily calm. All signs of emotion faded from her face. Resolutely, she opened the gate at the back of the boat and stepped into the tumultuous sea.

The same cabin door opened a second time. Caught by the twisting wind, it slammed against the wall. Dante Donadio, a successful businessman in his late forties and owner of the yacht, stumbled onto the deck and looked both ways, his black, slicked-back hair made unruly by the wind. His blood-soaked, white dress shirt became saturated in seconds as the wind lifted the silk tie hanging around his open collar and carried it away. Pressing a wadded-up linen against his upper right breast, he attempted to slow the bleeding. Growing weak from loss of blood, he grabbed onto the railing to steady himself. A second man emerged in an attempt to help. Dante forcefully pointed toward the front of the boat, giving the orders: drag her back.

Hanging on to steady himself, he staggered toward the back of the boat—his fierce anger competing with the violence of the sea. Nearing the stern, he stepped on what felt like a rock beneath his bare foot. With closer examination he found it to be a pearl. Several more caught his eye as they rolled with the movement of the boat. He followed the trail to the soaked dress lying near the open gate. He picked up the dress then desperately looked in every direction. Enraged, he screamed into the storm then threw the dress into the ocean. His assumption was quickly confirmed when the second man arrived at the stern alone. The object of his obsession had betrayed him. The impact of her treachery, coupled with the fatigue from loss of blood, caused him to collapse onto the deck.

Leaving behind the lights at the surface, Candace sank into the cold ocean. Her blonde hair trailed behind. Peace had come at last. This was the end and she was content. Just as she prepared to release the remaining air from her lungs, something unexpected happened. Her survival instincts kicked in. Using her arms and legs to fight her way back, she burst through the turbulent surface. She only had enough time to fill her lungs before a wave took her under, sending her body turning in every direction. Disappointed in her failure, she released the air from her lungs. She longed for the peace that death could bring, but the ocean had different plans. It wasn't long before she was thrust back to the surface. Fighting against her survival instincts, she refused to fill her lungs with air as she waited for the next wave to engulf her. Death was her choice and she wasn't going to let anyone take that away from her. Not even the mighty ocean. Instead of sucking her under, the next wave lifted her higher in the air, causing her to gasp and fill her lungs with air. Fighting against her own will to survive had proven unsuccessful. She had no other choice but to fight the raging storm.

The lights of the distant yacht were still visible, but Candace made no attempt to swim in its direction. Instead, she fought to get as far away as possible. Swimming in a particular direction was out of the question against the ocean's power. The fierce waves made certain of that as they continued to carry her under, then return her to the surface as though it were a game.

After battling the forces of nature for some time, a light caught her eye. It appeared to be blinking through the storm. At first, she thought it might be the yacht returning, an idea more frightening than drowning at sea. Concentrating on the light, she realized it was a lighthouse beacon, warning sailors of a dangerous coastline, reef or rocks. She knew the boat had been traveling within sight of the coastline when the storm hit. The lighthouse meant land was within reach—a notion that lit the flame of possibility. Keeping her eyes focused on the light, she used it as a guide. The odds of her making it to shore were slim.

Jolted awake by fear, Candace sat up and tried to catch her breath. Her heart was pounding as she worked to stop the alarm going off in her mind. "It's only a dream," she told herself. Or more precisely, a memory. She had no idea if Dante was alive or if the wound she inflicted had claimed his life. The fear of him finding her would follow her for the rest of her days. At least the mystery had been solved. For the first time since she woke up in the lighthouse, she recalled the details of the night she jumped from the boat. Candace made a conscious decision to step off the boat. The idea of ending her life had been brewing for days, but she didn't know if she'd have the courage to go through with it. An inherent fight for survival overpowered her desire and she failed to seal the deal. It didn't help that the ocean seemed to be against her death wish. Maybe Ruby did have something to do with it after all.

CHAPTER 13

Although it seemed like she arrived only yesterday, one week had come and gone since she washed ashore. For the past seven days she'd slowly pieced together the events of the dreadful night. Now she was trying everything she could to forget. But something inside refused to accommodate. In search of ideas for helping Rose, she continued to study the psych books. She'd made very little progress with her 'student,' so she continued to search for answers. Truth be known, she was also searching for help in piecing her own psyche back together.

Lying near the edge of the cliff, sandwiched between two warm quilts, the sun, the surf and the gentle breeze created the perfect environment for relaxation. She couldn't have asked for a more peaceful moment. Rolling over, she saw Will at the top of the lighthouse washing the windows. The sight of him enhanced the tranquil moment so she continued to study his actions.

Glancing down at Candace, Will was surprised to find her staring at him. So surprised, he accidentally dropped his spray bottle of window cleaner over the side. Trying to catch it, he slammed his head into the railing, sending him backwards in pain.

"I got it," yelled Candace from below.

Hurting too badly to respond in an intelligible way, Will waved his hand while watching her run toward the bottle.

"Are you all right?"

"I'm good," he lied, pretending to clean the window without any spray.

"I'm coming up."

While Will waited for her to arrive at the top of the stairs, he checked his forehead in the reflection of the glass to see if he'd broken the skin. It wasn't clear enough to tell. Before he could move, Candace cleared the last step and caught him in the act. "Let me look at it," she said, climbing through the glass door.

"It's nothing."

"There's definitely a red mark. No treatment necessary. Unless you need something for the impending headache," she said, handing him the bottle. "Maybe you should tie a rope on it and hang it from your waist."

"I'll take that under consideration. Sorry to interrupt your studies."

"I'm on my last book. They're so depressing." Distracted by something out at sea, she quickly reached inside the window and picked up a pair of binoculars setting on the window ledge.

"What do you see?"

"Just a sailboat," said Candace, breathing a sigh of relief.

"Anything useful?"

"What?"

"In the books."

"A misleading hope or goal," she said, placing the binoculars back on the window ledge.

"What do you mean?"

"That's another definition of will-o'-the-wisp. 'A misleading hope or goal.' I came across it today in the psycho-babble that I'm reading. It made me think of Ruby and Rose. She's spent all these years sheltering her daughter in that house, shielding her from the outside world. And now her goal is to get someone else to take care of her through marriage."

"I'm sure she has her reasons."

"Ruby mentioned protecting Rose as a child. Do you know from what?"

"Her husband was the town mayor for a long time. One day he had a breakdown at City Hall. He left his office and ran down Main Street, screaming that people were after him. No one could get close. He wouldn't even let Ruby touch him. He ended up at the state mental hospital and was there for over fifteen years until he died recently."

"Recently?"

"A couple months ago. It was a private, graveside service."

"When Ruby told me she lost her husband, I thought she meant he passed away when Rose was a child."

"She did lose him, mentally."

"Did Rose see his meltdown?"

"She was pretty young so I'm not sure how much she'd remember. It happened right after I graduated. Before I left for college."

"So she saw her father's breakdown?"

"City Hall is near the school. From what my grandmother said, the mayor ran from the building screaming at the top of his lungs. I guess he suffered some kind of psychotic break. His white shirt was ripped and stained with blood from self-inflicted wounds. People tried to help him but he kept fighting them off. It took three policemen to subdue him. They had to handcuff him to keep him from hurting himself or anyone else. The children were at recess and they saw the whole thing through the fence. They all knew the mayor was Rose's father. Some of the kids started laughing at Rose and making fun of her. The recess aide finally got them calmed down and back in the building but at that point the damage had been done. My grandmother kept Rose in her office until Ruby arrived. For months after that, Grandma tried to get Ruby to bring Rose back to school, but she chose to homeschool her instead."

"What happened to the mayor?"

"They took him north to the hospital where he was diagnosed. He never came home."

"Do you think it's genetic?"

"What do you mean?"

"Does Rose have the same problem?"

"You think she has a mental illness?"

"I've spent all this time trying to reach her and have nothing to show for it. Her behavior's far from normal."

"So what's the diagnosis?"

"Reading a few books does not make me an expert," said Candace as she crawled through the opening. "Anyway, I'm not getting paid to diagnose her." Poking her head back through the doorway, she shared a thought. "I was thinking about Joe. He seems like he'd make a nice husband."

"Are you looking?" joked Will.

"For Rose," she replied, then began her descent down the spiral staircase.

"For Rose..." he laughed, until he realized she was serious. "For Rose?"

Hollering from halfway down the stairs, she offered her explanation. "It's not like there's a lot of eligible bachelors her age."

"I don't think that's a good idea!" he yelled after her. "Candace?" Needing to convince her that Joe was not an option, he crawled through the door and followed her down the stairs. "You won't fix Rose overnight."

"Ruby doesn't want her fixed. She wants her married. That's the only way I'm getting my money."

"What if you can help her get better?"

"I've tried to help her, but it's no use," responded Candace as she pushed play on the cassette player. "I could use a break from reading. Do you want me to practice with you?"

As the Latin introduction music played, he and Candace slid the table to the side to create more room. Moving a chair, Will continued the conversation. "So not only does Ruby pay for your plans, but Rose does too?"

"It's Ruby's plan. I'm just getting paid to carry it out. That money's my ticket to happiness."

"Everyone knows you can't buy happiness."

"There's nothing wrong with trying."

Before Will could counter her argument, the dance teacher's voice entered the conversation. *"The tango's complex figures enhance the tease between you and your partner."*

"Can we focus on the dance?" she asked, manually placing his hand around her waist.

Will raised his other arm to hers and took hold of her hand. "Sounds like Ruby's not the only one with a misleading hope or goal."

"What's that supposed to mean?" she responded as they began going through the proper steps while the dance teacher counted them off.

"What's your definition of happiness, Candace?"

"Same as everyone else."

"That's a long definition."

"Can we just focus on the steps?"

"I don't know a lot about much, but I do know what makes me happy."

Fed up with his insinuations, Candace dropped his hand and fired back. "Living in a nowhere town, saving lives and fixing sinks?"

"That's part of it."

"And being alone?"

"You and I can change that."

Confused by his statement, Candace stepped back from Will, thinking he was referring to them getting together. For a split second, she allowed herself to consider the possibility.

"With all the dance lessons you've been helping me with," he added, clarifying what he said. "I'm bound to impress her."

"The tango's intrigue manifests itself through non-verbal communication," guided the dance teacher as Will lifted up his hand, inviting her to rejoin him.

"You're talking about Jill." Candace placed her hand back in his and allowed him to wrap his other hand around her waist. "The perfect girl."

"Those are my family's words."

"Aren't you the pot calling the kettle black?"

"What does that mean?"

"I'm talking about your own will-o'-the-wisp. Your little scheme for getting what you want is not that different than mine."

"You know what I like about fixing sinks, Candace?"

"Please, enlighten me," she said with a heaping dose of sarcasm as they moved to the counts of the dance teacher's voice.

"It's simple. There's either a problem with the water going in or the water going out. I fix a leaky faucet, I unclog a drain and someone's happy."

"People's lives aren't fixed that easily."

"I get that. But the sink never drains without removing the clog." To make the point more dramatic, Will dipped Candace, supporting her in his arms while he stared into her eyes.

"Dialogue, shared through body language is key to interpreting the dance," advised the dance teacher.

"You think I need to talk about what happened out there. The night I washed ashore. You think I need to share my feelings."

"Become absorbed in each other. Follow your heart and don't retreat," continued the dance teacher.

Losing her patience, Candace forced him to lift her to her feet. On her way to the door, she hit the stop button on the tape player, silencing the instructor's unwelcome advice.

Will followed her outside, determined to get some answers. "You want to know what I think? I think you're an excellent swimmer."

Candace kept walking as Will relentlessly followed. "Very few people could have made it that far in that storm and in that water temperature, yet you made it to shore and lived."

"Try swimming in a blender cause that's what it was like out there."

"Being a strong swimmer had to help."

"I don't want to have this conversation."

"There's a confidence that comes from being a strong swimmer, not to mention a skill set."

"What does that have to do with anything?" yelled Candace. She could feel herself spiraling out of control. She had no idea where the fury was coming from but it showed no sign of slowing.

"I'm trying to help you get to the bottom of this."

"Bottom of what?"

"How did you end up in the ocean, Candace?"

"That's none of your business!"

"You're right, but I'm still asking the question."

Stopping abruptly, Candace turned and screamed at her accuser. "I am an excellent swimmer. Captain of my high school swim team. It's just one of my super hero abilities. I leap from boats, swim to shore, pretend to have hypothermia so I can give tango lessons to desperate men trying to woo the woman of their family's dreams!"

"Oh, that's hilarious. Really. Hilarious!" Will turned and walked back toward the lighthouse. He made the mistake of trying to get her to talk about the night she washed ashore before she was ready.

"Say it! Just say it!" she shouted after him.

Confused by what she wanted, Will turned to face her. "What do you want me to say?"

"I failed! I can't even end my life right."

"Is that how you ended up in the ocean?" asked Will as he narrowed the gap between them. "You tried to end your life?"

"Why else would I jump off a boat in the middle of a storm?" Candace turned to walk away, but Will grabbed her hand and turned her back. "Why would a strong swimmer choose drowning to kill herself?"

Incapable of arguing his point, Candace stared at Will in silence.

"I don't think you failed, Candace. I think you fought for your life and won."

"So what's my prize?"

"A chance at happiness."

"Do I look happy?" she yelled then turned and walked away.

The frenzied anger in her voice told Will he'd opened a can of worms that should have stayed closed, at least for a while longer. Unfortunately, common sense had gone out the window. "You're chasing your own will-o'-the-wisp," he said, using her words against her.

"What did you say?" asked Candace as she turned back.

"'A misleading hope or goal.' Isn't that what you told me it meant? Isn't that what you're doing with Rose?"

"I was hired to do a job based on Ruby's terms. Nothing more!"

"You could make it more."

"Stay out of it, Will!" yelled Candace as she walked away.

"I'm just trying to help!"

"You're not helping!"

"And you're not listening!"

"Leave me alone!"

"You're chasing a light, thinking it's going to lead you to happiness."

Fuming at Will and his accusations, she refused to stop walking or even respond.

"Why not let happiness find you?" Will waited for an answer but none came. His intention was to help, but instead he turned up the heat. As he watched her walk toward the wood pile, he made the assumption that she needed some space so he walked toward the house. Just as he reached the door, he heard his truck engine start. It was half full of wood that he had split that morning. Turning back, he saw her tear out and speed down the gravel road. "Candace!" She was leaving with his only mode of transportation and without a license to drive. Grabbing her bicycle, he got a running start, leaped onto the seat and pedaled with all his energy.

Driving recklessly down the highway, Candace's tears were fueled by anger. Will opened a door she had no desire to enter. His words forced her to be honest with herself. "Why would a strong swimmer choose drowning to kill herself?" A hostage to her own mind, she painfully relived the night she jumped off the boat. There was shock at first, hitting the turbulent, cold water. It didn't take long to find relief beneath the surface. The weightlessness of her body allowed serenity to envelope her. She had forgotten what it felt like to have control and the freedom that comes with it. In a very honest way, she was angry at herself for surviving. It appeared Will knew her better after only a week than she did.

Finding herself in a comfortable bed the next morning came as a shock. A turn of events she had no idea what to do with. Although her circumstances had changed, she was still haunted by the fear of Dante's return. She had nothing. Literally. Where would she go? What would she do?

Then a second chance came in the form of an arrangement between two desperate people. The money Ruby offered was Candace's only hope for salvaging some semblance of a life. But at what expense to Rose? Years earlier, her own desperation to be cared for caused Candace to make the worst decision of her life. "Rose's situation was different," she told herself. She would find someone to do exactly what Ruby wanted: care for Rose. Candace could disappear with enough money to start anew and Rose could continue living in her own little world. It was as simple as that. No harm, no foul. Still, Will's words echoed in her mind. "A misleading hope or goal." Refusing to let him derail her plans, she fought to get his voice out of her head.

Seeing the words on the town's faded sign only intensified her anger. Welcome to Will-O'-the-Wisp Point. It was as though Will was standing in front of her, still leveling his accusations. Slamming on the brakes, she skidded to a stop on the side of the road and rested her forehead against the steering wheel. Unbearable feelings of failure, shame, guilt, fear and anger fought for dominance in her heart and head. Internally, she had no way of stopping it. Then she remembered the splitting maul in the back so she acted on an impulse and left the truck.

Grabbing the maul, she choked up on the handle then zeroed in on the words fueling the fire. Her first swing bounced off the wooden sign causing strong vibrations in the handle. Shaking her hands, she gripped it closer to the end then raised the eight pound blockbuster and swung it over her head. Her form was nothing like she witnessed watching Will split wood, but she didn't care. With the third strike, she made a large indentation and it felt good. Each swing brought increased satisfaction and eventually wood chips started to fly. Her pace increased with the exhilaration she felt. The release of her anger was exemplified by her loud screams and guttural groans.

Out of breath, Will arrived and leaned the bike against his truck. He wasn't sure what to make of the scene playing out so he waited for it to run its course. It wasn't an emergency so he decided to keep a safe distance.

With the sign in pieces, Candace finally lowered the heavy weight to the ground and leaned on the handle. Sweat dripped from her face as she tried to catch her breath.

"Feel better?"

Picking up the maul, she walked toward Will and leaned it up against the truck. "You're right. It is good therapy," she said without apology. Grabbing hold of the bicycle handlebars she headed toward the road leading to town.

Will waited for her to ride away, but she just stood there next to the bike. A few days ago he would have tossed her bike into the back of his truck and took her home. But this appeared to be a turning point for her and he wanted to see where it would lead.

"Freedom to do what I want, to go where I want, and to be who I want to be," she said, staring straight ahead. "That's my definition of happiness." Refusing to wait for a response, she got on the bike and rode toward town.

Will smiled to himself as he watched her disappear down the highway. She was finally starting to open up. This he could work with. Picking up the maul, he brushed the splinters from the head and tossed it into the back. Before he could crawl inside, a truck pulled off the road behind him. "What happened to the sign?" asked his friend, Jack, as he got out of the truck and walked toward him.

"Looks like a case of vandalism."

"Seems a bit extreme for our little town."

"Extreme pretty much covers it."

"This oughta liven up the next city council meeting."

"They could use some livening up."

"Have you found out any more about your guest?"

"We've talked a bit."

"I hear she's working for Ruby."

"She's helping her with a project."

"Any word on where she came from?"

"Not yet."

"She doesn't seem to be in much of a hurry to get back."

"I guess not."

"I better get on the road. I'll see ya at the tree lighting tonight."

"Wouldn't miss it," said Will. "Is your wife making the eggnog?"

"She started tweaking the recipe weeks ago. Can't you tell?" Jack responded, patting his belly.

"The rivalry between her eggnog stand and Mrs. Hoot's hot chocolate is getting a little out of hand."

"Don't I know it," said Jack as he got back in the truck and drove down the road.

Taking one last look at the destroyed sign, Will shook his head and crawled into the truck. "Out of all the beaches in the world, she picks mine to wash up on." Starting the engine, he followed Jack down the road toward town.

CHAPTER 14

Candace arrived at Ruby's home, leaned her bike against the porch and took a deep breath. "I can do this." Confidently, she entered the house. Finding the living room empty, she walked toward the staircase. A sticky note attached to the end of the banister caught her attention. She read it then continued up the stairs. "Questions. The books said to use questions," she reminded herself. Candace slowly opened the door to find Rose searching through a pile of books on the floor. The ripped open box setting next to the books told Candace they were probably new to her collection. "Hello, Rose."

Rose quickly got up and backed away from Candace, losing all interest in her new books.

"How are you today? Have you had lunch? Your mom left a note saying she had to run to the store." Candace noticed a change in her countenance when she learned her mother was no longer in the house. "Would you like me to help you put these books away?"

No response.

"You sure have a lot of books. What's your favorite?" Desperate for more questioning material, Candace looked to the amateur oil paintings on the wall. They were all of coastal scenes and had a simple beauty to them. "Did you paint these, Rose? They're lovely."

Running out of questions about her room, Candace broadened her scope. "It's a beautiful day out there. What do you say we open the curtains?" One by one, Candace made her way around the circular room, opening the heavy curtains as she went. Rose reacted by backing against the wall to avoid being seen. "What is it Rose? Is it the light?" Seriously wanting to know what was going on inside her head, Candace moved toward her as she continued her parade of questions. "What are you so scared of, Rose? What frightens you so much that you lock yourself away from the world?" Determined to get to the root of the problem, Candace made the conscious decision to delve deep. Coming face to face, she paused before whispering the hardest question of all. "Is it because of your father?"

Pushing Candace aside, Rose spoke out loud for the first time. "Be quiet. Be quiet!" She continued to yell the same words as she ran from window to window, grabbing the curtains and pulling them shut. After the last curtain was closed, she turned and yelled directly at Candace. "No more voices! I have to stop the voices!"

Stunned by her reaction, Candace intercepted her before she could run out the door. "Then start talking! Until you do my voice is all you're going to hear." Staring into Rose's eyes, she could see the intensity. A battle between her mind and heart was playing out. She could tell Rose wanted to talk but fear would not allow it. "Talk to me, Rose. Say anything. Yell at me if you want."

"I'm home," hollered Ruby from the living room. Her voice traveling up the stairs giving Rose renewed hope for escape. Quickly, she darted past Candace and out the door. The sound of footsteps hurrying down the stairs at a stampede pace meant another loss for Candace. Sitting down on the chair next to the door, she listened to the conversation between mother and daughter. "Come here, Rose. I'm home now. It'll be all right. Why don't we go into the kitchen and see if we can find a snack?" Candace shook her head as she walked out of the room, shutting the door behind her. Glad to find the living room empty, Candace walked toward the couch. She thought of Rhue-wyn's book safely tucked inside her bag. She wanted to continue the story but wasn't sure if she or Will were supposed to be reading it. Plopping down on the comfy couch, she leaned her head back to rest her eyes.

WAKING UP AN HOUR LATER, Candace had to adjust to her surroundings. She had planned to shut her eyes for only a few minutes, but her body had different plans. The house was quiet as she checked the time. It was 3:00 in the afternoon. Time to be done for the day—not that she'd accomplished a whole lot. At this rate, she'd be old and gray before she got the money. Attempting to pull on her jacket, she felt the effects of swinging the splitting maul with such vigor. She shook her head when she realized she had more in common with Rose than she thought. They both had overreacted that day.

The sound of pans hitting the floor in the kitchen coaxed her from the couch. Entering the kitchen, she found Ruby picking up a set of stackable stainless steel mixing bowls. "Practicing juggling?" joked Candace as she picked up the remaining bowls and placed them on the counter.

"With all the practicing I've been doing lately, I could join the circus."

"Coming to work for you is a circus."

"Touché."

"Sit down while I put these away."

"Leave them for now," said Ruby as she pulled a heavy sweater off the back of the chair and put it over her shoulders. "Come with me to the backyard. Will you bring that box with you?"

Candace looked into the box of tangled Christmas lights as she pulled it into her arms. Then she followed her employer onto the large patio and waited till Ruby made herself comfortable in one of the chairs surrounding the table.

"Take a load off."

"I've been taking a load off for the past hour."

"What a lovely fall afternoon. Sweater weather beats needing a parka any day. Hopefully, the cold temperatures continue to hold off for a while longer."

"What are we doing out here?" asked Candace as she sat down, placing the box on the table between them.

"I want to drag Santa and his reindeer out this year. It's been too long since they've seen the light of day. We'll put them over there where they used to go."

Candace looked in the direction Ruby was pointing. The backyard was large with overgrown plants and bushes cluttering the border along the wooden fence. It would take a great deal of work to return the landscaping to its original beauty, but that's not what Ruby had in mind. "Would you mind helping me get the Christmas decorations out of the shed?"

"Sure. Wouldn't you rather put them on the front yard for everyone to enjoy?"

"I'm putting them up for Rose."

"I see," said Candace, knowing she only kept the curtains open on the window facing the backyard.

"Speaking of Rose, I'm beginning to notice a change."

"There's been no change, Ruby."

"Of course there has."

"No, there hasn't."

"You're making progress. Keep doing what you were sent here to do."

"Quit saying that!"

"You'll find someone to care for her. I have every confidence."

"You're asking for the impossible," responded Candace, standing up from her chair. "You sit in your big house, dusting your antique furniture and polishing your silver, dreaming of a future for Rose that's never going to happen. Not the way she is now."

Ignoring Candace's argument, Ruby turned to the box and began untangling the strings of old Christmas lights. "I'm not even sure if these lights still work."

"Don't change the subject, Ruby. We're talking about your daughter."

"Yes. My daughter. I know what's best for her."

"How can getting her married be what's best for her?"

"She needs to be cared for."

"Why, Ruby? Tell me why," demanded Candace.

"It's urgent that we find someone who will care for Rose. That's all you need to know."

Noticing Ruby's reaction and shortness of breath, Candace backed off the questioning and quietly responded. "No one wants this job over as much as I do, but I don't see that happening anytime soon."

Tossing the tangled mess of lights back into the box, Ruby stood up to challenge her observation. "I haven't seen one gentleman caller since I hired you!"

"Gentleman caller? Are you nuts?"

Ruby staggered before she could respond. Quick to her feet, Candace caught her before she went down and helped her back to her chair. "Don't accuse me of being crazy. Not in this family."

"I'm sorry. You should have Will check you out."

"Not a word to Will."

"Have you seen a doctor?"

"The doc referred me to a cardiologist up north."

"Have you gone?"

"I can't leave Rose."

"I'll stay with Rose."

"She wouldn't be able to handle that," responded Ruby emphatically as she returned to untangling the lights.

"You'd be surprised what people can handle when they're forced to," argued Candace, speaking from her experience.

"I know my Rose."

"It might actually be good for her to spend some time without you around."

"How could that be good for her?"

"I can't do my job when she's practically paralyzed waiting for you to save her."

"That's what mothers do."

"Are you sure about that?"

Candace's questioning of her parenting skills was more than Ruby wanted to deal with so she changed the subject by reverting to happier times. "This yard holds so many memories. Laughter, conversation, luncheons with friends, parties with so many people you'd wonder where they all came from, entertainment, balloons, even a small circus once. We had some grand parties when my husband was—"

"Quit changing the subject. You need to take this seriously," advised Candace, cutting her off mid-sentence. "Rose doesn't need a husband for a caretaker, she needs help."

"I know what she needs."

"How can you? You've never been in Rose's situation. You have no idea what she needs."

"A quick assumption when you've only known me for a week."

"True. But looking around this house, it's hard to imagine you've ever wanted for anything."

"It's time for you to leave." Ruby slowly pushed herself from the chair and walked onto the grass. She would do her best without Candace's help. "I'll see you tomorrow."

Unwilling to drop the topic, Candace followed as Ruby made her way across the yard to a large shed in desperate need of a paint job. "I'm not going to drop this."

Reaching the shed, Ruby knew she needed to end the conversation. "Take it. Take it all. My furniture, my silver, my china, my crystal, anything you want. I used to have everything I wanted. Now all I have are my memories... and my Rose. I won't see her institutionalized. She'd die being locked up like..."

"Like... her father?" asked Candace, hoping to understand.

Surprised by the personal observation, Ruby silently turned and reached for the latch.

Candace placed her hand over hers, determined to help her understand. "The only difference between your daughter's room and one at the State Mental Hospital is the location. A cell is still a cell."

"Let me make one thing very clear. Rose does not have a mental disorder. She was only six when her father was taken from us. She saw it happen right in front of her, in front of the whole town. I wanted to protect her from all the gossip and cruel assumptions after my husband's public breakdown and subsequent diagnosis. By the time she became a teenager, things had died down enough that I thought she would be okay dealing with the public. I tried to get her to come shopping with me or to the park. Anywhere. She refused to leave the house. I was concerned that she was heading down the same road as her father. I asked one of the psychiatrists that had worked with Wally for years to visit with Rose. It was difficult for her, but after observing my daughter for a weekend, he diagnosed her with anthropophobia. It can be found in certain disorders, but by itself it's just a phobia. The safeguards I put in place to protect her created the perfect environment for the phobia to develop. As the years have passed, she became even more reclusive."

"That answers a lot of questions. Thank you, Ruby. I know how difficult that was for you to share."

"She's twenty-one years old and you're her only hope."

"Please stop saying that."

"I hardly know you, Candace, but I believe in you."

"I don't know what else I can do for her."

Refusing to listen, Ruby began walking to the house. "I need to get dinner on. Rose will be hungry."

"I'm serious, Ruby," implored Candace as she watched Ruby enter the house.

Candace had a decision to make. The gate was nearby and her first inkling was to run as fast as she could. At the same time, she felt a new kinship with Ruby. Candace had been so focused on Rose that she hadn't taken into consideration what her employer was dealing with. No wonder she wanted the Christmas decorations up in the backyard. It was a reminder of happier times. Decorating for Christmas wasn't about Rose. It was for Ruby. Her memories were all she had left.

CHAPTER 15

Opening the double doors of the shed, Candace began moving things around to get to the large display pieces. Working hard not to break the antiquated decor, she packed each reindeer to the center of the yard where Ruby had pointed to and arranged them in perfect order from Rudolph to Blitzen. Santa's sleigh was a bit more cumbersome to fit through the door, but Candace struggled with it until she cleared the opening and finished off the festive scene. All she was missing was Santa himself. Returning to the shed, she found him in a large canvas bag. Dusting off the cobwebs, she unzipped it, showing Father Christmas the light of day for the first time in years. Next, she would require extension cords which she found coiled neatly and hanging on the inside wall of the shed.

The only thing left to deal with was Ruby's box of Christmas lights. Since the display had its own lights built in, she assumed they were for the trees and bushes behind the display. Looking at the large box setting on the patio table, she took a deep breath and walked toward it. "Too bad these lights weren't coiled as nicely as the extension cords," she said to herself as she placed the box on the grass and began pulling them out, stringing them into individual rows.

The sun was getting close to setting in the late afternoon and

Candace knew her time was running short. Pulling a ladder from the shed, she began the arduous process of stringing lights onto the grouping of decorative trees and bushes. They were way overdue for a pruning which made the job more difficult. Her determination would not let her quit until the last string of lights was tested and hung on the trees. It was well into dusk by the time she finished and growing darker by the minute. Standing in the middle of the yard, she surveyed her work with a smile. It felt good to have actually accomplished something.

Walking into Rose's bedroom, she found her laying on a stack of pillows, reading a book. "Get up, Rose."

Not wanting to accommodate, she continued to read as though no one else was in the room.

Refusing to take 'no' for an answer, Candace grabbed the book from her hands and pulled her to her feet. She walked her to the window facing the dark backyard and left her there. "Don't move," she ordered as she hurried back to the door. "I mean it, Rose. Don't move."

Curious as to what she was up to, Rose cupped her hands and placed them against her temples, peering into the darkness. She could see something down there but wasn't sure what it was.

Just as Ruby was pulling a casserole from the oven, Candace raced into the kitchen and passed by her on the way to the back door. "Come on!"

Placing the casserole on the top of the stove, Ruby turned off the oven and followed her out the door.

"Sit down," suggested Candace as she hurried to the corner of the house. She hadn't felt this level of childlike anticipation for years. Once Ruby was settled and ready, she looked to the turret window and saw Rose waiting like she was told. The fact that she actually followed her direction to stay near the window added to the excitement. Flipping the switch filled the backyard with magic. The North Pole instantly came to life.

Rising to her feet, Ruby walked onto the grass, her hands covering her mouth in awe of the beautiful sight. Swept back in time, the tears flowed freely as her heart filled with joy.

Candace approached and stood next to her. "Is it close to what it used to be?"

"It's perfect," exclaimed Ruby as she took in every detail from Rudolph's bright nose to the twinkle in Santa's eyes. "Thank you, Candace. Thank you!"

Glancing up at the turret window, she found Rose pressed to the glass, her smile showing the same reaction as Ruby. With a tap to Ruby's shoulder, Candace turned her attention to her daughter. They watched as Rose opened the window and pointed her camera at the display. It was an instant camera using self-developing film, so it wasn't long before Rose was examining the photograph. Ruby placed her arm around Candace's shoulders and gave her quick squeeze. "Thank you, Candace."

Ruby got exactly what she wanted, and Candace got more of what she needed. By stepping outside of herself to brighten their day, Candace brightened her own as well.

WALKING down the steps of the front porch, Candace grabbed the handlebars of her bike and pushed it along as Ruby followed her to the street. "It's too dark to ride that bike down the highway this evening."

"I have a light."

"Will should be at the town's Christmas kick-off party tonight. Get a ride home with him."

"I'm not sure if he wants to see me. We had a disagreement this afternoon."

"You and I disagreed earlier," said Ruby, "but we're still talking."

"This one escalated beyond a difference of opinion."

"If I know Will, he's already forgotten it."

"I'll probably just head home."

"You'll like our little holiday tradition."

"Actually, I hate the holidays."

"Because of your parents' death?"

Stopping in the middle of the street, Candace was shocked that Ruby knew such a personal detail of her life. "How do you know that?"

"Once I found out your last name, I did some searching on the internet at the library. I discovered the story in a newspaper article. I didn't know if you were the same Candace Hart until now."

"This Christmas will be five years since the accident," said Candace as she began to slowly push her bike.

"The article reported that they wrecked their vehicle in a snowstorm on their way to visit their daughter for the holidays."

"They were driving to the city to bring me home."

"Why?"

"I was desperate for help."

"How desperate?"

"I was in a bad place."

"How bad?"

Candace continued to push her bike down the street as Ruby walked next to her. She had serious reservations about opening the door to her past. In a way, she felt like she owed her some answers. After all, she'd asked the same thing of Ruby about Rose's condition just a few hours earlier. "I attended a two-year community college and got my associate's degree then left home starry eyed. After ten years in the city and more failed auditions than I could count, I hit rock bottom. I barely had enough money to make my rent, but I couldn't go home a failure. I was the hometown star and everyone expected me to be the next big thing. I continued to audition and every now and then I'd get a role in a corps de ballet of some small budget production."

"A what?"

"The ensemble ballet dancers in the background. I went to an audition one day on my lunch hour and the audition went long. I was late getting back to work so I got fired. In desperation, I called my parents and told them everything. They were coming to save me."

"Would you have gone back with them if they'd made it?"

"All I know is that I needed to regroup."

"What did you do after the accident?"

"I was devastated over my parents' death. I felt so much guilt.. I couldn't show my face in that town. I didn't even go home for the funerals. My uncle called and I told him to handle everything for the funeral and their belongings. That's the last time I spoke with any member of my family. I was so ashamed."

"Such heartbreak. I'm sorry, Candace."

"So am I. Every minute of every day."

"The article said it was a multi-car pileup, yet you think you're responsible," observed Ruby.

"They drove into that snowstorm because of me."

"Parents will go to great lengths for their children. That's our choice to make."

"It was a long time ago, Ruby, I'd rather not talk about it anymore."

"Time may lessen the impact, but you still have a hole deep inside. All these years I've held onto the hope that my husband would get better and come home from the hospital. I've wanted so desperately for everything to go back to normal. He died recently which ended that dream."

The conversation turned to silence as they continued to stroll down the street toward town square. "I feel there's something else that haunts you, separate from the guilt you feel over your parents' deaths," said Ruby. "You've been wearing it on your face since the day you arrived."

"No wonder people in this town think you're strange."

"I may be eccentric, but when it comes to reading people, I've only been wrong once."

"Now it's twice."

"That remains to be seen," she said with a twinkle in her eye.

Needing to change the topic, Candace saw the library in the distance. "I keep thinking about a painting I saw in the library. It depicted a woman walking on the beach at dusk, holding a lantern."

"I'm familiar with it."

"Is that the woman at the center of the will-o'-the-wisp legend? The mischievous fairy whose light leads weary travelers off the beaten path?"

"That's what they say," responded Ruby, slightly irritated.

"It looks like she's wearing a wedding dress of some kind. Is that why she waits for the captain's ship to return? It doesn't make any sense. He captured her then dumped her on a foreign shore, destitute and all alone. Why would she wait for him to come back?"

"The only thing the captain captured was her fascination."

"Did she love him?"

"As close as she could get, I suppose. Mostly, he intrigued her. According to legend, he hung a strand of pearls around her neck and whispered, 'come away with me and I will show you the world.'"

"She wasn't kidnapped?" asked Candace.

"They spent their weeks in each other's arms, until one morning when the sight of a new coastline stopped time as she knew it. The man she trusted bound her hands and feet and had his crew row her to shore."

"So it was betrayal."

"In her anger, she ripped the pearls from her neck and scattered them on the beach as she watched the ship sail away."

"Pearls," whispered Candace, placing her open hand around the bottom of her neck where her own strand of pearls once rested.

"My favorite part of the story is the one that's never told."

"Which part is that?"

"What became of the woman after being stranded on the beach."

"What did become of her?"

"She didn't pine away for the man who left her there. That's for certain. She picked herself up, wiped the sand off and found a way to live her life."

"How do you know that?"

"That's what strong women do, Candace. We pick ourselves up, dust ourselves off and go on."

"Do you think she still wanders the beach?"

"Every now and then, when the wind is blowing in the right direction, they say a voice can be heard calling to the sea."

"What does she say?"

"That's for the sea to tell."

Unexpectedly, the large Christmas tree in the town square lit up to a great applause. Candace was too intrigued by the story to pay attention. "Did the woman find happiness, Ruby?"

"Happiness found her." With that said, Ruby took a second look at the beautiful tree then turned and walked back toward her house. Candace watched her stroll down the street. Her answer echoed the same thing Will had said earlier that day. Still, Candace found it impossible to believe that it could ever be that simple.

Rather than ride her bike home in the dark, she gave into the tempting voices and music from the town square. Soon, she found herself pushing her bike through a crowd of Santa hat-wearing celebrants, young and old, drinking and eating with merriment. Booths boasted cotton candy, caramel apples, popcorn, eggnog and hot chocolate. On the back of a flat-bed trailer, decorated with straw bales covered in fake snow, large candy canes and ribbons, sat a small, hometown band performing holiday favorites. Candace began to wonder if she'd sized up the town correctly.

Continuing through the crowd, she saw a roped-off area with a few plastic reindeer and Santa sitting in the sleigh. The line of children was long, all waiting eagerly for their chance to sit on his lap and tell him their wishes. She recognized the "Ho, ho, ho" instantly with it's Irish accent. Captain Bob from the hardware store was Santa Claus. It made perfect sense. Pushing the bike forward, she nearly collided with a familiar face. It was Joe, dressed as an elf and carrying a water bottle. "Joe? Is that you?"

"Hey, Candace."

"I'm looking for Will. Have you seen him?"

"Check the buses. I heard him mention something about a loose seat."

"Buses?"

"Over there," he said pointing to the street. "Gotta run. Trying to keep Santa hydrated. That suit's a sweat machine." Then he disappeared through the crowd.

Looking toward the buses, Candace saw a light flicker inside so she walked her bike over and entered the bus. "Will?"

"Under here," he called from the back of the bus.

"What are you doing under there?" she asked, making her way down the aisle.

"Tightening the legs down."

"So you save buses as well?" she joked, sitting on the edge of a seat.

Crawling on his hand and knees to the aisle, he placed his ratchet in the toolbox then sat on the seat across from her. "Just keeping a promise I made to my grandma." The tone of his voice lacked the lighthearted nature that usually accompanied his answers. Anticipating the waters to be dicey after their argument, she decided to wade in carefully. "She taught you well."

"They both did," said Will, in a respectful tone as he placed the rest of his tools in the box. Uncertain of where to go from there, he looked to Candace and found her staring out the window at the people gathered for the celebration. "Looks like another good-sized crowd this year."

"The whole town must be here."

"The fishing industry for the small fisherman isn't what it used to be. A lot of families are struggling. Taking care of the kids is one thing our community does really well."

"It's impressive," agreed Candace. The last thing she wanted to do was get into another argument on the heels of their last one so she did her best to validate the town's good deed. As moved as she was with what she saw happening through the window, she couldn't allow herself to get sucked into it. The memories it brought back were too difficult. "Can I get a ride back to the lighthouse with you?"

"Of course."

"Are your ready to go?"

"Where?"

"Back to the lighthouse."

"The kids aren't finished yet," he said, closing the lid on his toolbox.

"Their parents are here, aren't they?"

"Sure."

"Then why can't we leave?"

"Tough afternoon at work?" asked Will, trying to understand why she wanted to leave so early.

"I'm not a big fan of Christmas. Why can't it be like every other holiday? The day arrives, you celebrate, then it's done. Why drag it out for so long?"

Will pointed at a child through the window who was sitting on Santa's lap. "That's why. They wait all year to tell him what they want."

"It doesn't really matter what they tell him. Santa doesn't exist."

"That's where you're wrong. See the elf with the notebook standing by Santa? That's Donna. She works in the hardware store, but tonight she's the record keeper. She writes down each child's name and what they ask for. Our town has a lot of poor families so we fundraise all year long, including tonight. Tomorrow, the committee members take the list and start purchasing the toys, all to be delivered on Christmas Eve. It's our version of a Christmas miracle."

"It seems like a false sense of reality. Like you're teaching them that all they have to do is ask for something and they'll get it."

"They know reality all too well. Tonight they can just be children asking Santa for a toy. There are worse things than Christmas spirit to teach a kid," said Will as he picked up his toolbox and walked down the aisle.

Candace left the bus in time to see him walking down the street toward his parked truck. She watched him put his toolbox in the back then walk toward one of the snack kiosks. Taking hold of her bike, she pushed it toward an empty bench away from the crowd and sat down, rubbing her hands together to keep them warm. Unexpectedly, a young girl about six years old hopped onto the bench next to her. She waved at Candace wearing a stretched out set of knitted mittens, three times the size of her hand. Unsure of what to do, Candace halfheartedly waved back. The young girl smiled in response then slid next to her. Tugging on her sleeve, Candace looked down to see her pull a hair clip out of her pocket. "It fell out," said the girl.

"Where's your mother?"

Without answering the question, the young girl handed the clip to

Candace then turned her back to her. "Just pull the sides back and clip them together," instructed the youngster.

Finding herself in an uncomfortable situation, Candace hesitated to help her as she looked around the crowd for possible parents. "Shouldn't your mother be doing this?"

"She's busy helping Santa. Don't you fix your hair?"

"I used to," replied Candace, finally giving in and using her fingers as a comb.

"Your hands are cold," reacted the girl.

"It's wintertime."

"Not till December twenty-first."

"It's starting to feel like wintertime," responded Candace as she clipped the barrette in her hair. "There. That's the best I can do without a brush." The little girl felt her hair and was happy with the stranger's work.

Candace returned to rubbing her hands together in an attempt to warm them.

Wanting to help, the little girl crawled onto her lap, picked up Candace's forearms and wrapped them around her waist. Then she took Candace's cold hands and slipped them inside her over-sized mittens next to her warm hands. Stirred by the young girl's act of kindness, Candace leaned over and whispered in her ear. "Thank you."

"My name is Michelle. What's yours?"

"Candace."

"What did you ask Santa for this year, Candace?"

"Nothing."

"Don't you believe in Santa?"

Candace controlled the urge to set the little girl straight. Will had a point: there are far worse things to teach a child than Christmas spirit. "I'm not sure what to ask for," she said, supporting the little girl's belief.

Hearing Candace's response, Michelle slid her hands out of her gloves and hopped off her lap.

"Where are you going?" asked Candace, hoping she didn't hurt her feelings.

"To ask Santa to bring me a pair of gloves."

"These are your gloves."

"They're yours now." With that said, Michelle smiled and ran toward the line.

The young girl not only warmed Candace's hands but her heart as well. She had forgotten what it was like to be young and innocent. Glancing at the crowd, she caught sight of Will staring at her. She wondered how long he had been watching. He smiled and lifted a bag of popcorn as an invitation to join him.

Michelle had touched her heart enough to pay the kindness forward. She could at least pretend to be merry. Walking toward his location, she was once again intercepted by Joe, carrying a tray of plastic cups full of eggnog. "Care for a drink?"

Inadvertently sucked into the Christmas spirit, she took him up on his offer. "I'll take two," she said, pulling out a few dollar bills from her pocket and laying them on his tray. "Thanks, Joe." Handing a cup to Will, she stood next to him in the crowd.

In return, he pointed the bag toward her and poured some popcorn into her mitten-covered hand. "Who would have thought that watching a bunch of kids experience a false sense of reality could be so heartwarming?"

"You made your point."

"Let the festivities begin," he said as he touched his plastic cup to hers.

She couldn't help but smile at the entire situation. Her day had been a roller coaster of extremes and she was glad to end it on a high note.

CHAPTER 16

A heavy fog rolled in from the ocean, limiting Will's visibility as he drove home from the town party. The heavy mist was so thick he could barely see the lines along the dark coastal highway. With vigilance they silently watched for signs of wildlife or approaching vehicles in the wrong lane. A feeling of impending doom washed over Will and he wondered if it would involve them or someone else. "I've got a bad feeling."

"About?"

No sooner had he expressed his concerns, his foreboding hunch was validated. "Will. Are you there?" came Joe's voice from the radio.

Grabbing the receiver, he responded to the call as he pulled off the side of the road. "Go for Will."

There's been an accident on the highway, three miles south of town. It's a bad one. Multi-vehicle."

"Roll out as many volunteers as you can. I'll meet you there." Will quickly turned the truck around and headed back. They hadn't made it far from town when the call came in. "When we get there, take the truck and head back to Ruby's for the night."

"How bad do you think it is?"

"With fog this thick, anything could have happened."

Arriving at the scene, an array of headlights pointing in all directions lit up the multiple car and truck accident. Although hard to see, damaged vehicles were scattered across the highway and into the ditches. Most were rolled onto their sides and tops, while some managed to stay upright after the collision. Volunteer firefighters worked to free people from their vehicles as wounded survivors in all directions called for help. It was nothing like Candace had ever seen. Parents searching for their children and children crying for their parents.

"Not that I need to say it, but drive careful on your way back," said Will as he left the truck and ran to the closest victim.

Candace made no attempt to get behind the wheel. Needing some fresh air, she rolled down the window, allowing a choir of panicked voices to enter the cab. "Help my children!" "My wife is bleeding!" "My husband is trapped!" Thoughts of her parents' accident stormed her mind. "It could have been a scene like this," she thought to herself. A woman resembling her mother in looks and age held her husband in her arms on the ground, desperately calling for help as she rocked him back and forth. The guilt Candace had felt for years manifested itself once again. There were so many people in need of help, yet she was paralyzed to do anything. A woman wearing an elf outfit staggered along the side of the road screaming, "I can't find my daughter! Help me find my daughter!" It was Donna, Santa's assistant. She was bleeding from a head injury as she teetered back and forth. A fireman rushed to her side and caught her just as she collapsed.

The woman's unconscious state allowed Candace to hear a tiny sound. She leaned her head out the window and looked toward the pavement but found nothing. Quietly she waited until she heard a whimper from farther down the ditch. Someone was down there and nobody knew it. Her first thought was to tell Will, but he had his hands full. Scared of what she might find at the bottom of the ditch, Candace searched the truck for a flashlight, finding one in the glove box. Then she made the brave choice to leave the truck and climb down the embankment. The heaviness of the fog impacted the throw of her light. Once she reached the bottom of the hill, she discovered an overturned vehicle. The lights and engine were off. But that wasn't where the sound was coming from. Hearing a tiny cry, she pointed her flashlight in its direction.

A child lay on her back, all alone on the side of the embankment. Instinctively, she raced to her side, only to find it was Michelle, the young girl who gave her the mittens. Her clothes were torn and her legs and face were scratched and bloody. Thankful she was alive, Candace removed her jacket and laid it over the girl's quivering body. "Michelle. It's me, Candace. From the Christmas party. Do you remember, Michelle?" Having trouble breathing, all Michelle could do was whimper out the answer, "Uh-huh." That was enough for Candace to know she was alert. "You're going to be fine, Michelle. I'm going for help. I'll be right back."

Candace ran up the hill, losing her footing on the steep embankment, but she finally made it to the road and ran straight toward Will. "There's a little girl in the ditch. She must have been thrown from the car. Hurry, Will."

Leaving the stable patient he was attending in the care of his assistant, Will grabbed a spine board from the ambulance, a towel and his medical kit and followed Candace. Sliding down the wet grass, they arrived at Michelle's side. Candace held the light with one hand and Michelle's cold hand with the other while Will performed an exam, asking questions about her level of pain. She was cold and in shock from being thrown from the car. He didn't have an appropriate-sized cervical brace for the child so he rolled up a towel and placed it around her neck to stabilize her spine as much as possible.

"It's going to be all right, Michelle. Will is taking good care of you." Her only response was more whimpering so Candace continued to reassure her. Glancing up, Will saw the look of concern on Candace's face. He'd seen signs of compassion and kindness in Candace but not on this level.

"Mommy," said Michelle, her first understandable word.

"Everything's okay, Michelle," assured Will, wishing he could confirm that her mother was fine. Without skipping a beat, his focus turned to the next step which required help from Candace. "I need you to slide the board under her while I roll her onto her side."

"I can do that," she responded in complete confidence as she propped her flashlight up against a rock to use both hands.

Gently Will placed his arms across the little girl's body and cupped his hands around her opposite side. "Ready?"

"Yeah."

As Will slowly rolled her onto her side, Candace pushed the board beneath her then helped lay her back down. Will took over at that point while Candace went back to holding the light. "Are you doing okay, Michelle?" asked Will, securing her body to the board.

This time, her quiet, "Uh-huh," sounded less frightened.

Candace watched Will's hands work with proficiency as he safely secured her small frame to the board. He was gentle but exact. Candace could see that caring for others wasn't just a job for him, it was his gift.

The sound of sirens approaching meant more help had arrived. "EMTs and an ambulance from a town south of us," Will said with relief. "We'll take all the help we can get."

Once he had Michelle securely strapped to the board, they each took an end and carefully made their way up the slick hill. As they approached the blacktop, a curious driver waiting in traffic used his cellphone to capture video of Michelle's rescue. He kept recording as Candace and Will packed her toward the ambulance, even capturing the reaction of the young girl's mother, "Michelle! Michelle!" as she broke free of the EMT helping her.

The taping abruptly ended when a highway patrolmen moved the gathering crowd back. A reporter and his cameraman showed up to document the terrible accident, but the highway patrolman kept them behind the barrier. While they were waiting, the driver who videotaped Michelle's dramatic rescue shared the footage he caught with the reporter. The night would not be a total loss.

With Michelle in the care of Will and her mother, Candace returned for the medical bag. While at the bottom of the ditch, she scanned the area for more victims as well as inside the overturned car.

By the time she made it back to the treatment area, Michelle had been loaded into one of the ambulances along with her mother. Candace waved as they closed the doors to the back. It was an extremely satisfying end to a frightening situation. Then something wonderful happened: Candace felt her heart return to life. It had been beating enough to keep her alive but hadn't felt deeply for years. Her concern for Michelle caused an intense ache, induced by an overwhelming dose of compassion. That aching evolved into elation seeing her reunited with her mother.

"Candace," yelled Will from the other side of the road. "I need my bag." Jumping into action, she hurried toward him, weaving through victims receiving care. The rush of adrenaline she experienced from helping Michelle was still pumping through her veins. Tonight was about saving lives and helping those in need. Her level of physical and mental acuity had piqued and showed no signs of receding. She was truly alive for the first time in years. She also felt a part of something.

Kneeling on the ground, she assisted Will as instructed. She was surprised how much she had to offer. The use of two more hands made a big difference when help was spread so thin. Looking around, she recognized volunteers from town: Joe, Captain Bob and others she'd only seen in passing. Some of them labored, prying victims from their vehicles while others worked to make people comfortable till they could be seen by a medical professional. One ambulance left the scene while another returned. Will had said that taking care of the kids was one thing the community did well. From Candace's viewpoint, saving lives could be added to the list.

Looking back at Will, she could tell he was thirsty as he wiped the sweat from his forehead. He was just finishing up with his patient so Candace took the opportunity to run to her bike in the back of the truck and grab her water bottle out of the basket. She returned just as he was heading to the next victim. "Here," she said, handing him the water bottle and taking his medical bag in trade. With a smile, she did her best impersonation of him. "Your body needs that water. If you're smart, you'll drink."

Will laughed at her recitation of the advice he'd given to her when she refused to eat or drink the morning after she was rescued. "What goes around comes around, I suppose." He guzzled the water quickly, then handed the bottle back to her when they reached his next patient. Falling to their knees, they went right to work. Candace anticipated what he needed before he even asked, impressing Will with her attention to details. Remaining focused on his patients, he stole glances of Candace each chance he could. Little did he know, she was doing the exact same thing, until their eyes met.

All at once, the controlled chaos became the back story, swirling around their newfound interest. Their sole focus was what they recognized in each other's eyes. They saw each other as a man and a woman, rather than rescuer and rescuee. Nothing was shared verbally, but enough was said to connect the dots from the past week. Biased by their own plans, they had overlooked what was naturally occurring. But in that moment, amid the commotion, there was no denying their impassioned connection.

"Will!" yelled Joe. "They need you over here."

"This woman's ready to be transported!" he responded, ending their enchanted window in time.

Will rushed to his next patient while Candace helped Joe pack the woman to the ambulance. Working separately helped to clear their heads but it couldn't replace what they shared.

IT WAS TWILIGHT when Will pulled into Ruby's driveway. There was enough light to see but the sun had yet to show itself. Turning the engine off, they both sat in silence. The rush Candace was on had completely dissipated. She wanted nothing more than to crawl into a comfortable bed and sleep the day away. Ruby's couch for a couple hours would have to do.

Will, on the other hand, was headed back to the clinic to continue assisting the doctor and his staff with the patients. "Thanks for the help tonight."

"I've never experienced anything like that. So many people in pain, calling for help."

"You handled it well. On the highway and at the clinic."

"Just following your lead."

"We make a good team," said Will.

Thinking he might be implying more than just a rescue team, Candace opened the door to the truck. "I'll grab my bike out of the back."

"I'll get it for you," said Will, thinking he may have spoke out of turn as well.

Leaving the cab, he beat her to the bed of the truck, lifted the bike out and placed it on the ground between them. Again, they waited in silence. There were things to be said but neither was sure what those things were or even what it meant.

"Ruby leaves the back door open, so I'll sneak around the house," said Candace as she leaned the bike against the porch railing.

"I'll drop by later."

"Don't worry about me. When you're done at the clinic, head home and get some sleep. I'll be fine."

Will watched her walk away until she disappeared around the corner of the house. Confused by what he was feeling, he jumped in the truck and backed out of the driveway. He wanted to say something but the timing didn't seem right. Then again, he hadn't seen any signs of her wanting to say anything either. There was only one thing he could do: go back to saving lives. It was much simpler than dealing with his personal life.

From behind a bush near the back fence, Candace watched his truck drive down the street. She wondered why he didn't say anything to her. "Maybe the light of day had changed things," she thought to herself. Why was she even thinking about this? Getting into another relationship was the last thing she wanted. She needed her head to make her heart understand. More confused than ever, she chalked it up to being vulnerable from lack of sleep then continued into the backyard.

CHAPTER 17

The kitchen was empty when Candace walked into the house. There was enough natural light from the window to make her way through the room without making any noise. She assumed Ruby and Rose would still be asleep. That notion changed once she entered the living room and saw Ruby on the couch holding the telephone in her hand. The coffee table was covered with small piles of neatly-folded laundry with the basket still half full. "Are you all right, Ruby?"

Sitting with her head back and eyes shut, Ruby softly changed the subject. "How is everyone?"

"All the worst victims have been transported north. There's one patient left waiting for the ambulance to return. The rest involved were able to be helped at the clinic."

"Have you had any sleep?"

"I'm good," exaggerated Candace, more concerned with Ruby than her own self. "Are you sure you're all right?"

"I can't seem to fold the laundry."

"Let me help you with that." Making her way to the couch, she took a closer look at Ruby. Her pale skin color, beads of sweat on her forehead and obvious lack of energy caused concern for Candace as she began folding the clothes. "Is Rose still asleep?"

"Yes."

"Why are you up so early?"

"I'm usually up around 5:00."

"Are you waiting for a phone call?"

"What makes you think that?"

"You're holding the phone in your hand."

Looking toward her lap, Ruby saw the phone lying in her hand. "I've already made the call."

"What's going on, Ruby?"

"I'm not well."

"Who did you call?"

"The doc. After all these years, my heart is finally giving out."

"All these years?" curiously asked Candace, pausing from folding the laundry. "You talk like you're a hundred years old."

"Time is a funny thing. One minute you're going to live forever, then a tragedy breaks your heart and the idea of living forever is a punishment worse than death."

"Whatever's going on with your heart is most likely fixable. People don't die of a broken heart, Ruby."

"You're so young. So was I once."

"I know what a broken heart feels like."

"That was obvious the day I met you. I've just been around a lot longer."

"I suppose when I'm looking back in twenty or thirty years, I'll have a different perspective as well."

"The stories I could tell of the things I've seen."

Confused by what Ruby was really saying with her cryptic dialogue caused Candace to return to the situation at hand. "What did the doctor say when you called?"

"I need to take a ride."

"Where's this ride taking you?"

"North."

"To the hospital?"

"Yes."

"Who's driving you?"

"I'm catching a ride up in the ambulance with Joseph when he returns for the last victim. He should be back anytime. The doc figures it's better to ride in the front than wait until they have to put me in the back."

"A smart man."

"I was ready to go, Candace."

"You're not talking about the ambulance are you?"

"I was ready to be done with this life. But Rose still needs me."

"I'm not ready to lose you either. You made the right decision."

"You'll need to stay with Rose."

"Of course."

"There are things I have to tell you."

"We'll figure it out."

"I keep some cash in a tin in the cupboard above the stove. Use it for food and necessities."

"All right."

"Rose doesn't like raisins, dates or figs. No dried, squishy fruit."

"Okay."

"She loves milk. Plain or chocolate."

"I'll make sure she gets her milk."

"And she detests cashews."

"Ruby, she'll be fine."

"She needs you, Candace."

"I told you to quit saying that."

"It's true."

"When will Joe be here?"

"Any minute. He's stopping here first before he gets to the clinic. The doc wants to listen to my heart while they're loading the last accident victim."

"Do you have everything you need?"

"Yes," she answered, pointing to the bag next to the door. "How do I explain this to Rose?"

"You don't. Leave it to me."

Before Ruby could argue the point, Joe burst through the door wearing his fireman uniform. "Good morning, Mrs. Stratton. Are you ready to roll?"

"It appears I have no other choice, Joseph," responded Ruby, slowly sitting up.

"Are you awake enough to drive?" asked Candace as he neared the couch.

"Neither snow, nor rain, nor heat, nor gloom of night—"

"That's your postal job, Dear," said Ruby, cutting him off before he finished.

"I guess I am a little tired."

With both their help, Ruby stood up and walked toward the door. "Not to worry. I've got enough stories to keep you awake for days, Joseph." Ruby's humor lightened the moment but didn't make the situation any less difficult. Once outside, the mother looked toward her daughter's second-story window before she allowed Joe to help her into the passenger seat of the ambulance.

"She'll be fine," assured Candace as she placed her hospital bag and purse on the floor next to her feet. "I'll take good care of her." Candace waved as they backed out of the driveway and onto the street. She took a deep breath as the distance between her and the ambulance widened. Taking a look up at the turret window, she worried about how Ruby's absence would affect Rose. Things could go from bad to worse in a hurry. She had to be prepared for whatever may come. "Who am I kidding?" she asked herself. "There's no way to prepare for someone like Rose."

With that conclusion in mind, she entered the house and made her way up the stairs. Quietly, she opened Rose's bedroom door, finding her fast asleep. The curtains were in the same position: the curtains on the window facing the lighthouse were drawn open while the rest were shut. It was still dark enough in the room to see the effect of the lighthouse's beam as it passed through each time it rotated. An occurrence, she imagined, most people wouldn't like when trying to sleep. Candace concluded that Rose needed the beam to light her room with every rotation. Taking another look at the curtain placement caused her to consider another possibility. She began to wonder if it was about letting in the light or keeping something out.

Circling around the bed, she noticed an old-fashioned candy jar on the nightstand but she couldn't tell what it contained. Curiously, she picked up the jar and walked toward the window. She waited for the lighthouse beacon to pass by and light its contents. They appeared to be wishbones, large and small. It was safe to say that domestic fowl were a favorite at the Stratton home. Placing it back on the nightstand, she lifted the lid and reached in with her hand. As she was pulling several out, Rose reached out and grabbed Candace's fistful of bones, holding on tight until she released them.

"Good morning, Rose," said Candace as she placed the lid back on the jar. Not wanting to wake up, Rose disappeared beneath her covers.

"Good morning. How are you?" Candace said as she walked toward the door pretending to mimic Rose. "I'm fine, and you?" The mock conversation continued until she left the room and shut the door behind her. Walking down the stairs, she tried to think of the best way to tell Rose about Ruby's trip north. She gave up thinking once she reached the living room. Her brain was still trying to process all that had happened in the past twenty-four hours. She needed to slow her mind from the rapid pace it was moving. Then she remembered the book in her bag: Rhue-wyn's story. With a smile on her face she brought it into the light and found where she left off. Relaxing into the cushions of the couch, she drifted away to a distant land and time.

The port's activity had quieted for the day as the rest of the sailors climbed from the rowboats to the dock. The captain bid them passage into town and with hoots and hollers they raced each other down the street. The captain then made his way toward the ledge and the beautiful woman leaning against the railing.

"What brings you to our small port, Captain?"

"My ship is overdue for some mending. We've come for lumber and a safe shore to drop anchor while we make the proper repairs."

"You speak with a foreign accent. From what land do you hale?"

"Originally, Iceland to the north."

"Iceland sounds terribly cold."

"It can be. The sea is now my home."

"A vast home indeed," she replied, fascinated by his answer.

"Are you coming down or shall I make the climb?" he asked with gallantry.

Her normal coquettish response would have been to wait for him, but she chose a different answer that surprised even herself. "Would you consider it unladylike to meet halfway?"

"Not in the least."

"First, I must know your name."

"Captain Kristjanason," he responded as he began walking toward the foot of the concrete stairs.

"That's quite a mouthful," she replied, keeping up with him from above.

"Then call me by my given name, Andri."

"Welcome to Wales, Andri."

"I've been to this port on many occasions."

"So you're familiar with our town?" she asked as she reached the top of the stairs.

"Quite." Without warning, he ran to the top of the stairs before she could take the first step. Coming face to face, he lifted her hand and kissed the back of it. "I don't remember the scenery being this breathtaking on earlier visits."

"A lovely way to say 'hello,'" commented Rhue-wyn flirtatiously, knowing she had him spellbound.

"Inspired by a beautiful lady."

Staring into his eyes, Rhue-wyn was intrigued. It was as though his eyes were bottomless pools of water. The piercing blue color transfixed her for a moment, causing her to look away to clear her head. There was something familiar about him but she couldn't put her finger on it.

"Shall we begin with a meal?" he asked, extending his arm.

She accepted by wrapping her arm around his and together they walked down the street. Captivated by the stranger, Rhue-wyn wanted to know everything. Fortunately, she had the ability to get whatever her heart desired.

"Your name is strange to me. Tell me about it."

"In the Icelandic naming process it's common to use the patronymic system of taking the father's first name as the child's last and adding 'son' to the end if you are male. Less common is the matronymic system. It was my mother who raised me alone so she gave me her given name, Kristjana, combined with the word son. Kristjanason. Now that you know my name, might I have the privilege of knowing yours?"

"I have but one name. Rhue-wyn," she said proudly, placing the emphasis on the second syllable.

"A vibrant name like Rhue-wyn should require no other."

She'd never loved her name as much as when it trickled off his tongue. "Is it your wisdom or your charm that earned you the position of captain at such a young age?"

"Ownership of my vessel entitles me to be captain."

"You've done well for yourself."

"The transportation of goods is a lucrative business."

"What port do you call home? Surely, you have property somewhere?"

"Do you hear that?" asked Andri, stopping Rhue-wyn in the street.

"Hear what?"

"The sound of my stomach growling."

Ceasing the inquisition, she took him to her favorite dining hall. After a wonderful meal, they built a fire on the beach then wrapped themselves in a blanket to ward off the night chill. They stayed up all night staring at the stars while Andri told tales of his adventures in far-off lands.

A week had passed since the mysterious ship and its captain arrived in port. While the men on the ship made the necessary repairs, Andri and Rhue-wyn spent much of the time together on shore. One day he asked if she would like a tour of the ship. Jumping at the offer, she grabbed his hand and ran toward the boat about to depart with more supplies. The anticipation of boarding his ship grew with each stroke of the men's oars. Soon she was standing on the main deck staring back at the coastal town she currently called home. It seemed so small and inconsequential when considering the vastness of the ocean. The lure of sailing to remote destinations with the man who had enchanted her grew with each breath of sea air.

Just as she once longed to go beyond the forest walls, she now desired to go further than the shoreline of her own land. A tour of the ship at the captain's hand revealed a smooth operation. Everyone had a duty to perform and they took their jobs seriously. She felt the respect they had for their captain and the love they had for their way of life. In Rhue-wyn's fanciful imagination, it was freedom at its finest.

The last stop on their tour was the captain's quarters. It was everything she envisioned it to be. Decorated with furniture and artifacts from all over the world, she touched each one as she made her way around the room. Being ignorant to other cultures, she could only appreciate the exquisite designs and detailed handiwork. Everything from the tapestries to the furniture engendered wonderment.

While her back was turned, Andri lowered a strand of pearls over her head, allowing them to come to rest against her chest. "Come away with me and I will show you the world," he whispered in her ear as he fastened the clasp. Turning to look in the mirror, she rubbed her hand along the string of pearls then glanced back at the man standing behind her. Receiving presents from men was a routine occurrence in Rhuewyn's life, but the feeling that accompanied this gift was nothing she had felt before. Here was a man who could give her everything her heart desired. He could give her the world. Rhue-wyn knew she'd be a fool to turn him down. Turning in his arms, she whispered, "Yes," and with a kiss they sealed the deal.

"The repairs are nearly complete. We set sail in two days. We need time to restock the ship. That should give you enough time to gather your things and say your goodbyes. I will inform the crew."

"But what of the wedding?"

"Wedding?" asked Andri.

"Isn't that what a respectable woman would do?" asked Rhue-wyn coyly. She had no commitment to legal constraints but the image it would portray interested her.

"Then a wedding you shall have," exclaimed Andri, slightly confused by her request. "We'll hold it here, aboard the ship."

"At sunset."

"If that's what your heart desires. Leave all the details to me," he said with a kiss to the back of her hand. As Andri left the captain's quarters, Rhue-wyn *thought of who she would want to invite to the wedding. No one in the town came to mind. She had no real friends outside the forest. Her only use for humans was selfish entertainment. She already said goodbye to the ones that mattered most years ago when she left her home in Ffos Anoddun. Although she longed to return, she refused to go back without the most adventurous stories to tell. Traveling the world as a captain's wife would ensure a triumphant return to the forest she loved and those who inhabit it. She would be the talk of the forest for centuries to come.*

Walking toward the bed, she leaped backwards and landed dead center. "What makes Andri different from all the other men who romanced her?" she asked herself. Was it the mystique that surrounded a man of the sea or possibly the confident manner in which he pursued her? Needless to say, there was something about him difficult to resist. Having never fallen in love, she couldn't decide if she was in love with Andri or the future he offered. To be honest, she wasn't sure if she was capable of falling in love. From what she understood during her walk among mortals, true love was supposed to be selfless. Not a characteristic Rhue-wyn could attest to. Because of this, the concept of love bewildered her.

Standing up from the bed, she straightened her dress and walked toward the door. She had made her decision and that was that. She loved being in Andri's arms. It was as close to love as she'd ever been and she would treasure every moment of their adventure together.

The book was compelling but Candace's sleep-deprived body and mind finally gave out. She could have slept the day away but the subconscious thought of being Rose's caretaker woke her within an hour. Looking around the room, she was quickly reminded of reality and her current circumstances. She still had no idea how to reach Rose. Maybe a hot shower would help her think more clearly. With no clothes to change into, she decided to rummage through Ruby's closet for something to wear. While looking at the lotions and creams on Ruby's dressing table, a wild idea struck. If Rose saw herself as the adult she was rather than the child-like persona she had maintained for years, it may help them better relate to each other. At this point, she would try anything to help them connect. Checking the time, she assumed Rose would still be asleep so she ran into the kitchen, grabbed a handful of cash from the tin and left through the back door.

From her bedroom window, Rose watched Candace leave the porch and cross through the backyard. She breathed a little easier knowing the intruder who had invaded her life had left the house. Falling to her knees, she turned her attention away from Candace as she reached beneath the bed and pulled out a wooden box. Crafted from a light-colored wood, the box measured 10x7x4 inches deep with a full-grown beech tree engraved across the lid. A keyhole built into the front of the box kept the contents hidden from the world. Reaching between the mattress and box springs, she pulled out a key and unlocked the box then lifted the lid. Inside were numerous pictures taken with her instant camera. They were neatly organized using homemade file cards with descriptions written across the top. Walking her fingers through the different categories, she came to the section she wanted. Pulling thirty or so pictures from between the dividers, she turned around and used the side of the bed for a backrest.

It didn't take long for a smile to appear on her face as she looked at each picture. Most were taken from the viewpoint of her window and were all of the same subject: Will Bloom. Will working in the yard, Will eating lunch fixed by Ruby, Will talking with Ruby, Will painting a fence, Will arriving in his truck, and more. The quality of the pictures wasn't great but they allowed Rose to have Will in her life.

Placing the photos on the floor beside her, she crawled to her feet and looked out the window. The air was clear and the sun's position was just right, making the lighthouse extra visible. She placed the nearby binoculars to her eyes to get even closer. She was too far away to spy any details but that didn't keep her from using her imagination. Her mother had told her of the terrible accident on the highway last night so Rose assumed he was fast asleep. Thinking of his heroic actions made her smile even more. For all intents and purposes, Will was the only man in her life, even though he wasn't actually in her life.

For Rose, however, he was the light that brightened her days just as the beam from his lighthouse lit up her room at night. Turning back to the box, she returned her stack of photos, locked the box and slid it under the bed. Then she tucked away her key and hopped into bed. As she drifted off for a morning nap, fantasies of Will accompanied her mind.

CHAPTER 18

The air was crisp as Candace made her way down the street and past the park. Still unfamiliar with all the shops in town, she continued down Main Street hoping to find what she was looking for.

"You're out early this gran' morning," remarked Captain Bob, approaching from a side street, carrying a bouquet of artificial flowers. "And without your bicycle."

"It's parked at Ruby's."

"What brings you out so early, Lass? I would expect you to be sleepin' after last night."

"I could say the same for you," replied Candace.

"I'm on a mission of deadly importance."

"Me too. I'm looking for a store that sells cosmetics."

"Mae's Grocery has some female accoutrements, but your best bet's gonna be LeBlanc's across the street."

"LeBlanc's?"

"LeBlanc's Embellishments and Remedies," explained Bob. "'Tis a drugstore and more. So much more."

"A pharmacy sounds perfect," said Candace as she started across the empty street.

"Just so happens I'm headin' in that same direction," replied the captain as he accompanied her.

"Do you think they're open?"

"The door always opens by 8:00 sharp."

"It's only 7:30," replied Candace with disappointment.

"Then it's a donut in the bakery and one for the road."

"I'm kind of in a hurry."

"If I know the beautiful shop owner, and I have for years, she's probably in the back toolin' around," said the captain as he stepped onto the sidewalk.

"She?"

"The lovely Fae LeBlanc. She's our local celebrity. She won the state beauty pageant forty years ago. After the glitz and glamour wore off, she came home to run the family business," he reminisced, pressing his face to the glass to see into the lit back room. "Her folks retired to Florida years ago and she's been runnin' it ever since."

While Captain Bob knocked loudly, two women approached Godfrey's Bakery next door and paused before they entered.

"Top of the morning, ladies," said Bob.

"She doesn't open till 8:00, Captain," responded one of the women.

"Oh, she'll be openin' for us."

"And what makes you so special?" one woman asked, pointing the question toward Candace.

"Come out dancin' with me and I'll show you," cut in the captain, just as the door unlocked and opened.

"Incorrigible!" exclaimed the second woman.

"But oh, so lovable," he responded as he escorted Candace through the open door then stuck his head back out. "Good day, ladies. And let me know if you feel like kickin' up your heels."

The captain's insinuation left the women outwardly appalled, yet inwardly intrigued as the door to the drugstore closed. "I heard he had a different woman in every port."

"You know as well as I do... for the past forty years, he's only docked at two ports. Will-O'-the-Wisp and the fishing port twenty miles south," said the second woman, trying to clear up the hearsay.

"Nonetheless, sailors are all the same. Gallivanting around the world. Looking for adventure."

"He was the captain of his own fishing boat, not a sailor on the high seas," argued the second lady as she opened the door to the bakery.

"We'll see what everyone else has to say," argued the first woman as she entered the bakery and made her way toward the group of middle-aged ladies gathered for coffee and morning gossip.

In the store next door, Captain Bob tucked the flowers behind his back as he followed Candace and the store owner to the front. "Don't let those ladies be botherin' you. They think it's their duty to keep everyone informed," he advised.

"There are men in this town who do the same thing. Gossip is not gender-biased," said the beautiful shop owner as she picked up her cup of tea and saucer and took a sip.

"Such good citizens," replied Candace.

"They're small in numbers compared to the rest of us," said Fae.

"Damage is still done."

"Unfortunately, yes. Since the captain has clearly misplaced his manners this morning, allow me to introduce myself. I'm Fae LeBlanc."

"Candace Hart."

"Top of the morning to you as well, my dearest Fae," commented the captain.

"Beware, Candace. It's a well known fact that the Irish can argue either side of a question. Often at the same time."

"I'd accuse you of malarkey so early in the morning," replied the captain, "but your beauty has softened my tongue."

"A silent mouth is sweet to hear," replied Fae.

"Using an Irish proverb against me can mean only one thing... I'm in the dog house. Most likely about last night."

"Do not speak unless you can improve the silence."

"Another one. You're on a roll, my dear. Will flowers improve my luck?" he asked, handing her the bouquet of random artificial flowers.

"They might have if they came with a scent."

"You know quite well the florist doesn't open till 9:00."

"Are you telling me I'm not worth the wait?" she asked, making him work for it.

"I don't mean to interrupt," said Candace, "but I'm kind of in a hurry."

"Please excuse my lack of customer service. What's so urgent?"

"It just so happens we have an emergency," answered the captain.

"Upset stomach, fever, a cold coming on?"

"I need some makeup," said Candace.

"A true emergency," announced Fae, setting down her cup as she picked up a basket from the stack. "Follow me." As the ladies made their way to the cosmetic section, Captain Bob got detained by the perfume samples—sampling each one to find the right scent for his fake flowers.

"In this aisle you'll find everything you need and more," said Fae.

"I don't need much."

"Not with that beautiful face."

"I'm actually here for a friend."

"Someone needing to look younger?"

"Someone needing confidence."

"Take your time. If you have any questions, just holler," said the shop owner as she walked toward the captain to rescue what was left of her perfume samples.

Candace studied the different brands, types and shades with Rose in mind. She quickly decided against foundation. She wanted to keep it simple. Rose had flawless, porcelain skin—most likely due to her lack of sun exposure. Candace wanted to add a touch of color to show some life, so she chose a soft peach for a blush. She also wanted her eyes to stand out, so a tube of black mascara and a soft color palette of eyeshadows went into the basket. Finally, the lips. A beautiful coral pink captured her attention. "Perfect." One final item: a pack of makeup removal wipes.

Before she left the aisle, Candace accidentally caught her reflection in a mirror. Her appearance was real and unrefined. It was the woman she was beneath the facade she'd been forced to wear for the past five years. Frightened at first to see herself in such an imperfect state, she looked away. Dante never would have stood for such imperfection. And she never would have let it happen. The consequences would have been dire. She showered, styled her hair and applied her makeup each morning before he woke up. Even in the dark of night he insisted she look as beautiful as possible. She literally trained herself to sleep flat on her back so as to not mess up her hair or cosmetics during her sleep.

Curiously, she returned to the mirror. The longer she stared at the raw image, the more she liked what she saw—her hair not styled, her face void of makeup. In a way, the blank canvas of her face symbolized a fresh start to her life. Soon it became impossible to hold back the smile waiting to form: another feature she hadn't seen staring back at her for a very long time.

Turning her attention to the cosmetics, she located her favorite shade of lipstick, a rosy pink. It wasn't the designer tube of creamy red she was forced to grow accustomed to in recent years, but the shade she used to wear when she lived life on her own terms. Tossing it into her basket, she confidently walked toward the counter. It was time to add some color of her choosing.

Approaching the counter, she unloaded her basket next to the cash register. "Is there a clothing store in town?"

"I suppose you could call it that," responded Fae. "If it's rustic work clothes or everyday casual wear you're looking for, there's a small department store on the next block."

"They got everything a man could need, except someone to keep them warm at night," said the captain with a wink to Fae LeBlanc.

"Those days may very well have sailed, my seafaring friend."

"Friend. When did that happen?"

"When you stood me up last night."

"I was a wee bit busy switching hats from Santa to volunteer firefighter."

"A phone call would have been nice."

"How far away the stars seem, and how far is our first kiss, and ah, how old my heart," exclaimed the captain.

"Even Yeats won't get you out of this one."

"How about dresses?" asked Candace, interrupting the domestic dispute once again.

"Thank goodness. I've been dying to upgrade your wardrobe since you walked into my store. I realize style is a personal thing, but are those men's clothes you're wearing?"

"My luggage got lost. I'm borrowing Will's clothes."

"You poor dear. You won't find many dresses in town this time of year," answered Fae. "Your best bet is forty miles north."

"Too far to bike."

"I can order anything online and have it here in a few days."

"Is that how the women shop in this town?"

"Some. Most ladies come in and order here."

"No internet?"

"They come for her keen sense of style," mentioned the Captain.

"Really?"

"I may have left the pageant world, but I keep my ear to the ground when it comes to fashion. What are you looking for?"

"A young adult dress. Obviously not for me. Nothing glitzy or too revealing, size four or smaller."

"You may be in luck," said Fae as she walked into the back room, talking loudly so Candace could still hear her. "I ordered a party dress for one of my customer's teenage daughter, but the girl hated it. Probably because her mother picked it out. I have yet to return it." Walking around the corner she held the powder blue gown up in a clear dress bag for Candace to have a look.

"It's adorable," said Candace as she unzipped the bag and touched the satin fabric.

"I don't think 'adorable' was what the daughter had in mind."

"The conservative style is perfect for Rose."

"Rose Stratton?"

"Yes."

"I heard Ruby brought in a professional to help her daughter."

"I'm just a friend trying to help."

"When I was a teenager entering pageants, Ruby taught me how to walk like a lady and talk like a lady. But more than that. She taught me the key to confidence and how to woo a judge's eye. I'd drop by each day after school just to attend my own private finishing school."

"Ruby must have been pretty young then."

"Probably in her thirties. She's always been blessed with youthful beauty. I'd kill to know what she uses on her skin."

"Have you ever asked?"

"She buys basic lotions here every month, but it can't be that. She's got a secret to her youthful beauty. I hope someday she'll share."

"You should've seen her back in the day. When Wally Stratton snagged her as his wife, every man in town was wonderin' what star she arrived on," reminisced the captain as he eavesdropped on the conversation.

"And every single woman in town was heartbroken. Especially Louise Godfrey."

"She and Wally had tipped their toes in the pool of romance, but that ended when he met Ruby," added the captain.

"It's only been recently that she's begun to show her age. Even now, she's still as beautiful as ever," noted Fae, impressed by the fact.

"How old would that be?"

Fae looked at the captain for help, but he shrugged his shoulders, unable to answer the question. "Not an inkling here."

"Interesting," replied Candace, trying to equate all the details in her mind. "So how much for the dress?"

"It just so happens I'm having a seventy-five-percent-off sale today."

"My lucky day."

"And Rose's as well. We could all use a bit more self-assurance."

"Everyone except the lovely Fae. She's fillin' the room up with self confidence."

"Flattery will only get you so far, Captain."

"You've seen nothin' yet."

"You wouldn't happen to have a curling wand I could borrow?" asked Candace, feeling like a third wheel in need of an exit strategy.

"Take this one," she said, picking one off the shelf. "I've got more coming in this week. And if your luggage doesn't show up soon, please come back and see me."

"Thank you," she said as she walked away. Just as she reached the door, Candace decided to help the captain out by giving Fae something to think about. "It's not often you find a man who quotes poetry." Then with a wink she opened the door and left the shop. Candace felt a spring in her step as she walked down the sidewalk, but it didn't last long. Passing by Godfrey's bakery, two women left the store at the same time and strolled along beside her. "Are you the psychiatrist working with Ruby Stratton's daughter?"

"We're quite concerned about the girl," said the second woman, feigning sincerity. "How is she doing?"

"Her name is Rose but I'm pretty sure you already know that. If you're so concerned, why don't you stop in and see her?"

"We wouldn't want to get in the way of her treatment," said the first woman as they walked along.

"The whole town's concerned about her condition," added the second woman.

"We have been for years."

"And what condition would that be?" asked Candace.

"You would know better than us," discreetly replied the first woman. "Her 'mental' condition."

"We don't blame the child for her problems."

"We realize it's genetic. From the father's side, of course."

"Not that Ruby's completely normal."

Candace stopped on the street to gather her thoughts. The last thing she wanted was to give them anymore scuttlebutt to use against Ruby and her daughter. So she chose instead to share her professional diagnosis as the psychiatric doctor they believed her to be. "Now that poses an interesting question."

"Yes?" they replied in unison.

"In regard to genetics... will your children turn out to be as nosy as their mothers?"

It took the women a few seconds to understand the accusation. Flabbergasted, they turned and stomped back toward the bakery.

Candace watched them move down the street, whispering back and forth at a rapid rate as though the world were coming to an end. "It appears this doctor thing has its perks."

Turning back, she caught her reflection in the store window. Fae had a point. Maybe she should probably try to find some women's clothing at some point. Will's clothes continued to serve a purpose both practically and therapeutically, but they were a far cry from the designer clothing she had worn for years. In Dante's world, everything was for show. It didn't matter whether she was on his arm at an upscale event or sitting at home. Her so-called assistant, warden to be more exact, picked her clothes out for her every day and night, from top to bottom. Once she was dressed, Dante would scrutinize everything from the clothing to accessories until perfection was reached. Those days were over. Proudly, she continued down the street in the same baggy jeans and blue flannel shirt she had been wearing for the past twenty-four hours. Her outfit was far from perfect. That's why she loved it the most.

CHAPTER 19

Entering Rose's room, Candace found her still buried beneath the covers. Trying to make as much noise as possible, she crumpled the shopping bag before placing it on a chair next to the dress bag.

Once she left the room, Rose popped her head out from under the covers and looked at the bags. She didn't dare leave her bed in case Candace returned. Hearing footsteps approaching, she disappeared again beneath the blankets.

Packing a freestanding mirror into the room, she placed it in front of the bookshelf and window facing the door. Then she moved a small rotating chair from the desk and set it in front of the mirror, but facing away. "You'll never guess what fun I have planned for us this morning."

"Go away," came a muffled voice from under the blankets.

"You've got five seconds to get up, take a shower and brush your teeth."

"I bathed last night."

"Then all you have to do is brush."

"Leave me alone!"

Yanking the covers from the bed, Candace removed the barrier between them, leaving Rose vulnerable and exposed.

"That's not five seconds," argued Rose.

"Time flies when you're having fun."

Wearing a girly flannel nightgown, Rose crawled off the mattress and stomped into the bathroom. Before she could get the door shut and locked, Candace stuck her shoe in the door and blocked it. "Door open, remember?" Candace gave her the privacy she needed, while keeping her foot in the door. After she finished her morning bathroom routine, Candace escorted her to the chair next to the mirror and sat her down.

"Where's my mother?"

"She had to run out for a while."

"I want to go downstairs."

"When we're done."

"Done with what?"

"Your makeover."

"My what?"

"Think of it as playing dress up."

"Playing what?"

"Dress up. Didn't you do that as a child?"

Not wanting to talk about her childhood, Rose remained silent as she watched her captor remove the makeup from the paper shopping bag and open the packages. Candace plugged the curling wand in to heat then tucked Rose's messy hair behind her ears. Kneeling next to the chair, Candace turned Rose's face toward her. "I need to you sit still while I apply some makeup."

"Mother says I don't need makeup."

"Have you ever worn makeup?" said Candace as she opened the eye shadow case and removed the brush.

"No."

"It's not that you need it, Rose... We're just enhancing the beauty you were born with," responded Candace as she proceeded to paint Rose's eyelids with a light color, just enough to compliment her eyes.

Next she pulled the applicator brush out of a tube of mascara and pointed it toward her eye.

Reacting to what she perceived as danger, Rose pulled her head away from the mascara brush. "You can't move, Rose."

"What's that for?"

"See?" said Candace, showing her the applicator brush. "It's like a comb for your eyelashes." Candace brushed a few strokes onto her own lashes as Rose watched with wonder.

"What if you stick it in my eye."

"I won't stick you in the eye."

"Do you promise?"

"Yes, I promise. Now try not to blink."

Feeling better about letting Candace continue, Rose moved her head back into position. At first it was hard to keep from blinking but the longer it took the more trust she felt.

Adding color to her cheeks brought life to Rose's pale face and the coral lipstick added the final touch. Her face was a masterpiece. "Beautiful," whispered Candace as she inspected the details. Getting up, Candace rotated her chair so she could see her reflection in the mirror. Using her feet, Rose rolled her chair close to the mirror and examined her face carefully. "Is that really me?"

"What do you think?"

"I don't know what to think."

Picking up a brush, Candace began to tackle the young woman's messy morning hair, carefully working through each knot and tangle. "Do you use conditioner?"

"What's conditioner?"

"I'll take that as a 'no.'"

It wasn't long before Rose's neck disappeared as her shoulders began to rise. A sign that her anxiety was increasing.

"I used to love it when my mother would comb my hair," shared Candace, hoping to distract her with a story. "She took her time with each stroke. Mom had the most gentle way about her." Noticing her shoulders receding, Candace continued. "My hair was about the length of yours and Mom would always let me choose what hairstyle I wanted to wear. I had four choices every time. Double braids, french braids, a low pony tail or a high pony tail. The only time she let me wear it down was to church on Sunday. Even then I had to pull the sides back in burettes or with a headband."

"Which one did you like best?" asked Rose, surprising Candace.

"Double braids that started at the base of my neck."

"Why?"

"Because they weren't as tight. How do you like to wear your hair?"

"Just brushed."

"Can I pull it back so we can see your face better?" asked Candace as she pulled the sides of her hair up to the top of her head to show Rose. A tentative nod gave Candace approval, allowing her to tie a hair band around the high pony tail. After a few tweaks and more brush strokes, she commenced curling her hair into curly tresses. The length of her dark tresses ended mid-back and maintained its curl nicely. "Your hair has tons of body."

"How can hair have a body?"

"It's a different definition. 'Body' means your hair has a lot of fullness and bounce to it."

"That's good?"

"That's great. It makes it easy to style." Putting the curling wand down, Candace looked at Rose's reflection in the mirror. "Done." She waited for a response from Rose but nothing came. She didn't want to force it so she unplugged the curling wand then walked to the dress bag. Carefully she unzipped the bag and removed the pale blue satin, knee-length, semi-formal dress. It had a round neckline, cap sleeves and a fitted bodice that tapered to the belted waistline. It whispered sweet and innocent. Turning around, Candace presented it to Rose. She waited patiently as Rose reached out and gently touched the fabric with her finger tips.

"Try it on. It's perfect for you," said Candace as she hooked the hanger over the mirror. "I'll be over here, looking out the window."

Before Candace made it to the other side of the room, she heard the hanger lift off the mirror. Smiling to herself proudly, she leaned on the windowsill and looked down at Santa and his reindeer in the backyard. It wasn't long before she heard the zipper slide down. Rose was sold. Looking up, Candace's eyes focused on the distant lighthouse and her thoughts turned to Will. She wondered if he was home or still at the clinic. Was he getting some much needed sleep or still aiding his patients? Assisting him through the night had changed things—a development she wasn't prepared for. A trust for him was growing, possibly born from watching him save lives and ease pain. The same thing he had done for her.

"I can't do it up."

Candace turned to find Rose struggling with the zipper. Crossing the room, she zipped the dress then looked over Rose's shoulder into the mirror. She was breathtakingly beautiful from head to her bare toes. The contrast between her dark hair and blue dress was perfect. She watched Rose's eyes take in every detail of her dress, makeup and hair. The serious look on her face was hard to read. The silent waiting was even worse. Then it happened—a smile. It wasn't a huge one, but big enough to give Candace a sign that she made some progress. Quietly, she picked up the lipstick she bought for herself and walked toward the door. Rose needed time and privacy to imagine the possibilities. At least that's what Candace hoped for.

Returning to Ruby's room, Candace stripped down and stepped into the hot shower. The pulsating water was therapeutic to her sore muscles. But that was nothing compared to the array of wonderfully-scented products Ruby had available. Clearly, she was one of Fae LeBlanc's best customers. Candace took in the fragrance of each bottle, finally settling on the one she really liked. The generic bar soap available for use in Will's shower/tub did the job, but it was nice to pamper herself. She continued her mini-spa by washing her hair with a silky shampoo. Another luxury.

After drying herself off, she found a blow dryer and styled her hair. Nothing fancy, just less of a wild look. Next came something to wear so she could wash her clothes. Ruby's closet selection was impressive. Too impressive. Pulling a pair of jeans from a drawer, she put them on with a t-shirt. The fit was perfect and Candace felt like a new woman. Leaning into the mirror, she applied some moisturizer and the lipstick she bought for herself. "Welcome back, Candace. It's been awhile."

CHAPTER 20

After folding the last load of laundry, Candace stacked the assorted piles of clothes, socks and towels back into the basket. Before she made it out of the living room, she heard a quiet knock on the door. At least she thought it was a knock. Scratches on the outside of the door came next. Placing the laundry basket back on the couch, she walked toward the window and gently moved the curtain. It was Will leaning his back against the door to remove his boots. A sense of relief washed over her. She knew exactly what triggered the uneasy notion as she unlocked the door and opened it wide. "I'm glad it's you."

"Were you expecting someone else?" joked Will as he walked through the door.

He had no idea how close to home that question came for Candace. She would always be expecting someone else: Dante. More reason to take the money and disappear.

"I wasn't sure if you'd still be sleeping."

Without either of them noticing, Rose opened her door and crawled to the railing to watch their interaction below—a familiar spot for surveillance. She was curious but not enough to overcome the fear of interacting with them.

"My sleep lasted about an hour," responded Candace. "Too much to do. How about you?"

"I'm headed home now. We had to clean up the equipment and put everything away at the firehouse after I left the clinic this morning."

"That accident was terrible."

"Worse than most calls we get. So how's Rose?"

"So far so good."

"How's she dealing with Ruby leaving?"

"She thinks she coming back soon."

"So you haven't told her yet?"

"I'm not sure how she's going to react."

"And when Ruby doesn't come home tonight or tomorrow or the next day or…?" The sound of the tea kettle whistle stopped Will from making his point.

"Have a seat. I'll be right back."

Anxiety instantly set in for Rose as she squirmed back into the room and quietly shut the door. Sitting with her back against the wall with her knees to her chest, she felt the familiar symptoms kicking in: heart palpitations, trembling, difficulty breathing, throat tightening. She had trusted a stranger and that stranger had lied to her. She used the tears rolling down her cheeks to scrub the makeup from her face, rubbing her eyes, cheeks and lips. Without a washcloth, all it did was smear. Her anxiety continued to build until the fear of approaching danger caused her mind to detach from reality. Jumping to her feet, she moved to the other side of the chest of drawers near the door and pushed as hard as she could. Her struggle ended in a solid barricade. No one would be allowed into her room until her mother returned. If she returned.

Returning from the kitchen, Candace moved the laundry basket to the floor and sat next to Will on the couch. "On the bright side, I did make a little progress with Rose this morning."

"When are you going to tell her?"

"I'll let the cat out of the bag after you leave."

"The cat!" responded Will, realizing he forgot. "I promised to get Mrs. Campbell's cat out of the tree."

"Isn't there someone else who can do that for her?"

"It won't take long," said Will, getting up from the couch. "I need to hurry so I can catch a nap before I head north. I haven't even packed yet."

"Packed?"

"The wedding's tomorrow afternoon."

"That came fast," commented Candace as she walked behind him to the door.

"I have to be there later this afternoon for the wedding rehearsal, rehearsal dinner, bachelor party, argument with my parents, mostly Dad. You know... standard wedding stuff."

"And Jill," said Candace, opening the door for Will to share how he felt.

"There is that."

Candace waited for him to say more but nothing came. "Have you considered what you'll do if Jill doesn't know how to tango?"

"I've already planned for that contingency. Whether or not she can tango won't matter."

"Oh, it'll matter."

"I'll just alter my strategy."

"You have a strategy?"

Resorting to humor as well as his narrator voice, Will put himself at ease. "I show up at the reception, wander through the crowd, mingling, chatting, loading my plate with finger foods, secretly enquiring if anyone tangos."

"Are your odds good?" asked Candace, unsure as to whether he was serious or joking.

"There's going to be hundreds of people there. Country club types."

"Do 'country club types' dance the tango?"

"Why wouldn't they?"

"You do know the tango is a dance that originated in impoverished areas of Argentina?"

"I did not."

"Even if there are some guests skilled in the tango, it's going to take a while to interview hundreds of women," responded Candace.

"Obviously, demographics will come into play in terms of age and agility."

"So there will be research involved."

"Of course. After I find a dance partner and clue the band to the right music, I'll start tangoing."

"With the partner you found through the research and interview process."

"You're getting hung up on the particulars. All I have to do is impress Jill from afar."

"Two strangers dancing the tango at a country club wedding reception should definitely get her attention," said Candace trying unsuccessfully to hold back the sarcasm.

"Women love dancing movies," whispered Will into Candace's ear.

"Again with the research. I didn't realize you were such a lady's man."

"I'm not. Why do you think I need a strategy?" he said as he reached for the door knob.

"All joking aside, Will. At least I hope we're joking. You do know you're not ready for a performance of the tango, right?"

"I guess I'll just have to win her over with my charm."

"Charm goes a long way."

"The truth is, Candace, I promised my brothers I would come with an open mind and spend some time getting to know her."

It was the response she expected a man like Will to give. He'd made a commitment and he would see it through. The least she could do was help him carry out his promise with less embarrassment. Putting aside her own confusing feelings, she took his hand and pulled him back into the living room. "Don't move."

"I really need to go."

"This will only take a few minutes," she said as she walked toward the Victrola. Lifting up the lid, she placed the needle on Ruby's old record and waited for the music to begin. The wind instruments came first followed by the strings and a soft voice singing the lyrics to an old Welsh folk song. Returning to Will, she removed his coat and hat. "Hold me."

"Hold you?" he said confused.

"Like we're dancing."

"I should probably get to that cat."

"Obviously, the cat's not going anywhere."

"True."

"You may not be able to tango but anyone can slow dance. Now take me in your arms."

Will touched his palm to the side of her waist as he had done several times during tango practice then took hold of her hand. The distance between them was wide enough to fit a second pair of dancers.

"We've already been through the 'how to hold a woman' lesson and this is not it," said Candace.

"Sorry," he said, nervous about getting too close after the evolution of his feelings at the accident scene.

"Loosen up. You're not a statue."

"I really should go, Candace."

"Just relax. Women like to dance with men who actually bend."

Moving his head from side to side, he made a concerted effort to relax, at least on the outside.

"Better. Slow dancing is really about one thing: moving to the rhythm of the music," instructed Candace as she moved him back and forth then began leading him in a slow circular pattern.

"That's it?" asked Will, hoping he'd instantly mastered the art of the slow dance.

"It's a start."

"What else is there?"

"Close your eyes."

Will took a nervous glance at his feet then back at Candace. "I don't think that's such a good idea."

"Don't think about your feet."

"I'm thinking about yours."

"Your shoes are off. I'll be fine. Now close your eyes."

Will did as she asked and closed his eyes, allowing Candace to study his face as she continued. "You may feel like holding her closer. Touching your cheek to hers."

He followed her suggestion and pulled her closer.

Candace's voice softened as she continued to tutor him, whispering in his ear. "The softness of her skin, the smell of her hair, the movement of her body as it moves with yours. They feed your senses. They create a rhythm of their own. Let it wash over you." In the beginning, her goal was to keep it platonic. Just one friend helping out another. But the more Will surrendered himself, the closer he pulled her toward him. It wasn't long before their bodies were pressed against each other. The danger of their dance becoming more than a teaching moment was fast approaching.

Giving into her own advice, Candace did the unthinkable—she closed her eyes. Wrapped in each other's arms, they moved to the music, allowing time to lose all significance. For the first time in as long as she could remember, Candace felt safe in a man's arms. She felt at peace. It wasn't long before even their breathing patterns matched.

Approaching the point of no return, Candace opened her eyes to reality. Abruptly, she pulled away from Will and stopped the music from playing. "That should help with Jill," she said.

Stunned by the abrupt ending to the dance, Will tried to collect himself. "That was... very informative. Thank you."

"You should get to that cat."

"Yes. The cat." Will walked toward the door, stumbling before picking up his coat and hat. "I'll stop by when I get back."

"Good luck," said Candace, her words barely getting through the open door before it shut behind him.

Crossing the porch, Will stopped at the top of the stairs. "What are you doing?" he mumbled to himself as he turned back to the door. With no immediate answer, he decided the best course of action would be to put some distance between them so he could think. But that didn't stop his mind from racing. Perplexed by the emotions he was experiencing, he hurried down the stairs in his socks. The cold, damp ground was an instant wake up call. Back up the stairs he went. The wet socks made sliding his feet into his boots a bit more difficult but his ill-fitting footwear didn't keep him from making a beeline for the driveway. Escape was his only plan as he hobbled to his truck, trying to force his right foot further into the boot. Tripping over his untied boot lace, he slammed his shoulder into the side of the door. This was not his day and it was only noon.

CHAPTER 21

Holding onto the paper tag at the end of the string, Candace swirled the submerged tea bag through the hot water. At the same time, thoughts of her experience with Will swirled through her mind. Coming to the realization that the tea and her mind had steeped long enough, she added some sugar and cream then placed the two dainty cups on a tray. As she carefully walked up the stairs, Candace kept watch over the tea, steadying the tray to keep from spilling it. Proudly she made it to the balcony without incident. The doorknob turned with ease but the door would not budge. She tried applying pressure with her shoulder, but it still wouldn't open. "Rose? The door won't open. Are you all right? Rose, open the door."

"No!" came an angry voice from the other side of the door.

"I brought you some tea."

"I don't want it!"

"What's wrong?" asked Candace, shocked at the turn around from their earlier experience.

"Where's Mom?"

"Let me come in and we can talk about it."

"Tell me!"

"I'll tell you when you open this door."

"Tell me!"

"Come on, Rose. This tray is getting heavy."

"Where is she really?"

"Open the door and I'll tell you."

"Tell me now!" Rose screamed from the other side of the door.

Taking a moment to weigh the options, Candace recognized she only had one choice. Tell the truth and wait for her to digest it. "The doctor sent her to the hospital." No response came from the other side. Candace continued to wait for something, anything. "Rose? Rose!"

"Leave me alone!" she yelled, sitting on top of the chest of drawers with her back against the door. "Go away!"

"Let me in, Rose. I can explain," pleaded Candace from the other side of the door.

Rose's anxiety turned to a growing anger as the streams of tears cut through her smeared makeup. She lost her father to the hospital and now it would take her mother as well.

"Open the door, Rose. I'll just sit with you until you're ready to talk. You have to trust me. I'm the only one you have right now."

A call for trust from the person who betrayed her was the last straw. Rose leaped from the top of the chest of drawers and began destroying her room. Grabbing onto multiple book spines, she yanked them from the shelves, leaving a trail of books behind her as she rounded the room. Nothing was off limits: pictures and knickknacks fell victim, blankets were ripped from her bed, the desk wiped clean of its contents. The sound of Candace pleading from outside the room only made her more angry. She was a tornado with no direct path. But even tornados fizzle.

Grabbing her container of wishbones, she stopped just before hurling it at the window. Instead, she pressed it to her chest and wrapped her arms around it. Empty and weak, she sank to the floor in sadness and eventually cried herself to sleep.

Candace waited for an audible sound to clue her into Rose's activity. The continuous silence gave her hope that she had settled down. Hopefully, she could process the information about her mother more rationally now. Walking down the stairs, Candace was beat. The couch broke her fall as she collapsed onto her back. Reaching between the cushions, she pulled out Rhue-wyn's book and opened it to where she left off.

> *The time for the sunset wedding had arrived. Word of the union had spread quickly through the town and Andri invited all aboard who wanted to witness the event. Through the window of the captain's quarters, Rhue-wyn watched the last boat full of curious townsfolk approach the ship. She had watched each boat arrive. On the laps of every woman set a tray of delectables for the buffet. Excitedly, she hurried back to the mirror and put on her final accessory—a collection of beautiful flowers shaped like a crown.*
>
> *Andri had bought her the most elegant gown in town. The one in the window that all the women desired yet no one could afford. She had never looked more beautiful. Everyone would be envious of her. The multi-layers of satin fabric were composed of different shades of gold with embroidery in the same hues. The dress itself weighed nearly as much as Rhue-wyn. Bows, large and small, were in abundance and the poet sleeves added an exquisite flare. The scoop neckline was the perfect setting for the strand of pearls Andri had hung around her neck. His romantic invitation still playing in her head. "Come away with me and I will show you the world."*
>
> *A gentle knock on the door pulled her attention from her reflection, followed by the announcement she had been waiting to hear: "We're ready to begin." One last look testified of perfection. Opening the door, she was elated by the large crowd that filled the main deck. A path of flower petals pointed the way through the crowd to Andri at the front. He was stunning. The ideal match to her beauty. As she walked through the crowd, the men seemed disheartened while the women were ecstatic with smiles from ear to ear.*
>
> *Andri took her hand in his and they stood in front of a captain from a merchant ship docked in the harbor. Andri had asked him earlier that the day to perform the ritual. The vows were simple and short then sealed with a kiss. A party with music and dance followed. Most of the townsfolk left after their*

bellies were full and before it became too dark to see. Some stayed to enjoy the music and dance.

After the final guests departed the ship, Rhue-wyn retired to the captain's quarters, while Andri made one last trip into town under the dark of night. He had one more piece of business to attend to before they set sail at dawn. Rhue-wyn had no concern for the business of a ship's captain so it made no difference to her. She was so tired from the day's events that she drifted off to sleep, well pleased with her current circumstances.

Candace followed suit, allowing the book to slide from her grip and come to rest on her stomach. Her body desperately needed sleep and she was happy to oblige. As she drifted off to sleep, she contemplated how the story contained in the old book came to life in her head. It was as though she was a bystander to Rhue-wyn and Andri's romantic wedding. "Come away with me and I'll show you the world," she whispered to herself as she tried to make sense of the connection. Abruptly, she lifted her head and popped her eyes wide open as she put two and two together. "Those are the exact words Ruby said to me."

Candace went on to conclude that Rhue-wyn was the woman who wanders the beach with the lantern—the woman at the center of the will-o'-the-wisp legend. Her imagination continued to spin, supposing that Ruby was a descendant of Rhue-wyn and Andri. "That's how she came to be in possession of the book." Closing her eyes, Candace laid her head back down. Pleased with her hypothesis, she quieted her mind enough to sleep.

THE SOUND of the house phone ringing woke her from a deep sleep. She stumbled across the room, grabbing the receiver by the third ring. "Hello." Candace was relieved to hear Ruby's voice on the other end. "How are you?" Ruby filled her in on the test results and upcoming surgery then asked about her daughter. "Rose is fine," she lied. "I've just made some tea and I'm heading upstairs." Ruby shared her concerns about Rose and reiterated her belief. "She needs you." Refusing to validate the sentiment, Candace instead reassured her that all was well. "We'll see you soon." As she hung up the phone, she felt perfectly justified in the deceit. The last thing she wanted to do was add more stress to Ruby's situation. As for Rose... she was done trying to help her.

"She needs you, Candace."

Looking around the room, she expected to see Ruby's ghost standing nearby, but the room was empty. The words must have originated inside her own mind. She wanted to argue with the voice like she'd done so many times with Ruby. She wanted to prove she'd done all she could to help Rose. She wanted to quit and walk away. Tired and frustrated, Candace was out of ideas and had no one to turn to for answers.

"She needs you, Candace," whispered her conscience a second time.

As she took a second to consider Rose's needs, something clicked. "I'm all she's got," she said thoughtfully. That realization changed everything. Rose needed a real friend.

After years of loneliness, trapped in a prison she allowed herself to enter, Candace knew firsthand what that need felt like. Maybe she and Rose had more in common than she thought.

A noise coming from Rose's room caught her attention. It sounded like the dresser being moved. She knew eventually, nature would call. Candace positioned herself to watch from the shadows of the dark living room. As soon as Rose entered the bathroom, she hurried softly up the stairs and squeezed through the entrance into the bedroom—not an easy task since she required more room than Rose. Once inside, she sat in a chair across the room and waited.

Once Rose re-entered the room, Candace waited for her to move the chest of drawers back into place. "Would you like some help?"

"How did you get in here?"

"The same way you did. The fit was a bit tight. Next time, could you make the opening a little wider?"

"You were watching for me."

"I'm concerned about you."

"Bring my mother home."

"Ruby called a while ago," said Candace as she moved closer with each response. "They're performing the operation tomorrow afternoon. She'll be home a few days after that."

"I don't believe you."

"I'm telling you the truth."

"She's not coming back."

"It's a common procedure. One of her heart valves has stopped working properly. They're going to replace it and she'll be back home in no time."

"You're lying to me."

"Why would I lie to you?" argued Candace.

"To keep me from knowing."

"Knowing what?"

"That she's not coming back."

"I'm telling you exactly what Ruby told me."

"You're lying!" yelled Rose, her back pressed against the wall as Candace drew closer.

"I'm not lying. Your mother will be fine. Better than fine."

"I don't believe you."

"Why?"

"People who go there never come back," responded Rose, unable to hold the tears of anger back.

"Of course they do."

"No, they don't!"

"That's what hospitals are for," said Candace, trying to use rational thought to calm her down. "They fix sick people and send them home."

"That's not true!"

"Yes, it is."

"Then why didn't they send my father back?" screamed Rose, her question stopping her opponent in her tracks.

Standing face to face, Candace had no response. Instinctively, she reached out and wrapped her arms around Rose before she had a chance to resist. Rose fought to free herself from the tight grip but Candace held on with all her strength until she calmed down.

"He never came back," muttered Rose. "He never came back." Rose repeated the same words over and over as she sobbed against Candace's chest. Years of anger and disappointment flooded out and all Candace could do was hold on tight.

CHAPTER 22

Still dressed in her gown, Rose sat in the middle of her unmade bed staring out the window at the lighthouse. Her beautiful dress torn, her face unrecognizable, her hair a disaster. Her mother would not have approved. She had lost control—a thought she wasn't proud to admit. Coming off the meltdown over her father, she found herself in a trance of sorts—numb to inner feelings or external stimuli. She'd born her soul to a stranger, leaving her hollow and empty.

Candace entered the room carrying a tray of food and a large empty bowl. She put the tray on the desk then walked toward the bathroom. Filling the bowl with warm water, Candace watched Rose through the two open doors, wondering what was next. Once the bowl was full she grabbed a washcloth and a hand towel then re-entered the bedroom. Placing the bowl on the night stand, she crawled onto the bed and sat next to her. A lot had happened since she arrived at Ruby's early that morning. The torn and stained condition of the once beautiful dress told the tale. "I'm going to clean your face, Rose." As expected, Candace received no response so she pulled the pack of makeup wipes out of her pocket and began.

With each gentle wipe, Candace paid attention to detail. The last thing she wanted was to cause her any more discomfort. It was strange stepping into the mother role, but the deeper she cared the more naturally it came. "I made us lunch. Sandwiches with chocolate milk." She waited for a response but Rose remained silent. "The amazing thing about sandwiches is that you get everything you need in each bite: bread, cheese, veggies, meat. All the major food groups. Someone reminded me of that recently."

Finished with the makeup removal, Candace dipped the washcloth into the warm water, then wiped the remaining solution from Rose's face. She did it twice to make sure her pores were clean. After drying her face, she rubbed some lotion between her hands and applied it to her skin. "Beautiful." Again, no response. Getting up, she picked up the tray and placed it on the bed between the two of them. "I hope you like turkey and cheese."

Candace shook her head at the turnabout. It wasn't long ago that she was in Rose's position being told to eat for her own good. What she now understood that Will did not was the fact that she didn't care about her own good. Rose was in that same place and nothing she could say would get her to eat. Their saving grace was the sound of the phone ringing. "Guess who's calling, Rose?"

Rose watched as Candace pulled the portable phone from her back pocket and handed it to her. "Answer it," said Candace.

"You answer it," she replied, pushing the phone away from her.

Candace pushed the button and spoke into the receiver. "Ruby Stratton's home."

Rose waited in anticipation.

"Yes, she's right here." Candace handed the phone to Rose. "It's your mother."

Pressing the phone to her ear, Rose's face lit up at the sound of her mom's voice. Candace couldn't hear what Ruby was saying. She could only hear Rose's 'yes' and 'no' responses.

After a few minutes, Rose told her mother that she loved her then handed the phone to Candace. They wished each other luck and that ended the phone call. Candace and Ruby had talked after Rose's meltdown over her father. Ruby knew exactly what to do.

Now Candace would see if the plan worked. Turning to Rose, she asked a question she already knew the answer to. "What did she say, Rose?"

"She'll be home in less than a week."

"Do you believe her?"

"I think so."

"Good. Now eat." Picking up half a sandwich, Candace followed her own orders and started to eat while Rose reflected on the conversation she had with her mother. A large hardback book on the floor caught her attention. "Castles of the United Kingdom." Sliding off the bed, she set her plate on the floor next to her and opened the cover. The book was well worn and many of the pages were marked with sticky tabs. Candace noticed notes written in the margins as she leafed through the pages. "I've always loved castles," she said, turning a page. "This one is beautiful."

"Have you been there?" quietly asked Rose, surprising Candace with her question.

"No. Have you?"

"Not yet, but someday."

"You must really love castles," commented Candace as she took another bite of her sandwich.

"The countryside is beautiful as well. It's very romantic."

"Romantic?" exclaimed Candace, allowing a laugh to escape before she caught herself. She could tell that Rose was embarrassed. "I'm sorry, Rose. I wasn't expecting that comment."

After a moment of silence, Rose found the strength to continue the conversation. "Victorian ladies used to scatter wildflower seeds from the windows of their carriages. You can read about it on page fifty-nine."

"Fifty-nine," said Candace as she turned to that page, amazed by her recall.

"The beauty becomes a part of you. When you leave it, you long for it."

"It sounds like you've been there," remarked Candace, finishing the first half of her sandwich.

"Mother told me all about England and Wales. I'm going there someday."

"Alone?"

"With someone."

"Ruby?"

"And someone else."

"Do I know this person?"

Rose slowly crawled from the bed and walked to the window facing the lighthouse. "I thought it would be nice to have a picnic on the lawn of the castle on page thirty-two."

Quickly turning the pages back, Candace searched for page thirty-two, her mind racing from this new side of Rose—one she didn't see coming.

"For years I've watched him from these windows and listened to his voice from my hiding spot at the top of the stairs."

Candace slowly closed the book as she realized who Rose was referring to: Will. It made total sense. He was kind and generous and the only man she saw and heard on a regular basis. He was there each time Ruby needed something done or repaired. It didn't hurt that he was handsome either. "Will is a nice man. It's natural for you to have feelings for him."

"But beyond that?"

"I think it's dangerous to put all your hopes and dreams in one person."

"All these years, thoughts of him have taken me beyond these walls."

"In your imagination."

"That's all I have."

Crawling to her feet, Candace walked to the window and stood next to Rose. "It doesn't have to be."

"What do you mean?"

"If you want to have a relationship with someone, you have to get out of this house."

"So you can get the money, right?"

"What?"

"You don't have to pretend to care. I overheard my mother and you on the porch that first day."

"The money's important to me, Rose. I've never said otherwise. Up until yesterday the money was the only reason I took this job. But you've grown on me. I even think we could be friends."

"You do?"

"Can I tell you a secret?"

"Yes."

"I don't have any friends."

"Why?"

"Long story."

"You can tell me."

"Someday. Maybe," said Candace, allowing herself to momentarily slip into her past. Refusing to stay there, she changed the topic. "You should eat that sandwich before it dries out."

Rose returned to the bed, picked up her sandwich and began to eat while Candace continued to stare at the lighthouse. Turning back, she noticed the jar of wishbones on the night stand. Still interested in the reason for such a strange collection, she joined Rose on the bed. "Why keep all those wishbones?"

"I'm saving them up."

"For what?"

"Don't you believe in wishes?"

"No, I don't."

"Why?"

"In my experience, they don't come true."

"That's because you've never been in love," said Rose, surprising her with such an accurate analysis.

"What makes you say that?"

"'When you love someone, all your saved-up wishes start coming true.'"

"Who told you that?"

"Elizabeth Bowen. She was an Irish writer who grew up in England. Her father went crazy too."

Candace watched Rose take another bite of her sandwich as

though everything she said was normal. It was clear she lived in an altered reality where everything she read was the truth. "Not everything you read is true. Not even about love."

"My mother knows a lot about love. And not just human love."

"What do you mean?"

"She told me that fairies can never fall in love."

"Why?"

"The source of their immortality is in their heart."

"How does Ruby know that?"

"She knows a lot about fairies."

"So why can't they fall in love?"

"Fairies risk becoming mortal if they give their hearts away. So falling in love is a venture they refuse to take." Rose nonchalantly reached for her chocolate milk and took another bite of her sandwich.

Candace, on the other hand, left the second half of her sandwich on the plate. She'd lost her appetite after discovering Rose's feelings for Will. Looking around to distract herself, she took in the terrible state of the room. "After you finish eating, why don't I help you clean up this disaster?" Rose nodded her head as she continued to eat.

CHAPTER 23

The high ceilings and tall windows surrounding the wedding party were grand to say the least. The gold hue created by the hanging chandeliers perfectly matched the wood-trimmed, gold upholstered chairs and gold satin drapes. It was the ideal setting for an upper crust family to gather for a rehearsal dinner. Will sat inconspicuously at the fourteen-seat dining table surrounded by family, dressed in his only suit—the one worn for weddings and funerals. He had finished the main course far too quickly which left him with nothing to do. He wished they would have seated him at the bridesmaids' and groomsmen's table. Making polite conversation with a close cousin was passing the time but not quick enough. At least it was a distraction from his father's endless praise of his two younger brothers. He'd lost count as to how many times they'd raised their glasses in praise of them. Truthfully, no one could be more happy for them than Will.

Growing up, he was the one who helped them with their homework, who bandaged their skinned knees and helped with their sports training. Their father, George Bloom, was too busy at work and their mother's societal responsibilities took her away more than they liked. His brothers were his best friends and he loved them selflessly. For that reason, he was proud of their accomplishments. On the other hand, it took their upward movement in status for his father to show the type of love that should have been unconditional.

Glancing toward the other end of the table, he noticed his mother's eyes were on him. With a wink, Alice Bloom let him know she was thinking of him. He winked back, letting her know he was fine. Pulling out his phone beneath the table, he checked to see if he had any messages. His screen was blank. This was the first time in over two weeks he hadn't eaten dinner with Candace. He was surprised at how alone he felt. The fact that a woman he barely knew was the one occupying his thoughts at a table surrounded by his family made it worse. Growing fidgety, Will needed some space to shake it off so he quietly excused himself and left the dining room.

Before he made it out the door, an arm slipped around his. He would recognize that touch anywhere. "I just need some air, Mom."

"Can't a mother take a stroll with her long lost son?"

"You know where I live. The same place I've lived most of my adult life."

"Yes, William. We're very aware of where you live."

"And what I do for a living."

"It's a noble profession," responded Alice.

"That's a surprise."

"It shouldn't be. I raised my children to shoot for the stars."

"Even if the stars they shoot for shine down on Will-O'-the-Wisp Point?"

"If you're happy, I'm happy."

"Are you dying or something?"

"Why would you ask such a thing?" asked Alice in disbelief.

"'If you're happy, I'm happy' is not your normal mantra."

"It could be if ALL my sons were progressing in life."

"I'm happy doing what I'm doing. That should count for something."

"Not entirely."

"And here it comes," said Will as he opened the door to the outside veranda, hoping to escape. Her arm remained clasped tight as he continued into the cold. The seating had been stored for the winter season leaving an open deck, so they walked to the edge of the patio overlooking the grounds. Although his mother had a blazer-style jacket over her evening dress, he removed his suit jacket and wrapped it over her shoulders for protection.

"Always the thoughtful one," she commented. "I'm sure that's a plus in your line of work."

"It helps," he responded as he leaned on the railing.

"I worry about you living in such a remote place. All alone," she said.

"I'm not alone, Mother."

"Jack Junior will not keep you warm at night."

"You'd be surprise."

"Can you at least try to be serious?"

"I love the lighthouse. I love my job. I love my dog. I'm happy."

"There's more to life than that."

"Grandma and Grandpa were happy there," reminded Will.

"That's my point, William. They had each other."

"And now that Sam and Henry are married, it's my turn."

"You were supposed to be the first."

"I was supposed to be a lot of things," said Will, pointing to his parents' expectations.

"I saw you talking with Jill at the wedding rehearsal."

"You and everyone else. We had a captive audience."

"Well?" asked Alice, hoping for something extraordinary.

"She's very nice."

"That's it?"

"Nice is important."

"It's going to take more than 'nice' to get you to the altar," said Alice, slightly frustrated.

"We'll see how the wedding and reception go tomorrow."

"Why wait? She's here tonight."

"Too bad I forgot my engagement ring," he replied, tongue in cheek.

"Not everything in life can be solved with a joke, William."

"Not everything in life needs to be solved."

"What's that supposed to mean?"

"I think I'm going to head back to the house and turn in early."

"Not until you answer my question."

"It doesn't matter if I answer your question."

"Of course it matters," replied Alice, slightly alarmed at his view.

"Do you know I've been learning the tango for the past couple of months?"

"Why?"

"To impress Jill."

"With the tango?" asked his mother, rhetorically.

"Dance choice aside… I've spent a lot of time, frustrating time, preparing to impress a woman I've never met. Do you know why?"

"Men have been known to go to great lengths for a catch like Jill."

"I didn't do it for Jill. I did it for my family. I'm a thirty-five-year-old man still trying to impress his parents."

"We just want what's best for you."

"How can you know what's best for me when you don't even know your own son?"

"William!" replied Alice, surprised by his accusation.

"I recently saved the life of a stranger. After just two weeks, she knows me better than my own parents."

"We just want to help."

"No, Mom. You want to solve the problems you see with my life."

"What's wrong with that?"

"I ease the pain of others on a daily basis. I save lives in traumatic situations. I fix sinks and garage doors. I replace satellite dishes and retrieve cats from trees. Those are problems to be solved. The way I live my life is not a problem. Get to know me and you would see that."

"I had no idea you felt this way."

"I'm finished being the son who's not good enough." Will finally said what he'd wanted to say for years. "This is who I am, Mom. I'm happy with who I am."

"What has gotten into you?"

"A storm named Candace blew in from the ocean and I haven't been the same since."

"Why do I get the feeling you're not referring to a weather phenomenon?"

"Oh, she's a phenomenon."

"Is she? And when were you going to tell us about her?"

"I worked an all-nighter on a bad accident. I'm running on fumes. I'm going to head back. Goodnight, Mother." With a kiss to Alice's cheek, he walked away.

Stunned by her son's revelations, Alice watched him walk to the stairs leading off the veranda. "What about dessert?" she asked in a motherly tone.

"I'm sure Henry will have no problem taking care of that for me," said Will as he walked down the steps. It wasn't long before he disappeared into the darkness.

It'd been at least six months since he'd last visited and Alice missed him more than she realized. There's a bond that comes with your firstborn and she felt it strongly with Will. She loved her son with all her heart, yet she struggled to understand him. It was as though he was born into the wrong family. Then something clicked. In the silence of the night, Will's words penetrated her heart. What if understanding had nothing to do with it? What if she accepted him for the brilliant, compassionate son that he was? What if she and her husband tried to fit into their son's life instead of expecting him to fit into theirs? It would mean a change of mindset and a lot of work, but anything worth doing requires effort. With that in mind, she hurried back into the dining room and sat down at the table, still wearing her son's off-the-rack suit jacket and proud of it. Her husband stared down the table at her. His eyes full of questions that would have to wait for the drive home.

GEORGE OPENED the front door to their home and allowed Alice to enter first. They were exhausted from all the festivities but in a good way. "What a day it's been," said George.

"A wonderful day. I'm going to return William's suit jacket."

"You mean you're going to check in on him. He is an adult," said her husband.

"He may be, but he's still my son." Before she started up the stairs, she handed Will's take-out dessert to George. "Slip this in the refrigerator for me."

"I'm going to the den. I'll be up after a while."

"I'll be waiting up. I want to finish our conversation about my talk with William."

"I won't be long." George knew that laying flat would be impossible until his acid reflux passed. After tucking his coat into the closet, he entered the kitchen and put his son's dessert in the fridge. Then he moved to the vitamin cabinet. Pulling out a bottle of antacids, he emptied several into his hand and tossed them all into his mouth. It would take more than the recommended dose to help him tonight. As he entered the den, he picked up the remote control and settled into the leather couch. He had the DVR set to record in case he didn't make it home in time to watch the news. He loved to close his day with the local broadcast from his favorite network.

To his surprise, Will entered the kitchen, holding his dessert in one hand and a fork in the other. "Mind if I join you?"

"Did your mother find you?"

"I've been out on the back porch doing some thinking."

"Maybe that cake will help."

"Can't hurt," said Will as he sat down on the other end of the couch and dove into his dessert.

"There's ice cream in the freezer."

"I'm good."

"So how are things in Will-O'-the-Wisp Point?" asked George, staring at the television while waiting for his son to answer.

"The local economy's hurting but we're making it work."

"Are tourists still coming in search of the woman on the beach?"

"Not since summer."

"Does her voice still travel in the wind?"

"Off and on. Can I ask you something about the woman on the beach?"

"Look at this," said George, ignoring his son's request as the story changed to coverage of the accident from the night before. Hearing no response from his son, he looked over and found him entranced with the footage. "Is this the accident you were involved with last night?" asked George as he turned up the volume.

The cell phone footage caught by a driver waiting in traffic showed Candace and Will carrying Michelle up from the ditch. George watched intently as his son did his job. The mother's voice in the background screaming for her daughter sent a chill down his spine. "Looks like it was a bad one." Not getting a response from his son, he continued to listen to the reporter share facts about the accident. The cell phone video ran on a loop as the reporter shared the details. "How long were you out there?" He received no answer. George glanced at Will who was engrossed in watching the footage. The look on his face suggested that it wasn't his own participation he was interested in. "William?"

"Most of the night. We were lucky. No fatalities."

"Thanks to you."

"Thanks to a lot of people."

"Including the woman helping you?"

"Her name is Candace."

"So that's Candace? Your mother mentioned you spoke of her," said his father as the news story ended.

"The dessert definitely helped," said Will, trying to avoid answering the question. "Good night." Will got up and left the room, leaving George with another clue to the puzzle he and his wife were trying to unravel.

Quickly, he grabbed the DVR remote control and replayed the news story on mute, studying Candace as well as his own son.

CHAPTER 24

Candace stepped out of Ruby's front door and onto the porch. Breathing in the crisp morning air, she geared up for another day. "It's a perfect morning for a walk." Turning back to the open door, she looked for Rose who she expected to be right behind her. "Come on, Rose." Rose stood petrified in the shadow of the doorway until she found enough courage to stick her head out and look both ways.

"Just one step. That's all," encouraged Candace.

Slowly Rose picked up her foot and moved it into the light of the doorway. Before she could step onto the porch, she heard whispering from up the street. Two women slowed their walk to a crawl as they focused in on Ruby's front porch. Rose couldn't understand the words they were whispering but the sound was supersonic to her ears.

"Come on, Rose. It's easy."

"I can't," she said, pulling her foot back inside the house.

"Do you want to get out of this house?"

"Yes."

"Then step onto the porch."

"Tomorrow."

"Today."

"I can't," she pleaded, the sound of the whispers growing louder in her ears.

"Yes, you can. It's a simple step, Rose."

"No, its not!" Rose ran into the living room and Candace followed, shutting the door behind her. Halfway up the stairs, Candace grabbed Rose by the wrist and stopped her. "What is keeping you in this house?"

"I just need more time!"

"You've had a lifetime," she countered, attempting to pull her down the stairs. "You need to take the first step."

Jerking her hand from Candace's grip, Rose stood firm on her decision. "I can't! Not today."

"Then when? Tomorrow? The next day? The day after that?"

"I'm not ready, that's all!" she yelled then ran up the stairs and slammed her bedroom door shut.

Unwilling to give up, Candace ran up the stairs and into her room. As expected, she found Rose sitting on her bed staring at the lighthouse. "Are you allergic to sunshine or just fresh air in general?" Not getting a response, she walked to the street side of the room, threw the curtains open and began opening the window.

Immediately, Rose leaped from the bed and slammed the window shut. "Keep it shut!"

Surprised but not curtailed, Candace reopened the window. "No."

Again, Rose shut the window and pulled the curtains closed. "It has to stay closed!"

"Why keep it shut? No one can see you from the street," said Candace as she reopened the window.

"It's too loud," answered Rose as she shut the window for a third time.

"What's too loud?"

"The window keeps the voices out."

"What voices?"

"The voices in the air."

"That sounds crazy."

"I'm not crazy!" shouted Rose in defense of herself.

"I didn't say you were crazy."

"I'm not crazy."

"Who said you're crazy?"

Rose pointed to the window as she backed away. "The voices. They say I'm crazy... like my father. I'm not crazy, Candace. I'm not crazy!" Running to her recently organized shelves, she grabbed a large, well-worn dictionary and shoved it into Candace's hands. "Look it up. Page seventy-six. Tell me if I'm crazy. Am I deranged in mind, insane, unsound, mentally disordered?"

"Calm down, Rose," said Candace as she tried to find the proper page.

"Out of mind, a lunatic, a nutcase?"

"I get the point."

"Demented, mad, unbalanced, delirious?"

"Rose, stop!"

"Neurotic. Psychotic! Catatonic!"

Candace dropped the book to the floor and grabbed onto Rose's upper arms. She could feel her shaking from fear. "Rose, you have to calm down."

"Am I crazy like my father, Candace? Am I?"

"No, Rose. You're not."

"Then why does everyone in town say I am?"

"Are those the voices you keep talking about?"

"Yes."

Candace left Rose and walked back to the window. She looked out and saw the two women still standing on the sidewalk, carrying on a conversation in front of Ruby's home. She realized the window opening and shutting probably added to their false narrative. She needed to nip it in the bud. "I'm going to open the window, Rose."

"No!"

"I need to hear the voices." Placing her finger over her lips, Candace asked Rose to be quiet so she could hear the two women below. As Candace opened the window, Rose backed away and sat on the bed.

"Do you think that psychiatrist is doing her any good?" asked the first woman.

"I doubt the girl will ever come out. I'll be surprised if she ever does."

"And with Ruby in the hospital, I don't know what will become of her."

"Poor child."

"It's really quite sad."

"You want to know what's sad?" asked Candace from the window.

Surprised at seeing her, the women smiled as though it were a friendly encounter. "I'm sorry, what did you say?" asked one of the women.

"Do you want to know what's really sad?"

"What?" asked the other woman.

"The two of you with nothing better to do than stand outside this house and talk about the people who live here."

Shocked and offended, the women looked at each other in disbelief.

"Do you realize that's a serious medical condition?" continued Candace.

In unison, both of them let out a gasp in response to her accusation.

"A condition that stems from a self-imposed sense of pomposity," said Candace as she pulled her head back into the window. But she wasn't done yet. Sticking her head back out, she finished her diagnosis. "And if you don't know what that means, you might want to make an appointment."

Grabbing onto each others' arms, they hurried down the sidewalk.

Straightening up, Candace shut the window and closed the curtain. Finally everything made sense. Ruby had taken sole responsibility for Rose's phobia. She told Candace how she kept her daughter inside after her husband's public psychotic break to protect her. Little did she know that her daughter had been hearing voices from the sidewalk all those years. No wonder Ruby couldn't get her to leave the house once she got older. The walls and closed windows kept her safe.

"Are you a psychiatrist?" asked Rose nervously.

"No."

"But they said..."

"People like that never know what they're talking about. They just think they do."

"I could never do what you just did."

"You're going to run into people like that your entire life. People who make themselves feel better by spreading lies, blame and exaggerations."

"Every time I hear them, it takes me back to that day—clinging to the fence, watching my father in the street, listening to the other kids laugh while my heart was breaking. The voices say I'm the same way. All these years I've been waiting for it to happen to me."

"Does what they say hurt? Absolutely. But you're hurting yourself more by letting it affect you."

"Growing up was torture."

"That must have been terrible," said Candace, placing her arms around her for support. "How can I help you get past this?"

"Teach me to be like you."

Candace pulled back, coming face to face with Rose. "You're Rose Stratton. You just haven't discovered who that is yet."

"Will you help me find out?"

"Do you want to know a secret?"

"Sure."

"Lately, I've been trying to find out who I am. What do you think about doing it together?"

"Yes, yes," she answered with enthusiasm, throwing her arms around Candace's neck. "Can I ask you something else?"

"Anything," responded Candace as she slowly pulled away.

"What's a self-imposed sense of pomposity?"

"You're going to love the library!"

Candace walked to the bedroom door. "Since we're not going for a walk, let's grab some breakfast." Candace left the room.

Rose walked to the window and peered around the edge of the curtain. It was the same concealed position she'd taken since she was a child, rarely allowing herself to be seen by the outsiders. Turning from the window, she pressed her back against the wall while Candace's advice played loudly in her mind. Her words were hard to hear. For years, she'd seen herself as a victim to the cruel world outside her house. To think that she had a part in her circumstances seemed wrong, but Candace was right. She'd allowed the voices to imprison her. Her windows weren't striped with iron bars but she'd made her room a cell nonetheless. Striking the curtains back, she slid the window open, allowing a fresh breeze to blow past her face.

"Come on, Rose," hollered Candace from downstairs. "Sandwiches await."

"For breakfast?" Rose walked toward the open door then turned back to take a new look at her room. What once served as her safe haven now felt claustrophobic. The deeper she let Candace into her life, the more her world changed. As much as she hated the process, it was time to take a leap.

CHAPTER 25

*L*ater in the day, Rose wanted to spend some time alone reading. Candace agreed to the idea since everything she knew to be normal had been stripped away. Curling up with a good book would allow Rose time to digest what had happened over the past twenty-four hours. Speaking of a good book, Candace was dying to read more about Rhue-wyn and Andri. Closing Rose's bedroom door, she raced down the stairs and ran to the couch. Within seconds she was lying on the sofa, searching the pages for where she left off.

After six weeks on the open sea, a shoreline came within sight. It was morning and the ringing of the bell woke Rhue-wyn from her sleep. The news came as a welcome relief as she rushed from the captain's quarters still dressed in her white nightgown and robe. As much as she enjoyed spending the time with Andri, she was ready to see something more than ocean and sky. Their adventure together would finally begin. Rushing to the front of the ship, she saw what appeared to be a deserted shore. They could be anywhere in the world. She had no idea of their location. Andri had told her it would be a great surprise so she had waited in suspense.

The men worked quickly to lower the sails and drop anchor as Rhue-wyn hurried back to prepare for going ashore. Andri intercepted her mid-ship and walked her to the side of the boat.

The men were lowering a smaller rowboat to the water's surface and two of them crawled down into the boat.

"Andri, I need to dress for the day."

"That can wait."

Uncertain of the plan, she waited with excitement to find out more as she peered over the ship's side. Hearing footsteps approaching, she turned to see three of his largest crew men standing behind her. One of the men held pieces of rope in his hands.

"Your adventure is about to begin," said Andri.

"You mean our adventure," she responded with enthusiasm.

"There has never been an 'our.'"

"I don't understand."

"I didn't arrive in your port on accident."

"Of course not. You came for repairs."

"An excuse to spend time with you."

"What are you saying?"

"Do you remember when I told you how lucrative the transportation of goods can be?"

"Yes."

"Thanks to a bounteous harvest, the women of your town and surrounding areas were able to hire my ship for transportation. They pooled their extra earnings along with their valuables without their husbands knowing and sent word by ship. I happened to be anchored near Liverpool. A deal was struck."

"What deal was that?" asked Rhue-wyn, her heart beginning to pound in her chest.

"You're the 'goods' being transported, my dear," he responded without a drop of empathy.

Looking at the three men waiting to bind her hands, she realized the whole thing was a trick, a ruse, and everyone was in on it. Suddenly the roles were reversed and Rhue-wyn felt for the first time what it was like to be the object of another person's mischief.

"Would you like to see the price paid for your abduction?" Two men walked up and placed a chest nearby. Opening the lid revealed jewelry with precious stones, silver goblets and frames, coins and more.

"Who are you really?" asked Rhue-wyn.

"You know who I am. Captain Andri Kristjanason. What you don't know is that I'm half huldufolk."

"You're half fairy. I knew I saw something familiar in your eyes that first day we met."

"Yet you didn't pursue it because you were blinded by what I had to offer."

"I've heard of the Iceland huldufolk and their ridiculous sense of morality. Where is your propriety now?"

"I'm half human."

"Then you're an outcast to humans and huldufolk alike. That's why you call the sea your home. You have no country to call your own."

"The world is my country," he yelled, silencing her accusations. "I was banished from my homeland for being half-human, half-huldufolk—a circumstance I cannot change. But you have been banished for the hurt you have caused for decades, all for your own amusement."

"You can't tell me that everything we shared was a lie," she said softly, after being emotionally stripped to the bone. "You're my husband and I am your wife."

"It's a common belief that captains can perform marriages aboard a ship, but it's not true. That's why I paid a captain of a merchant ship to marry us. We agreed to vows but none of it's legal and binding. The wedding was your idea. I just went along with it. I knew the only way to get a clever fairy like you aboard my ship would be on your terms."

Without hesitation, Rhue-wyn slapped him across the face. "You will live to regret this."

"No. I will live my life out and die as humans and huldufolk do. But you will go on forever on a distant shore, far from your homeland and the forest you love."

"Please don't do this to me," pleaded Rhue-wyn for the first time in her life.

"What is this?" he asked with amusement. "The enchantress begging for leniency? You will receive as much help from me as you have given to those hurt by your own selfish trickery."

"So you were never under my power?"

"Of course not. As a fellow fairy, I'm immune to your tricks. I prepared my men as well."

"What we had together has to mean more than that!" she cried.

"The only worth you are to me is the contents of this trunk." Then with a nod, two crewmen removed the trunk as the other men bound her hands and feet with the rope. "I've sailed this shoreline many times. Keep a watchful eye and you may see me pass by." With that said, he turned and walked away.

"I will never think of you again!" she yelled after him. He continued to walk away as they lowered her to the boat and headed to shore. The ride was long, bobbing back and forth with the motion of the sea. The sadness she felt confused her. She hadn't felt this type of emotion. An element of fear accompanied it—also new to Rhue-wyn.

A few people had gathered on the beach to look at the ship that had anchored itself nearby. Intrigued by what was going on, the foreigners enquired after the woman as the sailors dragged her onto the sand and untied the ropes. They told stories of the immortal enchantress and warned them of the cruel tricks she loved to play on humans. As the sailors boarded the boat and left shore, the people refused to help her out of fear and prejudice. Hurrying from the beach, they left her alone on the sand.

Rhue-wyn was so devastated she couldn't move. All she could do was watch the ship sail toward the horizon. For the first time in her centuries of life, she began to sob. She continued to lament until the sun settled over the horizon. With nothing to wear but her white nightgown and robe, she knew she had to find shelter. The only thing in sight was a grouping of trees near the shore. Staggering from the beach, she found a small opening tucked between several bushes. There she would spend the first night of her new life.

The next morning she awoke to the sounds of birds chirping in the trees. Thinking she was waking up in her forest home, her smile quickly faded once she opened her eyes. The truth of her situation came rushing back. The flood of new emotions she'd experienced yesterday; anguish, sadness and anger, to name a few, had been replaced with a numbness. Her hopes had been dashed and she was left with an empty vessel.

Closing the book, Candace wiped the tears from her eyes. She felt a deep empathy for Rhue-wyn, born of her own pain. She knew the emotions she was experiencing intimately. They had both been betrayed, albeit in different ways. Betrayal hurts no matter what the cause.

In a very real way, she was betraying Rose. Will's accusatory words rang in her ears. "You're chasing your own will-o'-the-wisp!" Candace had been putting the promise of a large sum of money over Rose's happiness. It was nothing short of selfish. Her excuse may have been self-preservation but that should never come at the expense of another human being. Ruby was right. She was the only one who could help Rose.

CHAPTER 26

The cathedral's High Victorian Gothic architecture was breathtaking with its hand-carved woodwork and stained glass. A string quartet was playing prelude—a version of *Canon in D*, while the attendees politely whispered to one another. The large sanctuary boasted a nearly three-fourths attendance as ushers continued to seat more guests. The city's elite were present and expected nothing short of perfection from a Bloom wedding. Checking his watch, Will finished his conversation with the priest at the front then left through a side entrance.

As he walked down the hallway, he ran his forefinger between his collar and neck for ventilation. It was a nervous reaction to being in an uncomfortable situation, as well as his perfectly-tailored tuxedo. Will was used to having more room to move in his clothes. He would do anything for his brothers but that didn't mean it was easy for him. Entering the dressing room, he found his brother Sam pacing the floor and Henry fidgeting with his tie. "Five minutes, guys."

"Soon you'll be looking at the happiest man on the planet."

"I give him a year," laughed Henry.

"Year and a half tops," added Will jokingly.

Excitedly, Sam threw his arms over his brothers' shoulders. "You guys."

"She's really great, Sam."

"Seriously. She is," agreed Henry.

"Thanks. That means a lot. Now you're the only one left, Will."

"Saving the best for last," he quipped.

"So Jill looked pretty hot at the rehearsal yesterday," noted Sam.

"You guys definitely looked like you hit it off," added Henry.

"She is beautiful. No doubt."

"I knew it," shouted Sam. "I knew you'd like her."

"You're stupid in love. You don't know anything. Now let's get you married," said Will, trying to change the topic.

"Anyone seen Dad?" asked Henry.

"I'll find him. You get your brother to the chapel." Entering the hallway, Will accidentally ran into Jill, knocking her off-balance. He caught her in his arms before she fell to the ground. "Sorry, Jill. I didn't see you," apologized Will.

"I was on my way to deliver a message. We're running a few minutes behind: an unexpected issue with the dress."

"I'll pass it along."

"Okay."

"Thank you... for letting us know."

"Of course," she responded. "I am the maid of honor."

"Yes, you are."

"And you're the best man."

"That I am."

Awkwardly, they stood in silence until Jill continued the conversation. "The rehearsal dinner was nice last night."

"Very nice."

"It's too bad you had to leave early."

"It'd been a long day."

"That's what Sam said. Being a paramedic must be very exciting."

"It has its moments."

"How much longer do you plan to do that?" she asked, hoping he was finally ready to move back to the city and begin a career with his father.

"As long as I'm physically able."

"Oh." Taken back by his answer, Jill wasn't sure where to take the conversation next. "Well... I guess I should get back."

"Me too."

Will watched Jill walk down the hall. He'd come to the wedding with a goal to impress her after spending nearly two months trying to learn a dance. They'd had several interactions during the wedding rehearsal but not enough to feel what he thought he would feel when they finally met. There was only one way to know. He didn't have the guts to try the tango in front of hundreds of people, but an empty church hallway might work. "Jill?"

"Yes," she responded, turning to face him.

As he hurried toward her, Will quickly found the track of music on his phone that he'd been using for practice when he wasn't near the tape player. Placing it in the outstretched hands of a religious statue, he hit the play button. "Would you mind dancing the tango with me?"

"The tango?"

"Yes," said Will as he took her in his arms. "Are you familiar with it?"

Intrigued by the invitation, Jill was willing to play along. "I took a Latin dance class in college. I think I can keep up."

With confidence, Will led her in the first step, then the second, and before long he was moving her up and down the hallway. He held her just as he was taught: not too loose and not too tight. Like Candace promised, Jill became putty in his hands. He only knew about half the steps so he continued to repeat what he had learned.

Down the hall, Henry opened the door. The sight of Will and Jill dancing stopped him from entering the hallway. He motioned to Sam to join him and the two brothers eagerly watched through a small opening.

"See! I told you they'd hit it off," whispered Sam.

"My money's still on the woman from the newscast that Dad told us about."

"If that's true, my soon-to-be wife's going to kill me. Jill's her best friend."

"What about Mom? She's already envisioning how their names will look on the invitations: Will and Jill," remarked Henry, highlighting the rhyme with a raised voice.

"They're coming back this way." Sam and Henry pulled their heads back into the room and shut the door just as the couple turned to dance in the other direction. Ending the dance with a twirl and dip, Will lifted Jill back to her feet. "Thanks for the dance."

"I look forward to more at the reception," she said as she walked down the hallway.

As much as he enjoyed the dance with Jill, there was something missing. Before he could put his finger on it, he heard his dad's voice coming from a half-open door down the hallway. He walked in and waited for his father to finish his call. Out of the corner of his eye, he saw Sam and Henry walk past the room on their way to the chapel. Turning his attention back to his father, he pointed at his watch.

"Why don't we push that to Wednesday of the following week and cancel the Harrison meeting. Keep me up to speed on the Franklin merger as well," said George, then he disconnected the call and stood up from the couch. "Are they starting?"

"In a couple minutes."

"It's about time," he responded as he walked toward his son. "Why do weddings take so long to begin? We still have the reception to get through."

"I think I'll cut out after the wedding and head home," said Will with great hesitation.

"All right."

"All right? What about our usual one-sided discussion on my failure to live up to your expectations?"

"I think I'll skip it this time."

"Are you the one dying?" joked Will as they reached the open door.

"Not that I know of," said George. "Your mother and I will see you tomorrow anyway. We're driving down to see what improvements need to be made to Mom's old school."

"Why the sudden interest in Grandma's school?"

"If she were still alive, we'd be celebrating her ninety-fifth birthday this Christmas. I suppose I'm feeling a bit melancholy."

"I think you'll like the improvements I've made on the place."

"That goes without saying, William."

"It usually does."

For the first time ever, George allowed his son's honest response to resonate. Rather than refute the facts, he changed the topic of conversation. "Seen Jack lately?"

"He still expects his boots."

George laughed out loud with great pleasure, placing his arm around his son's shoulders as they walked down the hall. "First, let's get your brother married."

"Then you'll buy the boots?"

"After I hear all about your girlfriend on the news."

"She's not my girlfriend."

"The look on your face last night said differently," responded George as they reached the side door to the chapel.

"She's a friend."

"Where did you meet?"

"She washed ashore one night."

"All right. I'll let you have your privacy," his father replied, thinking he was being facetious. "We look forward to meeting her."

"Before we go in, can I ask you a question?"

Checking his watch, George saw they were passed the starting time. "Make it fast."

"You mentioned the voice in the wind last night. When you were a kid growing up at the lighthouse, how often did you hear it?" asked Will.

"Usually when a storm was approaching. "

"Crying for help?"

"No. Singing. Always the same song."

"What song was it?"

"It sounded like a different language but it didn't seem to matter. Her voice was the most exquisite thing I'd ever heard."

"The summer before Grandpa died, he told me you spoke to her."

"That was supposed to stay secret."

"Did you?" asked Will.

"I used to sneak out of the house at night and sit on the edge of the cliff. I would imagine being the captain of a ship, sailing as far away from that boring town as possible. One night the moon was full which made it possible to see the beach. That's where I saw her."

"Her?"

"A shadowy figure carrying a light. I knew the trail from the cliff to the beach like the back of my hand so I rushed down, keeping my eye on the dark silhouette. A storm was fast approaching so I had to hurry before the clouds covered the moon."

"How old were you?"

"Thirteen."

"Weren't you scared?"

"I needed to know if the legend was real."

"And?"

"Just as I reached her, she turned around and lowered the lantern. The moon was at her back so I couldn't see any details, but I could tell by the silhouette of her face she was beautiful. Breathtakingly beautiful."

"Did you speak to her?"

"No. I just stood there," he said, drifting back in time. "I was transfixed watching her long hair dance in the wind."

"Did she speak to you?"

"Yes."

"Do you remember what she said?"

"Like it was yesterday. She asked, 'What do you seek?'"

"What did you say?"

"All I could do was repeat the question back to her. 'What do you seek?'"

"Did she answer?"

"'That's between me and the sea,' she said. Then she asked me again what I sought. I asked her if she was real. She reached out and placed the palm of her hand against the right side of my face. There was no doubt she was real. I may have only been thirteen but I instantly fell in love. She must have sensed what I was feeling so she leaned over and whispered in my left ear. I'll never forget how the side of her face felt against mine. Somehow it was magical. I swear, William, I thought my heart was going to burst through my chest. It was like my body went through a physiological change. I'd never felt anything like it."

"What did she whisper?"

"Save your heart for someone who can love you in return. And when you find that love, treasure her for the rest of your life."

"Mom."

"The best decision I ever made."

"Why haven't you told anyone?"

"I didn't want my experience to be tarnished by the retelling of it."

"What did you do after she whispered in your ear?"

"I watched her walk away."

"You didn't follow her?"

"The feelings lessened the farther she went."

"The legend is real," whispered Will beneath his breath.

"We better get in there," answered his father, looking at his watch.

Will followed his dad through the door, stopping in the front to take his place as best man between Henry and Sam. His dad continued to the front row and sat next to his wife as the string quartet played Debussy's *Clair De Lune*. The delicate beauty of the music was the perfect prelude as everyone waited for the bride to make her entrance.

Will had a perfect view of the room, including his parents. He couldn't get his dad's story out of his mind, especially the advice given by the woman on the beach. He noticed his father wrap his fingers around his mother's and place her hand on the top of his leg. For the first time, Will saw his father and mother as the loving couple, Alice and George, rather than a set of parents with their own expectations for his life. From an outside view, their marriage ran like a well-oiled machine. The bugs had been worked out years ago, resulting in what appeared to be a clockwork relationship. Will had never considered the deep love that lay beneath the surface.

Alice's voice was equal to his in every situation. He'd never heard his father speak ill of his mother nor talk to her with disrespect. She was his most influential advisor and best friend. For the first time in his life, he saw the great gift his father had given to him: how to treat the woman you love.

"You're starting a little early, aren't you?" asked Henry, referring to Will's tearfilled eyes.

Will turned his head from the crowd and wiped the water away before it rolled down his cheek. He hadn't expected such a physical reaction, especially when thinking about his parents. He loved them, but the ongoing pressure to measure up had caused a rift between them.

The sound of Mendelssohn's *Wedding March* began and Will breathed a sigh of relief: the sooner it started, the quicker this emotional ride would end. Watching his future sister-in-law walk down the aisle was a beautiful moment, but it couldn't compare to the smile on Sam's face. Will couldn't help but be biased: it was his kid brother after all. As the ceremony began, Will's thoughts drifted to Candace. Could he eventually see himself in the same setting with her standing by his side? The answer was yes, and it scared him. The last thing he wanted was a broken heart. Unfortunately, the odds of a different outcome were slim.

Looking past the happy couple, his eyes locked with the maid of honor, Jill. A smile quickly appeared on her face and Will responded in kind. He wondered how many of the wedding guests were curiously watching the two of them like a tennis match rather than the actual marriage ceremony. He didn't dare look. Things had been in the works for months to match the two of them up. Here stood a beautiful woman, completely in line with his parents' wishes. He knew ample details about her life and pedigree before going on a single date. In his parents' eyes, she was the perfect match for him. And in his own way, he had hoped it was true. Instead, he felt foolish as he considered the months of work he had gone to in order to impress a woman he'd never met. She was his own will-o'-the-wisp. A fact he would never have realized if a certain stranger hadn't washed ashore.

This mysterious woman's impact on his life was tangible. He'd only known Candace for a short time and knew very little about her. So why was she the one occupying his thoughts and not Jill?

With the start of the wedding recessional music, Will's attention returned to the couple making their way down the aisle as husband and wife. It was over as fast as it started. As he took Jill's arm and led her down the aisle, he did it knowing she was not the one for him. His choice was confirmed by the weight being lifted from his shoulders. Once they reached the line of cars waiting to take them to the country club reception hall, he graciously parted ways with Jill and found his brother Henry. "I'm going to head back home."

"You can't miss the reception."

"I've been here for everything important. The wedding photos are done. I did my job as best man. The 'I do's' have been said. The rest is just frosting."

"What about the toast? That's your job."

"I pass the goblet to you, younger brother," he said, walking backwards down the sidewalk. "Tell Sam I love him and I expect a visit from him and his wife after the honeymoon."

"I never got an invitation after my wedding."

"We're brothers, Henry. Do you really need an invitation?" hollered Will from down the street, then he turned and ran toward his truck.

"Dad's right. He's in love. It's about time." Smiling, Henry got into the car with his wife and parents and they drove away from the church.

CHAPTER 27

Night had fallen on Will-O'-the-Wisp Point as Candace ran down the porch steps. Looking up and down the low-lit sidewalk, she found it to be vacant of people. No one stayed out after nine o'clock so the coast was clear. Candace turned on her flashlight and motioned to Rose to join her. Nothing happened. She motioned again then whispered loudly. "Come on, Rose." Returning to the porch, Candace reached her hand through the open door. "I won't let go. I promise."

Still uncertain, Rose placed her hand in Candace's and stepped through the doorway. The air was crisp and Rose took a big helping of it into her lungs. She gripped Candace's upper arm with both hands as they walked down the steps together. It wasn't long before they were headed to the same sidewalk that had brought so many voices past her window. Stepping onto the concrete, she looked up at her room. The light was on but the curtains were drawn. This was all the 'voices' knew of her—a closed window on the second floor.

"There's a lot more to see tonight," said Candace as she gently pulled her forward. Rose continued her slow pace as they passed by each home lot. The neighborhood she had lived in her entire life came alive for the first time since she was a child. The houses were beautiful with their lit windows and porch lights still aglow. Several of the houses already had their Christmas lights hung. A dog's bark scared her briefly but Candace kept her moving. "No turning back now, Rose." It wasn't long until her speed increased to a steady walk. By the time they neared the end of the street, Rose's walk showed signs of confidence. Finding the well-worn foot path to the beach, Candace and Rose ran toward the moonlit ocean.

Bursting onto the beach, they both stopped once their shoes sank into the soft sand. Candace was breathing heavy, but Rose was gasping for air. Other than running up and down the stairs of her home, she'd never experienced such a distance. Bending over, resting her hands on her knees, she worked to catch her breath. The crisp air felt like shards of glass inside her delicate lungs. But that didn't stop her from grinning from ear to ear. This was what freedom felt like and she wanted to experience every aspect.

"Are you all right?" asked Candace, concerned they might need to call an ambulance.

"I'm fine. Better than fine," she replied, taking in the view of the dark ocean for the first time in years.

"We couldn't have picked a better night for this. The clouds are closing in, but I think we're safe for now," said Candace, sitting down on the sand.

"It's louder than I remember. I forgot how ferocious it sounds. It's wild and beautiful all at the same time."

"Beats four walls and a ceiling."

"The lighthouse is so much closer," noted Rose as she looked down the beach.

"In my mind, I've had thousands of conversations with him."

"The words will come when you meet the right person."

"You mean when I talk to Will for the first time?"

"If he's the right person," answered Candace, trying not to pop her fragile bubble.

"How will I ever find the courage to tell him?"

"Two weeks ago, I couldn't get you to say a word. Now I can't shut you up."

"He knows what people say about me."

"I know what it's like to live in fear. Sometimes you just have to jump and see what happens."

"I could never be like that."

"What do you want, Rose?"

"I don't want to be afraid anymore."

"Then say it."

"I don't want to be afraid anymore," she said quietly.

"Say it like you mean it!"

"I don't want to be afraid anymore," she said with determination.

"Now shout it to the universe."

Jumping up from the sand, Rose looked to the stars and yelled at the top of her lungs, "I don't want to be afraid anymore!"

Candace couldn't believe the change in Rose as she watched her spin out of control while yelling the same thing over and over to the universe. She applauded with her hands as laughter erupted from a place of pure joy. Leaning back, Candace placed her hands on the sand behind her to brace herself. She instantly felt something press against the palm of her hand. In the fleeting moonlight, she lifted her hand and pulled a pearl from the sand. Using her forefinger, she moved the pearl around her palm. "Could it be from the necklace worn by the woman abandoned on the beach?" she wondered. Her second thought was of the pearl necklace she ripped from her neck the night she jumped.

Shining her flashlight on the pearl, she saw no signs it was once a part of a necklace which meant it was natural pearl that had broken free from the shell. It had escaped its prison. The symbolism between the pearl and her own situation, as well as Rose's newfound freedom, screamed volumes. Candace turned the light off and held the pearl securely in her hand just as Rose collapsed next to her.

"That was amazing."

"Now say it like you believe it."

"I'm not going to be afraid anymore," she reiterated with great determination.

"Neither am I," said Candace as she squeezed the pearl with one hand and Rose's hand with the other. Lying on their backs, they watched the moonlight disappear as the dark clouds covered the last of the night sky. The universe was hidden from their sight. "Good thing we brought a flashlight. We should go before the storm hits."

"Wait," said Rose, stopping Candace from getting up. "I want to remember what rain feels like."

One by one, a few drops started to fall. Candace turned her head to see Rose's reaction. She'd never seen her so peaceful—more evidence of the progress they were making. It wasn't long before the small droplets turned larger, delivering more of a punch to their faces. Pulling Rose from the beach, Candace ran next to her holding the flashlight. By the time they made it down the long trail to town, the rain was coming in sheets.

Laughing and out of breath, Candace and Rose ran up the porch steps. "Let's take off our muddy shoes," suggested Candace. Soaked to the bone, they burst through the front door. Candace turned her back to Rose and removed her wet coat. "I'll put on the kettle while you get out of those wet clothes. Sound good?" While hanging her coat on the rack, she noticed a large muddy shoe print on the floor. "Rose?" Her young friend's lack of response sent a chill down her spine. Candace's deepest fear was realized when she heard a cold familiar voice.

"I could use a warm drink."

Candace turned to find Dante sitting on the sofa. He'd made himself at home with his dark dress coat laid over the back of the couch and his leather gloves neatly stacked beside him. His condescending sneer showed he'd taken ownership of the room.

"I think champagne might be more appropriate," he continued. "We are celebrating your apparent survival."

Hearing the door open behind her, she turned to see Dante's right-hand man, Albert, enter the house and lock the door behind him. "I pulled the car into the driveway." Taking a solid stance in front of the door, he wrapped his gloved hands together in front of him. He was a large man, capable of leveling his opponent with a single strike.

Candace's first instinct was to run, but Rose stood between her and Dante. She couldn't leave her behind. Candace knew there was only one thing to do: get Rose to safety. Stepping close to Rose, she whispered in her ear. "Run, Rose. Out the back. Run!"

Without hesitation, Rose ran from the room as fast as she could. Albert's meaty stature kept him from getting a quick start as he attempted to follow. Instinctively, Candace rammed her shoulder into his body as he passed by, throwing him off balance. Then she grabbed a letter opener from the nearby desk and tucked it into her back pocket as she ran toward the door. Before she could get it unlocked, the painful grip of his brawny hands around her biceps stopped her escape. Jerking her back to the center of the room, he asked, "Should I go after the girl?"

"No. I have what I came for." Rising from the sofa, Dante walked toward her, his smug face dripping with triumph. "I'm hurt. No phone call to tell me you're alive... to ease my pain and suffering."

"You don't know pain and suffering," replied Candace. Although her voice cracked from the trepidation of him moving closer, she leveled the accusation with exactness.

"Are you hearing what I'm hearing, Albert?"

"Maybe she hit her head on a rock when she washed ashore," he responded flippantly, trivializing what she'd gone through.

"Trauma is a possibility," said Dante, artfully adopting concern as he leaned his body against hers, lowering his head to examine her every detail. "Whatever the case... I'm feeling generous today."

Candace was trapped. The feel of Dante's warm breath on her face tightened that familiar knot in her stomach. Choosing to avoid direct eye contact, she turned her head to the side as a sign of disrespect—a small tactic but she knew it would send a message. She'd come too far to give up without a fight. "I want nothing from you, Dante."

"Don't be hasty, Candace," he responded, using his fingers in an attempt to straighten her wet, unruly hair. "I don't offer forgiveness very often."

"You've never offered mercy."

"How cynical you've become in my absence. Are you trying to ruin our happy reunion?"

His lingering closeness and the touch of his hands moving across her scalp and around the side of her face was almost more than she could stand. As he continued to move his head to maintain eye contact, she could feel the horror building inside her chest.

"I was in shock after you stabbed me and jumped from the boat," he said, feigning a wounded spirit. "I thought we had something special."

"You didn't even report me missing."

"You think I'd file a police report?" he said with a chuckle. "How would that have looked? Not to mention the inevitable investigation. I handle my own affairs. You should know that better than anyone."

"How did you find me?"

"It was fate. I saw you on the news. My little Candace, saving other people's lives. You seemed to fit right in. It's almost like you'd rather live here than where you belong."

"I like it here, Dante."

"This isn't your home."

"This feels more like home than being with you ever did."

"After everything I've done for you."

"Please, Dante. I'm trying to start over. You can't be here," she said calmly, trying to diffuse the situation.

"Why? Are you afraid this little town will find out the truth? That you're playing house? Pretending to be someone you're not?"

"It's not like that."

"It's exactly like that. How do you think I knew you were pretending to be a psychiatrist," he sneered. *"Dr. Hart?"*

"Who? I never told them I was a psychiatrist."

"You didn't tell them you weren't either. There's a lot of things you didn't mention. The kind ladies at the bakery filled me in on everything."

"It's just a job. I needed the money."

"I've given you everything you need."

"Don't you understand? I want my freedom!" yelled Candace, her voice trembling as the tears welled up in her eyes. "That's the only thing I want from you."

"You're mine, Candace. Until I decide differently."

"Why are you doing this?"

"I'm collecting on a debt. You can't expect to get pulled out of the gutter and be given everything your heart desires for free."

"For free? You took everything from me!"

"I don't know what's gotten in to you," said Dante as he wiped a tear from her cheek. "In time you'll see, I do what I do because I love you."

"You've never loved anyone but yourself."

"We all love in our own way," he said as he leaned down to kiss her lips. Candace wrenched her head to the side to avoid contact. Seeming amused by her defiance, he kissed her cheek and said, "Let's go home."

"Good," replied Albert. "This mausoleum is giving me the creeps."

"Wait! I'll have the money soon," implored Candace, nearing the use of her last resort—the letter opener hidden in her back pocket beneath her flannel shirt.

"You and I both know you'll never make it on your own," he chuckled, while putting on his coat. "You tried and you failed. I'm the one who picked up the pieces. Remember?"

"I'll pay you back as soon as I get paid."

"It's never been about the money!" snapped Dante.

Candace flinched, expecting to be struck but nothing happened.

Close to losing control, Dante flexed his fingers then slid his hands into his gloves. He needed the moment to collect himself. "What happened on the boat has changed me. I'm a changed man, right, Albert?"

"A changed man," echoed Albert.

"Things will be different this time."

"I don't believe you."

"You have my word."

"People like you don't change."

"Albert, let's take Candace home where she belongs."

"I won't go, Dante."

"Are you trying to provoke me?"

"No! I'm trying to tell you how I feel."

"Save it for the ride back," he curtly responded.

"I'm not getting in that car."

"It's time to go home." With a nod to Albert, Dante left the house.

Candace could feel the panic growing in her chest as Albert moved her toward the door. His hold on her upper arms made it impossible for her to reach the letter opener in her back pocket. Planting her feet firmly, she pushed back against him, refusing to take a step. But she was no match for his brute strength as he tightened his grip. The crippling pain shooting down her arms forced her feet into motion. The safety of Ruby's home would soon be a memory.

CHAPTER 28

Panic stricken, Rose ran from the backyard and into the alley between their house and the neighbor's property. Unsure of what to do or where to go, she kept running. The rain had let up as she made it to the park. She had to find help for Candace but didn't know where to go. The headlights of a vehicle driving down the street gave her hope. Quickly, she darted across the park to intercept the driver and ran into the middle of the road. The driver of the approaching pickup truck slammed on his brakes, skidding to a stop on the wet asphalt. Standing in the headlights only a couple feet from the bumper, Rose quivered in fear until she saw the driver emerge from the truck. It was Will. A familiar face was exactly what Rose needed.

"I didn't see you. Are you all right?" he asked, unaware that it was Rose Stratton.

"Candace...," uttered Rose, barely able to speak. "Candace said to run. I ran. I ran as fast as I could."

"Rose?"

She shook her head, affirming who she was as Will removed his coat and wrapped it around her.

"Where is she? Where's Candace?"

"With a man."

"Where, Rose?"

"At home."

"Did she recognize the man?"

"I don't know. She looked scared."

Wrapping his arm around her shoulder, he escorted her to the cab of the truck as he pulled his cell phone out of his pocket. "Get in the truck and lock the doors. Keep the engine going and the headlights on for safety. We're only a block from your house. I'm not going far. Don't let anyone in until I get back." After reassuring her as much as possible, he turned and hurried down the street, holding his phone to his ear.

Rose did as he said and crawled behind the wheel. The heat felt like heaven as she watched Will move quickly down the street. Although she was facing the direction of her house, she was too far away to see. The only thing she could do was wait for him to return.

Will had no idea what he was going up against, so he called in a favor. "Jack! I need backup at Ruby Stratton's house."

"Backup?" he responded, confused by the request.

"Get here as quick as you can!"

"Just leaving the harbor. Five minutes out."

Disconnecting the call, Will pocketed his phone and began sprinting the five hundred feet to Ruby's house. He was used to the adrenaline rush of emergency situations, but this felt different. It felt desperate. He'd only known Candace for a short while but the thought of losing her was a crisis in itself. Approaching the house, he saw a dark-colored Maserati Quattroporte parked in the driveway. His attention turned to the front door of the house as a man dressed in a long black coat walked across the porch toward the steps.

Seeing no sign of Candace, Will hoped the stranger was leaving of his own accord and the danger had been averted. His understanding quickly changed as a large brute roughly yanked Candace onto the porch. Will knew he had to stop them from getting into the Maserati. With an engine designed by Ferrari under the hood, he'd never catch them.

"Dante, don't do this!" pleaded Candace as she fought to free herself. Dante refused to respond as he walked down the three steps and waited at the bottom.

"Candace?" The sound of Will's voice brought their departure to a stop. Will stood on the yard within feet of Dante, uncertain of his next move. "Who are these men?"

Frightened for Will's well-being, Candace became submissive in Albert's hands, allowing him to move her across the porch to the top of the steps. "You need to go, Will. This is none of your business."

"I can't."

"Turn around and walk away," she pleaded.

"I told you, I can't. I'm here on official business."

"What are you talking about?" asked Candace.

"You live in my town, that makes you my responsibility."

"I don't need a doctor," she cried, trying to keep the moment from escalating for Will's own good.

"You need rescued and that happens to be a part of my job, as a paramedic and a friend."

Growing irritated with the exchange, Dante mocked Will's intentions. "Look at this, Albert. Our little Candace went and found herself a friend." He was an expert at maintaining his cool demeanor in public, but on the inside the fires of jealousy had ignited. "No one here needs rescuing. So go home, have a drink and forget you ever met her."

"She's coming with me and you're leaving town."

"No one tells me what to do," warned Dante. "Who do you think you are?"

"The guy telling you what to do. Now let her go."

"Or what?"

"I call the police and we make this official."

"Small town cops don't scare me."

"She's not going anywhere with you."

"Candace and I have an arrangement. A deal's a deal. She's bought and paid for."

"You're not leaving with her!" forcefully responded Will.

"Who's going to stop me?"

"I am." Will lunged at Dante and slugged him in the face.

Dante lost his footing and landed against the hood of his car, instantly reminded of the stab wound inflicted by Candace before her escape. The shooting pain heightened his lust for vengeance.

"Boss?" yelled Albert, unsure of the priority.

"I got this!" Dante pushed himself from the car and took a swing at Will, but his opponent's defensive moves kept him from making contact. He didn't see the second punch coming. The hit to the side of Dante's face was so hard it dropped him to the ground. Slightly disoriented, he could see Will moving toward him to finish what he started so he reached into his coat pocket and pulled out a pistol. "Back off!" The fight ended, allowing Dante to get back on his feet. It took him a moment to regain his composure. He wasn't used to being at the receiving end of a double punch.

"Get out of here, Will!" pleaded Candace. "Just go!"

"Not without you."

"We're leaving! One way or another," warned Dante, keeping the gun aimed in Will's direction.

Using the car as a barrier, Albert pushed Candace past Dante and opened the back door. "Get in."

More worried about Will than herself, Candace tried again to convince him to leave. "Just go, Will. I'll be fine."

"I'm not going anywhere and neither are you." Will advanced toward the car with the intent of confronting the man holding her captive. The henchman let go of one of Candace's arms and pulled his gun as well. "I wouldn't," warned Albert.

"She's not worth getting yourself killed over," said Dante. "Turn around and leave her to us. You could never control her anyway."

"I wouldn't try," responded Will defiantly.

The freeing of Candace's arm made it possible for her to reach the letter opener in her back pocket. Within her grip, she slid the weapon up her sleeve to keep it hidden. She didn't dare use it with two guns aimed at Will.

Before anyone made another move, a pair of headlights lit up the driveway as Jack Segal slammed on his brakes, stopping catawampus in the street. Will mentally breathed a sigh of relief knowing he had backup. Dressed in his Coast Guard uniform, Jack left the truck, pulling the sidearm from its holster. Positioning himself in the center of his lit headlights, he remained calm and collected as he took control of the situation. "Do we have a problem here, boys?"

"He's not taking her, Jack," said Will.

"I'm collecting what belongs to me," piped up Dante, trying to see through the bright lights from the other side of the car.

"If it isn't Dante Donadio," replied Jack, leveling the playing field. "You're a long way from your yacht."

"This isn't the ocean, old man," said Albert.

"I've got news for you... The United States Coast Guard is wherever I am. And right now there's a fleet parked in this driveway, so unhand the girl."

"You know this guy?" asked Will.

"Stay back," ordered Jack, then he returned his attention to Dante. "Let her go, Donadio."

Albert looked to his boss for their next move, but Dante was too busy plotting how to regain control of the situation. "This has nothing to do with either of you. She accidentally fell off my yacht and after a long search I finally found her. It's obvious she's suffering from some form of amnesia. I need to get her home so she can receive proper medical attention."

"Is that right, young lady?" asked Jack.

"I told you she can't remember!"

Candace's first instinct was to back up his story like she had done for the past five years. It was always an accident of some kind. Within a matter of minutes, Candace had returned to the same situation she was in before she jumped from the boat. Rubbing the palm of her hand on the side of her pants, she felt the pearl in her pocket. A montage of moments shot through her mind: the pearl necklace she ripped from her neck before she jumped from the boat, the woman with the lantern abandoned on the beach, Rose dancing freely, yelling her mantra to the universe.

"I need you to answer the question, ma'am."

"I don't want to be afraid anymore," she whispered. A simple sentence to recite, but difficult to achieve, especially in her current circumstance.

"What did you say?" asked Dante with a threatening tone.

Staring straight into Dante's eyes, she repeated the sentence loudly, with courage and strength. "I'm not going to be afraid anymore." Then she turned to Jack to answer his question. "I jumped to end my life... or save it. One of the two."

"No one jumps into the ocean during a November storm to save their life, Miss."

"At the time, it seemed better than the alternative."

"That's all I need to hear," Jack responded. "Let her go. I'm not going to say it again."

Dante grabbed ahold of Candace and shoved her between him and the car. Placing the gun to her head, he defied Jack's orders and raised the stakes. "Get in the car, Albert."

"Don't you move," countered Jack.

"Now!" yelled his boss. Albert opened the front seat passenger side door and slid across the seat into the driver's position.

"Jack, do something!" said Will.

Worried Candace would get caught in the crossfire, Jack held his position.

"Start the car," ordered Dante as he moved his hostage toward the open back door. Candace fought back. With little wiggle room, she landed an elbow to the side of his face. Shocked by her audacity, he shoved her against the trunk of the car. He never considered she would fight back. What started out as a simple retrieval had escalated into a criminal act. Nothing he could do could change that.

"Take your hands off her!" yelled Will.

"We're leaving and she's coming with us," said Dante, matter of factly.

"How much is that boat worth to you?" asked Jack.

"My yacht has nothing to do with this."

"I asked you a question."

"It's none of you business."

"You just made it my business. I'm about to get on this radio and have your multi-million dollar vessel impounded up north as part of my investigation into why you lost a passenger overboard and didn't report it. Who knows what a thorough search will uncover? Add that to an attempted kidnapping and you're looking at some decent prison time."

Dante took a moment to consider what Jack was threatening. He knew they would find evidence of drugs aboard from the many extravagant parties he had hosted. That would open the door to a deeper search into his life and business dealings. The last thing he wanted was to have his reputation damaged. Or worse yet, go to prison. Although he amassed his wealth through questionable and illegal ventures, he'd built a facade of respectability as an investor to the arts. After weighing his options, he recognized that Candace could be replaced more easily than his fortune and social status. But his extreme narcissism overruled common sense. The thought of losing anything was intolerable.

"How much is that boat worth to you, Donadio?"

Placing his mouth next to her ear as Candace struggled beneath his weight, Dante whispered, "Tell them this has all been a mistake and get in the car. I'll let you go when we get back to the city. You'll never see me again."

"You're lying like you always do," she replied, her voice trembling.

"I promise. We'll go our separate ways. You owe me this."

"Just let me go now."

"Even if I do, you'll always be waiting for me to collect," he whispered. "Always looking over your shoulder. You'll never be safe. Do this one thing and we're even."

Candace took a moment to consider what he was saying. She wanted to believe that it could end that easily. That she could get her life back with no fear of him waiting in the shadows. But he had broken every so-called promise he'd ever made to her and she knew this would be no different. "I don't believe you."

"Then do it to save your paramedic's life."

Candace stared across the trunk at Will. The last thing she wanted was to bring her problems to his doorstep, but that's exactly what she'd done. She could see the worry in his eyes. He'd saved her life once but was helpless to do it again.

"He's only a couple feet from Albert," continued Dante, whispering in her ear. "One round to the chest and he's gone."

Candace knew the only way to end the situation peacefully was to do what Dante asked. It was her turn to save Will. "Okay," she whispered. "Just don't hurt him. Please, don't hurt him."

Dante straightened up and allowed Candace to as well. He waited for Candace to speak.

"This has all been a big misunderstanding," said Candace. "I'm leaving with Dante."

"Don't do this!" yelled Will.

"It was an accident. I fell overboard that night. It was my fault. I just want to go home and forget this ever happened."

"That's no longer possible, young lady," said Jack. "He's committed a crime by bringing a weapon to the scene and holding you hostage."

"I won't press charges. You're risking your life for no reason."

Her performance was so believable that Dante felt confident enough to tuck his gun back into his jacket. He knew Albert had his back if things didn't go the way he expected them to. "There we have it." Dante produced a smile to cover his malicious intents as he waited for Jack to concede.

"Please, Mr. Segal, put down your gun and let me go home," she concluded.

"Don't believe her!" pleaded Will. "He's forcing her to say that."

"You don't have to do this, Candace," said Jack. "We can protect you."

"I don't need protection anymore," she responded, tightening her grip on the letter opener. Then she crawled into the car and slid over behind the driver's seat.

Will rushed to the door, but she locked it before he could grab the handle. Refusing to look at him through the window, she stared straight ahead.

"Candace, don't do this!" he screamed, banging on the glass. "Get out of the car!"

"As always, Jack, it's been a pleasure," said Dante, then he joined Candace in the back seat.

Frustrated, Jack lowered his gun. "Let her go, Will."

"No! Candace, get out of the car!"

The car backed out of the driveway with Will walking beside, still banging on the window. "Don't do this! Please, Candace. I love you!" Those were the last words he spoke before the car drove away. All he could do was watch the taillights drive down the street as Jack caught up to him.

"I'll call it in. We'll get him."

"Before or after he beats her to a pulp? Or worse?" said Will as he started toward the truck. "I can't let her leave town with him."

"Will, wait! Look."

At the end of the block, the car started to chaotically zigzag back and forth until it left the road and slammed into a large tree in the park. The back door opened and Candace dove onto the ground—the bloody letter opener clutched in her hand. She got to her feet and ran like her life depended on it.

Will took off toward her on a dead sprint. Jack followed but at a slower pace. His knees wouldn't allow anything faster.

Candace rushed into the security of Will's arms. After a few seconds, Will pushed her to arm's length to check her out. Fortunately, the low beams from Will's truck, still parked in the street near them, provided enough light for him to see. "Are you all right?" "Did he hurt you?" Looking down, he saw the weapon still clasped in her hand.

Realizing she still had the letter opener, she dropped it to the ground. "I'm a little shook up," said Candace, staggering a bit.

Her rapid breathing told him she was most likely heading into a state of shock. Will wrapped his arms tightly around her to provide the safety and physical support she needed to mitigate the onset of trauma. "What happened in the car?"

"You told me you loved me," said Candace, her face pressed against Will's chest. "I couldn't go back. I've come too far to go back."

Jack finally caught up with them lowering his phone from his ear. "The police and emergency services are on their way. What happened, Candace?"

"I'm trying to keep her from going into shock, Jack." Using his head, Will pointed toward the evidence lying on the ground near them. "Why don't you find out for yourself?"

Jack pulled out a folded white hanky and carefully picked up the letter opener. "They're going to need you on the scene, Will."

"Doc's physician assistant is on call in my absence," said Will. "Officially, I'm still on vacation."

"Take care of her." With that said, Jack hurried toward the accident scene. The sound of approaching sirens was the sign Candace needed that it was finally over.

Will and Candace remained in the street, separated from the accident scene. As the adrenaline began to wear off, she could feel the raw emotion of what happened. Anger and hurt were eventually replaced by a feeling of triumph. The tears flowed, but this time they were tears of joy. There would be much to work through in the coming months but not having to look over her shoulder would make it easier.

"How are you feeling, Candace?" whispered Will, still holding her tight.

"Someone once told me that drowning is a silent death that rarely attracts attention," she said somberly. "I was drowning long before I jumped off that boat." Then she pulled away from Will and asked a question impossible for him to answer. "How did I let myself get to that point?"

"I don't know, Candace. I fix sinks, remember?" he responded, trying to lighten the situation.

With exuberance, Candace wrapped her arms around his neck and held him as tightly as she could. "You saved my life."

"You saved your own life. Jack and I were just backup."

"I'll never be able to thank you for all you've done for me."

"You already have," replied Will, enjoying the opportunity to hold her in his arms. "Why are you soaking wet?"

"We got caught in the rain." Candace pulled away from Will. "Rose. I have to find Rose."

"She's safe."

"If anything had happened to her..."

"She's fine. And she speaks."

"I know. Isn't it wonderful?"

"I can't believe it. What a surprise."

"Speaking of surprises, what are you doing here?"

"I came home a little early."

"You didn't stay for the reception?"

"I realized Jill's not who I'm looking for. I'm pretty sure I knew that all along."

"What are you going to do about it?" asked Candace, acting on his recent declaration of love.

Now it was Will's turn. He'd rehearsed what he wanted to tell her all the way back from the wedding. In a moment of desperation, he'd jumped the gun by telling her he loved her. He had planned to suss out how she felt before exposing his own feelings. He had no idea if she felt the same in return. The idea of Candace wanting to spend the rest of her life living in a one bedroom lighthouse seemed like a fantasy. She'd set out to find her own kind of happiness and the last thing he wanted to do was get in the way of that. The only way to know would be to ask. "You already know how I feel," he said. "It's your turn to say something."

Without a word, she kissed him, reciprocating his feelings. He eagerly responded by kissing her back.

CHAPTER 29

Rose watched through the windshield of Will's truck in disbelief. The sight of them together pierced her heart as she continued to watch them kiss in the glow of the headlights. She had trusted Candace with her secret love and now her only friend in the world was betraying her. Tears rolled from her eyes as she sat in silence witnessing the treachery. She had to get away from both of them. The fog rolling in provided the perfect cover for Rose to escape unseen. Quietly she opened the door and snuck across the pavement. Within seconds, she had disappeared into the darkness.

Candace pulled away from Will. "We can't do this now."

"Why?"

"Because of Rose."

"I told you she's fine."

"You don't understand."

"No, really. She's right there. She can see us from the truck."

Shocked by the news, Candace slowly turned toward the truck. "No. No!" she cried, running toward the truck.

"What's wrong?" asked Will once he caught up with her.

"She's gone," exclaimed Candace in horror.

"She's probably back at the house."

"What have we done?"

"What are you talking about?"

"She's in love with you."

"In love with me," repeated Will with laughter. "We don't even know each other."

"You're the only man in her life."

"I'm not in her life!"

"I'll explain later. Right now we've got to find her. Get in!"

Quickly, they drove down the street and pulled into Ruby's driveway. Candace ran from the truck before he shut off the engine. Bursting through the doorway, she began a desperate search. "Rose. Rose!"

Will entered the house as Candace ran up the stairs. "Check in the kitchen." Will entered the kitchen calling her name and continued into the backyard. She was nowhere to be found. Running back into the living room, he met Candace at the bottom of the stairs. "She's not in the kitchen or the backyard. Where would she go?"

"The only other place she's been is the beach."

"I've got some flashlights in the truck. I'll radio Joe and get him down there."

"What if we don't find her in time?"

"In time for what?"

"I'm scared of what she might do."

"We'll find her."

Running from the house, they made their way down the trail to the beach. The clouds had parted, allowing the full moon to add some light to the search. "Rose. Rose!" Their voices calling her name in all directions as they ran down the beach. "She could be anywhere," said Candace, beginning to panic.

"We're almost out of beach. There's a trail that leads up to the cliff. I'll head up there while you keep searching down here. Joe should be here any time."

"What if—"

Will cut her off, "we'll find her. Stay calm and keep looking."

As Will ran toward the trail, Candace took a moment to compose herself. "Stay calm. Don't panic." Returning to the search, she pointed her flashlight in every direction as she moved down the beach, calling her name. "Rose, where are you? Rose!" Within a few minutes she reached the end of the sand. Shining her flashlight over the rocks in the water she searched for any sign of Rose. Eventually, the rocks led to an outcropping of rock that extended to the cliff above. Straining to see through the fog, she thought she saw something next to the rock wall below the cliff. "Rose? Is that you?" she yelled, trying to raise her voice over the roar of the crashing waves.

"Leave me alone!" yelled Rose.

"I can't do that!" The noise of the ocean made it difficult to hear without yelling at the top of their lungs.

"Don't come out here!"

"I'm going to have to unless you come to me!"

"Stay away!"

"Let me help you!"

"No!"

"You have to trust me!"

"I'll never trust you!" screamed Rose.

Candace knew there was only one thing to do. She had to get to Rose and bring her safely back. Hanging the flashlight around her neck, she stepped onto the first rock. They were slick and jagged as she stepped from one to the other. The waves crashing against them made it more difficult to traverse. She needed both hands to stabilize herself. Every few steps she pointed the flashlight toward Rose to make sure she was moving in the right direction. Reaching a gap between the rocks, Candace jumped into the surf. She found herself in cold water up to her waist as she pushed her way toward the next closest rock. As she pulled herself onto the rock, she found herself within ten feet of Rose.

"Stop or I'll let go!" warned Rose in desperation.

"Don't you dare let go, Rose!"

"What does it matter to you?"

"You're my friend. One of the only friends I have."

"You lied to me!" yelled Rose.

Slipping off the rock, Candace caught an edge with one hand then pulled herself out of the water and back on top. Needing to rest, she responded to Rose's accusation. "I didn't lie to you, Rose. Do I feel something for Will? Yes. And I probably should have told you that. I never dreamed anything would have come of it," she said, gathering the courage to leap to another rock. "I never meant to hurt you, Rose."

"But you did."

"I care for both of you and that doesn't come easily for me. But if loving Will means hurting you then I'll go away. And you can go back to your room and back to your fantasy." Not getting a response, Candace leaped onto another rock then took a moment to get her balance.

"I don't want that anymore," said Rose. Her voice no longer strained with anger.

"Then let me help you. Please, Rose. Let me help," pleaded Candace as she shined her light on the distance between them. They were within five feet of each other and for the first time, Candace believed she could turn this around.

Wanting her help, Rose reached out as she took a step onto a rock leading to Candace. Unable to secure her footing, she slipped and fell into the water just as a mighty wave slapped against the outcropping.

"Rose!" screamed Candace. With new found fortitude, Candace jumped to the next rock and then the one after that. Soon she could see Rose's limp body in the water. Leaping in next to her, she cradled her head in one arm as she wrapped her other arm around her chest. "Help!" she screamed just as another waved engulfed them. With Rose being unconscious, there was no way she could get her back to the beach by herself. All she could do was hope that Will would hear her. Keeping Rose's head above water, she used her other hand to blink her flashlight on and off as a signal for help.

Halfway down the trail, Will saw the flashlight blinking near the outcropping of rock. The trail was slick from the rain and although he slipped several times, he continued as fast as he could. In the distance, he saw a vehicle driving down the beach. It had to be Joe. Picking up his radio, he made contact with him. "They're in the water below the cliff."

Joe reached the end of the beach before Will. "How did she get across those rocks in the dark without killing herself?" he asked rhetorically as Will approached.

"Let's get her back."

Joe quickly tied one end of a long rope to the bumper of the fire truck then pulled out two helmets and several life jackets.

Will refused the gear. "There's no time."

"This life jacket may be the difference between saving lives or losing them."

"I hate it when you use my training against me," said Will as he put the life jacket on and grabbed a second one. Joe did the same and followed with the other end of the rope. Working together, they were able to make their way over the dangerous rocks and through the water faster than Candace.

"I'm losing her. Help me!" came a faint call from Candace, barely audible over the crash of the surf. "Hurry!"

With the rope tied around his waist, Joe leaped into the water next to Candace and took Rose in his arms. "What happened?"

"She slipped on the rock. I think she hit her head," responded Candace as Will helped her on with a life jacket.

Will bent down and did his best to examine the wound on the back of Rose's head while Candace held the light. The crashing waves made everything more difficult as they put the life jacket on Rose. "The only way to get her back is to float her around the rocks," said Joe. "Get Candace to shore."

"Let me help!"

"We'll take it from here, now come on," said Will, extending his hand to Candace. "You can help by getting a spine board and blankets out of the truck."

Candace accepted his hand and made her way back to shore. Will quickly returned and took hold of the rope. He gathered the slack as

Joe made his way around the sharp rocks, the waves pounding against them.

Moving her passed the last rock, Joe scooped Rose into his arms and carried her out of the water. Candace helped him lay her friend gently on the spine board then she stepped back to make room for the two of them to work. Will checked her vitals and found them to be good. He examined her eyes for responsiveness. Using a stethoscope, he listened to her heart and lungs. The only thing that had him concerned was the lump on her head, but that was the doctor's department.

"Rose, can you hear me?" asked Will. "Rose?"

"Rose?" asked Joe, surprised by the new information. "As in Rose Stratton?"

"I think she's coming around," said Will.

Watching intently, they breathed a sigh of relief as she slowly opened her eyes. Confused at first, she took in the two men's faces as well as the pain she felt. "My head hurts."

"You've got a good-sized bump there and most likely a concussion," said Will as he checked the mobility of her arms and legs, asking for levels of pain.

"You're going to be okay," added Joe.

"That's good," replied Rose. "Where's Candace? Is she all right?"

"She's here," responded Will, moving aside to give her space. "She's the one who saved your life. She kept you afloat till we could get out there."

"I'm here, Rose," said Candace as she fell to her knees beside her.

"Don't go away," she pleaded.

"You're not getting rid of me that easily. Looks like we need each other now more than ever."

"Do you think you can make it into the cab of the truck?" asked Will.

"I think so," responded Rose as she sat up. "I'm a little dizzy."

"Allow me," said Joe. He reached down and scooped her into his arms as Candace and Will ran ahead to open the door. Once Joe set her down in the cab, Candace laid a rescue blanket over her. Joe returned with an instant ice pack, crawled onto the seat next to her and held it over the bump on her head. She was in good hands.

Standing in the darkness next to the truck, Candace could no longer hold back the tears of relief that they'd found Rose alive. She needed a moment to quietly react to nearly losing Rose, so she walked away from the truck. If the outcome had been different, she never would have forgiven herself. She would have held onto the guilt just as she had done with her parents' deaths for the past five years. The degree of physical exertion mixed with emotional strain had taken a toll. She was spent. Dropping to her knees, she looked to the moon through the parting clouds for reflection.

Returning from the rear of the truck, Will saw Candace on the ground and rushed toward her. "Are you all right?"

"Yes."

"Are you sure?" he asked again, kneeling next to her.

"I'm absolutely sure." Reaching out to Will, she took hold of his hand, thankful for someone to share the moment with—someone she trusted. "For the first time in five years, I'm able to let go of the guilt I've carried about my parents' deaths. It's all because of Rose. I could have drowned trying to rescue her, just like my parents died on their way to rescue me. They chose to drive in that snowstorm because they loved me, just as I chose to cross the jagged rocks because I care for Rose. That's what I want to remember when I think about my parents... their selfless love for me. Not the anger and guilt I've carried in my heart for so long."

Will took her in his arms and held her tight. "Everything's going to be okay. I promise."

"I think you're right," she responded, wishing the moment they were sharing could last forever.

"We need to get Rose to the clinic." Candace agreed allowing Will to help her into the front passenger seat of the firetruck. After securing all the doors, he crawled in behind the steering wheel. From the light inside the cab he could see she was still crying. "Can I help?"

"Tears of gratitude. But thank you."

"Just another day at the beach."

The light-hearted comment was exactly what she needed. "You really are good at your job," she said.

"It's not a job if you love what you do." Will pointed to the back seat where Joe sat next to Rose holding the cold pack on her head. "I love a happy ending. Let's get out of here." Will started the truck and headed down the beach.

Hours later, Candace sat at the edge of Rose's bed watching her sleep. The lighthouse beam lit the room with each turn. She felt a kinship to the beacon—a deep bond. It had been her guide during the storm as well as a place of healing after being rescued. Rose turned over, drawing Candace's attention away from the window. She smiled as she looked at her jar of wishbones setting on the nightstand. *When you love someone, all your saved-up wishes start coming true.* The statement had a whole new meaning now. She had finally found the courage to give her heart away, not just to Will, but to Rose and Ruby as well. It wasn't easy to open her heart but her survival depended on it. And now her wishes were coming true. So much had happened in the past few hours that she could barely process it all.

With Rose safe in her bed and sound asleep, she left the room. Before she retired to Ruby's room for a well-deserved night of sleep, she picked up Rhue-wyn's book from the couch. Although reticent, she had to find out what happened next. Collapsing onto the bed, she opened the book and began to read.

> *Three days had passed since being abandoned on a foreign shore and Rhue-wyn had barely moved from the spot. Every now and then, some onlookers from the small village nearby would sneak a glimpse of her then run away. Humans no longer held an interest for her. She was numb to their antics. In fact, life no longer held an interest for her. As a fairy, she possessed a natural tendency to play tricks on humans. She had used her enchantment for her own gain and amusement for hundreds of years. To Rhue-wyn it was just a game. Never out of malice. She had no idea what humans experienced after*

she was through with them. That innocence ended the day Andri betrayed her. She felt the treachery deep within her core. For the first time in her life, she understood the cruelty of causing others pain.

One day a shadow fell over her, providing a break from the mid-day sun. Rhuewyn turned to see a woman in her late thirties, holding two glasses and a pitcher of lemonade.

"May I sit with you?" she asked.

"If you dare."

"I just made some fresh lemonade. Would you care to share it with me?"

"Thank you."

The woman handed her the pitcher of liquid refreshment then sat down next to her on the sand. Holding out the glasses, she waited for Rhue-wyn to fill them both. The slightly tart taste of lemon on her dry tongue was heaven to her senses. It was the best lemonade she had ever tasted. She emptied her glass quickly and asked for more. The woman was happy to oblige and filled her glass to the top. Feeling satisfied, she slowed her consumption.

"My name is Iris," said the stranger.

"Thank you for your kindness, Iris."

"May I ask your name?"

"Rhue-wyn."

"That's an unusual name. Very beautiful."

"It has served me well."

"I heard you arrived by ship."

"Yes."

"Will the ship be returning?"

"No."

"May I ask why you wait here?"

"I have nowhere to go."

"I don't have much and my home is small, but I can offer a roof over your head and food in your stomach."

"What will your husband think?" asked Rhue-wyn, pointing to the ring on Iris's left hand.

"I lost my husband and my two sons to the sea two years ago when their fishing boat went down in a storm."

"That must have been devastating."

"Indeed it was. I am alone now and would welcome company."

"But I'm a stranger to you."

"You were a stranger until we shared lemonade."

"And now we're friends?"

"Friendship goes both ways. I'm merely offering it. What you do is your choice."

"I could use a friend."

"Then dust yourself off and walk with me." Rhue-wyn did as Iris suggested and they talked all the way home. Iris didn't live in the village with the local folks. Her home was near the wharf. It was all she could afford. She repaired fishing nets for a living and it wasn't long before Rhue-wyn acquired the skill as well. Working together, their profits doubled. For the first time in Rhue-wyn's life, she learned what it was to feel human, to earn a living, to clean a home and cook a meal. Iris introduced her as Rhue, her niece who had recently been widowed. The story allowed Rhue to wear a scarf around her head and conceal her face. The last thing she wanted was a village of fishermen enchanted with her.

After the initial introductions, the only time Rhue left the house was at night, when she would wander the shoreline, taking in the evening air. The years passed and Iris aged as humans do. Rhue-wyn did not. On the day of her friend's funeral, Rhue wore a black net over her face so as to not be recognized. Iris left the ownership of the house to her longtime friend so she would always have a place to call home. The fishermen in the village valued the quality of Rhue's net repair and continued to bring them to her house. They would leave the damaged nets on the doorstep. Rhue-wyn would mend them and return them to the same spot. Their payment was always on time and slipped through the crack beneath the door. Once again, Rhue-wyn found herself alone in the world. But she was content with her circumstance.

Candace turned the remaining pages in hopes of finding another chapter, but the rest of the book was blank. Slowly, she closed the cover and slid it away from her. So many unanswered questions ran through her mind. Questions that would never be answered. No sequel would be written nor movie made to tie up the series. Her story left Candace wanting so much more. During the time they spent together, she'd developed a kinship with Rhue-wyn. Now it felt like her friend had moved a thousand miles away, never to be heard from again. Closing her eyes, she decided to imagine a happier conclusion—an ending worthy of such a unique character. Sleep came quickly. The denouement would have to wait for another day.

CHAPTER 30

It had been over a week since Ruby left for the hospital. Today she was returning home. Inside the turret room, Rose stood at her window staring at the sidewalk below. All the curtains in the room were open, allowing the sunlight to brighten the room. It had snowed the night before and the white layer that covered the ground added to the brightness. Candace hurried into the room with a brush and several hair ties. "Sit down so I can do your hair."

"I won't be able to see the street if I do," argued Rose.

"I refuse to let your mother see you looking like you just rolled out of bed. Now sit."

With a huff, Rose sat on the chair, stretching her upper body as far as she could while Candace brushed her hair.

"How do you want it? The last three days it's been the same style."

"Double braids are my favorite."

"Variety is the spice of life, Rose," advised Candace as she continued to brush her hair.

"Can you make it a grown-up style?"

"Of course I can," she replied, brushing her hair into a high pony tail then twisting it around. "How does a bun sound?"

"Really grown up," replied Rose with a big smile.

The change in Rose was astounding, especially in such a short span of time. For a woman in her early twenties, she still had many child-like qualities but her rate of growth was impressive. No longer did Candace see fifty-two thousand, four hundred, twenty-seven dollars and sixteen cents when she looked at Rose. Now she saw a friend. In the end, that's all Rose needed—a friend she could trust and who would love her without sanctimonious judgment.

"When will she be here?" eagerly asked Rose.

"Any minute. Sit still and let me finish."

"Do you think she'll be surprised?"

"I haven't said a word."

"Do you think Will or Joe told her?"

"We're all in on the secret."

"I can hardly wait!"

"You have to wait long enough for me to finish."

"Go faster."

"I think I liked you better when you refused to speak."

"That's a joke, right?"

"Yes, Rose. That's a joke," said Candace, handing her a mirror. "I'm finished."

Rose was enthralled as she looked at her reflection in the mirror. Using her free hand, she gently touched her hair, marveling at her appearance. "She's not going to recognize me."

"The hairstyle's only the tip of the iceberg."

Rose jumped from the chair and returned to her post at the window. "I see her car coming down the street. She's here!" With childlike exuberance, she ran from the room with Candace following close behind. Down the stairs they flew and through the living room. "Hurry, Candace," yelled Rose as she opened the front door and ran onto the porch.

"I'm right behind you."

Rose jumped off the porch and ran to the middle of the driveway. She couldn't wait to see the look on her mother's face when they came to a stop. Candace waited on the porch to allow Rose to be the sole focus. This was a mother/daughter moment and Candace was thrilled to be a bystander.

∽

Will turned into the driveway and drove Ruby's car toward the house, stopping within inches of Rose.

"Is that my daughter?" asked Ruby from the front seat.

"It sure is."

"Before she could reach for the door, Rose pulled it open. Then she hugged her mother like she'd never done before. Ruby was speechless. She had hoped to see some change but had no idea a transformation of this magnitude was possible.

Will smiled at the greeting then turned his attention to Candace on the porch. Although she had her fingers covering her mouth, Will knew she was smiling. Noticing Ruby trying to get out of the car, he snapped into paramedic mode. "Wait! You're not going anywhere without your walker."

"I told you I don't need a walker."

"The only way you're getting from this car to that house is with a walker. Now don't move until I get it out of the back seat." Will hurried around the car, opened the rear door and retrieved the folded up device. Snapping it open, he placed it near her open door. "Let me help you."

"I can," said Rose. And she did just that.

Reluctantly, Ruby took hold of the walker and started for the porch. Will followed, carrying her hospital bag and purse. When she got to the stairs, Candace bent down and lifted the walker up while her daughter helped her up the steps. When Ruby reached the top, she took Candace in her arms and held her tight. "I told you Rose needed you," she whispered into Candace's ear.

"It turns out I needed Rose just as much," whispered Candace. "I needed both of you."

"Sorry to interrupt the reunion, but duty calls."

"Thank you for everything, Will," called Ruby from the porch.

"Anytime," he responded as he walked to his truck parked along the street. "Make sure you use that walker. Those were the doctor's orders."

"Will," called Candace. "Remember to meet your mom and dad at the school at noon."

"Thanks for the reminder." Before Will got into the truck, he leaned his arms over the side of the bed and watched them enter the house. "They're going to be at it all day." A notion that was pleasing to Will as he hopped in his truck and drove down the street.

Ruby was delighted to see a Christmas tree lit and decorated as she walked into the living room. Everything was dusted and polished and neat as could be—a task she was having a difficult time keeping up with before her surgery.

"We rearranged some of the furniture to make it easier for you to get around with your walker," said Rose.

"I see that."

"Everything will go back in place when you're fully recovered," confirmed Candace.

"Actually, I'm thinking about having a yard sale."

"Will said the doctor doesn't want you to overdo it. Gaining back your strength needs to be a gradual process."

"Advice given to all his patients," said Ruby, brushing the advice aside. "I'm sure it's all relative."

"Relative or not... I'll be here to help."

"Good. Because spring is only a few months. A grand time of the year for a good cleaning and a yard sale."

"Would you make us all some tea, Rose?" asked Candace as she helped Ruby to the couch.

"I'd love to," she said, hurrying toward the kitchen.

"You aren't allowed in the kitchen till I clean up from the breakfast mess. Rose and I had Alice and George Bloom over for breakfast this morning. They're staying at the Inn on the other side of town. We filled in for Will since he left last night to pick you up."

"How did Rose do with two complete strangers in the house?"

"It was a good test run. She did fine. I jumped in when needed but she was able to give simple answers to any direct questions."

"It's as though my daughter has experienced a metamorphosis."

"She's still Rose," said Candace as she sat down next to her. "And we still have a ways to go."

"How did you do it?"

"She did most of it. It's hard to know what we're made of until we're pushed to our extremities. Once we hit that wall, we either recoil or find a way over it. Rose busted right through."

"With a push or two from you."

"I stirred things up for sure. Rose was the one who made the decision to no longer live the way she was living—if you can call it that."

"Just as I hear you did. Will caught me up on the way home."

"Yes. We both came to that point."

"To one degree or another, we all come to that point," agreed Ruby.

"When I woke up the day after Will rescued me, I was angry. I couldn't even end my life right. Then you offered me a ridiculous amount of money and suddenly I had a ticket to freedom. I'm ashamed that I was willing to marry Rose off to a total stranger to secure my own future. Not my finest moment."

"Desperation is a powerful catalyst. We're not so different, you and I. It took being pushed to my limit to realize that sheltering Rose all these years was not the right thing for my daughter. I desperately wanted to protect her. I just went about it in the wrong way."

"Misleading hopes or goals," said Candace.

"Yes," agreed Ruby. "We followed our own will-o'-the-wisps."

"Speaking of that," said Candace, standing up from the couch and walking to the book shelf. "While you were away, I discovered this book." Candace pulled it from the bookshelf and returned to the couch. "This is the diary of the woman on the beach, isn't it? The woman with the lantern or so called will-o'-the-wisp. How did you end up with it?"

Ruby took the book from Candace and held it carefully in her hands. "It's been in my possession for a long time."

"That's how you know so much about her story. About Rhue-wyn."

"That's a name I haven't heard in a while."

"Was she real?"

"Yes."

"And you knew her?"

"That I did."

"She must have known you well to trust you with such a personal keepsake."

"I've thought about destroying it over the years to keep the secret safe, but I haven't been able to do it."

"It should be published."

"To what end?"

"To enrich the legend."

"This book was written during a time of great introspection for Rhue-wyn. Andri's betrayal changed her life dramatically. It was a disruption she never anticipated. She knew nothing would ever be the same again."

"Publishing this book would make it real."

"So more investigators can converge on our little town in search of a woman finally able to live her life in peace?"

"Are you saying Rhue-wyn's still alive? If that's the case, I'd love to meet her."

"Maybe one day I'll introduce you. Of course, that all depends on whether or not you plan to stay."

"I did get a job offer from Fae LeBlanc. She needs part-time help in her store. I'm also thinking of teaching dance."

"So you plan to call Will-O'-the-Wisp Point home?"

"I may have reached that point, yes. I've grown in enlightenment over the past few weeks, but not in wealth. As long as I have free room and board, I'm staying."

"Speaking of which... will you hand me my bag, please." Candace did as she requested and placed the bag on the couch next to her.

Ruby searched through the bag until she found her checkbook. "I have something for you." Ripping a check from the pad, she placed it in Candace's hand. "I wrote it out ahead of time in case surgery went the wrong way. Fifty-two thousand, four hundred, twenty-seven dollars and sixteen cents. You earned it."

"Rose isn't married. That was the deal."

"If Rose chooses to get married, it will be in her own time and by her own choice."

"Take it, Ruby," said Candace, trying to give it back.

"It's yours to do with what you will. Your ticket to happiness."

"I'm done doing the chasing," said Candace as she ripped the check in half then in quarters. "This time I let happiness find me."

"That's the magic of a good story. Where one chapter ends, another begins."

Rose entered the living room carrying a large tray loaded with a tea set. She placed it on the coffee table then sat between her mother and Candace.

"Look who's waiting on who?" said Ruby.

"We're going to take care of you until you're all better. Right, Candace?"

"As long as the guest room is available," responded Candace, opening the door for an invitation.

"There's no guest room here. You're family. That room is yours for as long as you want."

"Yes!" squealed Rose.

"Will can finally get his bed back."

"He'll miss you staying there," said Ruby.

"I have a feeling he'll be dropping by a lot more," joked Rose, hinting toward Will and Candace's romance.

"Oh, really, Rose." Ruby's curiosity was piqued. "What have I missed since I've been gone?"

Candace watched Rose and Ruby's light-hearted interaction as mother and daughter. It was a happy ending after many difficult years. Candace felt the same about her own circumstances. Out of the ashes of her old life, she had found a family to love, and in turn, be loved. She'd found a man she could trust, who would love her selflessly for who she was. She'd found a community of people, although not perfect, willing to be there for each other when they needed it most. But most importantly, she had found her own inner peace and strength. She had no idea what the future held and that didn't matter. She would welcome each new day with a smile and always be grateful for those who took the time to care for a stranger who washed ashore during a storm.

CHAPTER 31

Four months later welcomed a beautiful spring day to Will-O'-the-Wisp Point. Blossoming buds and blooming flowers transformed Ruby's backyard into a garden paradise. The trees and bushes had all been pruned and several coats of paint brought the old fence back to its original beauty. Laughter filled the air as Michelle and other children ran with balloons in one hand and ice cream cones in the other. Platters filled with finger foods decorated the tables as well as punch bowls full of liquid refreshments. The Stratton backyard had once again come to life after being dark for so many years.

Jack arrived just as Candace walked out of the back door carrying a platter of food. "Good afternoon, Candace. Can I help you with that?"

"I've got it. I'm so glad you and your wife could make it."

"We wouldn't miss it. We're late 'cause she had to get her pasta salad just right."

"I'm sure it's delicious as always," said Candace as she waved to her across the yard.

"Have you seen Will?"

"He's carrying luggage to the car."

"I'll be right back." Jack walked into the house and entered the living room just as Will reached the bottom of the stairs carrying a large bag. The tapping of his fancy leather cowboy boot against the hardwood floor drew Will's attention to his feet.

"Looks like Dad finally came through."

"These boots were worth the wait," he said happily. "I got an update on the Donadio case today. Dante's going away for a long time. They've seized his assets and shut down his illegal enterprises. The evidence of crimes just keeps mounting. Candace won't have to worry about him anymore. I thought we should wait till after the party to tell her."

"I'll let her know. Thanks, Jack."

"Now if you'll excuse me, the buffet is calling." As Jack walked onto the back porch, he couldn't help but smile as he passed by Rose and Joe. "Well, I'll be," he said to himself as he made his way to the refreshment table.

Sipping from her glass, Rose sat completely entranced by Joe's vast knowledge of the US Postal Service. It was something she'd never read about so she found the topic very engaging.

"It's called, 'Deserting the Mail' and it's a misdemeanor," said Joe. "Postal workers have gone to jail for hoarding people's mail."

"Really?" replied Rose.

"The maximum penalty is a year in prison."

Candace also smiled at the cute couple as she passed by—two unique souls brought together by natural attraction. The future was theirs to plan in their own time and in their own way. The lively look on Rose's face was worth more than any amount of money.

As she continued through the crowd, Candace heard Captain Bob and Fae LeBlanc furthering their plans to take his boat out on its maiden voyage. The news came as no surprise. Plans had already been made for her to watch the store the following week. Catching Fae's eye over the captain's shoulder, Candace struck a pose to show off the floral sundress she had ordered. Fae nodded her head to show approval.

Looking to the corner of the yard, Candace saw the librarian teaching Louise and some of the other ladies from the bakery the dance steps Candace had been teaching her. They were jazzed up with the librarian's personal disco flare which brought an even bigger smile to Candace's face.

Spotting Ruby across the lawn, she weaved her way through the guests until she arrived at her side. Then she slipped her arm around the host's shoulders and led her away from the group.

"I have something for you." Candace placed a ring with a beautiful pearl setting in Ruby's hand. "I found that pearl on the beach the first night Rose left the house."

"What a rare discovery."

"An oyster puts in a lot of work to produce a pearl. It's a going-away gift to remind you how far we've all come."

"You were meant to find this," said Ruby as she placed the ring on Candace's finger. "I have Rose as my reminder."

"Are you sure?"

"I insist. It's your token to treasure."

"At first I thought it might be from Rhue-wyn's necklace when she was abandoned on the beach," admitted Candace. "Maybe when you get back from your trip you can introduce me to Rhue-wyn. I'm dying to know the rest of the story," said Candace excitedly.

"The most interesting part of the story is the ending."

"How can the story have an ending if she's immortal?"

"Eventually, she met a man and fell in love."

"I didn't think fairies were capable of that."

"They're capable of love; they just don't risk it."

"But Rhue-wyn did?"

"Her love was so pure and so selfless, that it changed the physical nature of her heart. On the day of their marriage, her heart began to beat like a human heart and she began to age."

"Are you saying Rhue-wyn has grown old?"

"Let's not call her old, but she has aged beyond her prime."

The festivities seemed to stop for a moment as Candace finally found the courage to ask. "You're her, aren't you? You're Rhue-wyn."

Before Ruby could answer, Will hollered from around the house.

"All your bags are in the car, Ruby. You better get going. It's a long ride to the airport, even with Joe driving."

"Just sharing some mutterings of old recollections," she hollered back to him, then turned to Candace and took hold of her hands. "My recollections. Distant memories so easily awakened. Rose will soon know as well. As my daughter, she has much to explore within herself. Going back to Ffos Anoddun will be a good place to start. Returning to my homeland will be good for me as well." With a reassuring squeeze, Ruby let go of Candace's hands and walked toward the house. "Come along, Rose. Our adventure begins."

Spellbound, Candace watched Ruby walk toward Will still waiting at the corner of the house. She had so many questions, so many curiosities. She desperately wanted to stop her from leaving, to stop time so she could learn more. "How could Ruby drop a bomb like this before leaving town for a month?" she whispered to herself in astonishment. Looking around the yard, Candace realized she was the only one in the entire town who knew Ruby's secret. The woman at the center of the will-o'-the-wisp legend trusted her with the truth.

The guests' reactions to Ruby's call captured her attention. She watched Joe take the drink from Rose's hand, and like a gentleman, help her from her chair. As they walked through the small crowd of friends and neighbors, they were greeted with well wishes for safe travels. Rose stopped in the middle of the crowd and look up at the turret window. Candace knew exactly what she was thinking. "You're no longer a bird in a cage," whispered Candace. "You're ready to test your wings at altitudes you never imagined possible." Candace continued to watch with curiosity as they approached. "Was Rose a fairy too? If so, what gift does she possess?" Questions raced through her mind, stirring her imagination.

Rose ran to Candace and hugged her tight. "Goodbye, Candace."

"You're going to have a wonderful vacation," replied her trusted friend as she wrapped her arm around her waist and escorted her from the backyard. "Did you pack your book on castles?"

"I plan to talk Mom into visiting as many of them as possible."

"A month should give you plenty of time. I expect lots of postcards."

Rounding the corner of the house, Rose ran to Will and gave him a hug then crawled into the back seat of the car parked in the driveway. Joe walked around the car and got in the driver's seat, leaving Will, Candace and Ruby to say their goodbyes.

"You and I will continue our conversation when you get back," said Candace smiling as she wrapped her arms around Ruby. "I'll take good care of the house while you're away."

"Be safe and stay out of trouble," mentioned Will as he gave her a hug as well.

"Not to worry, I doubt the Wales countryside has changed too much since I left," she responded. "But then again... it seems like that was over a century ago." With a wink to Candace, Ruby was escorted to the car. Will helped her into the back seat while Candace studied the pearl on her ring. "Rhue-wyn's finally returning home to the forest she loved," whispered Candace as the car drove down the street.

Will returned from the driveway and kissed her on the cheek then wrapped his arms around her, holding her tight.

"People are probably watching," said Candace with a cheeky tone.

"Let 'em watch." Then he kissed her, oh, so romantically.

ABOUT THE AUTHOR

Xann-shapella Smith had the opportunity to study playwriting and screenwriting at Brigham Young University and has brought her plays to the stage on many occasions. Her love for great storytelling has produced scripts that span many genres, including: drama, romance, comedy, fantasy, adventure and science fiction. After years of writing screenplays, she made the decision to broadened her horizon in terms of storytelling and became an author. Xann resides on a small farm where the beauty and solace that surround her provide the perfect atmosphere for creating stories as far as the expanse of her imagination. Writing has been one of the great loves of her life and telling a good story is one of her passions. Xann-shapella's writing is a skill that rewards her in abundance each and every day and a passion she loves to share with audiences everywhere.

For more books and updates:
www.xannsmith.com

Made in the USA
Monee, IL
31 October 2020